*Then a new
king, to whom
Joseph meant nothing,
came to power in Egypt.
"Look," he said to his people,
"the Israelites have become far too
numerous for us. Come, we must
deal shrewdly with them or they
will become even more numerous
and, if war breaks out, will join
our enemies, fight against us and
leave the country."
So they put slave masters over them
to oppress them with forced labor, and
they built Pithom and Rameses as*

store cities for Pharaoh. But the more they were oppressed, the more they multiplied and spread; so the Egyptians came to dread the Israelites and worked them ruthlessly. They made their lives bitter with harsh labor in brick and mortar and with all kinds of work in the fields; in all their harsh labor the Egyptians worked them ruthlessly.

The king of Egypt said to the Hebrew midwives, whose names were Shiphrah and Puah, "When you are helping the Hebrew women during childbirth on the delivery stool, if you see that the baby is a boy, kill him; but if it is a girl, let her live." The midwives, however, feared God and did not do what the king of Egypt had told them to do; they let the boys live. Then the king of

Egypt summoned the midwives and asked them,
"Why have you done this? Why have you let
the boys live?"
The midwives answered Pharaoh, "Hebrew women
are not like Egyptian women; they are vigorous
and give birth before the midwives arrive."
So God was kind to the midwives and the people
increased and became even more numerous.
And because the midwives feared God, he gave
them families of their own.

—EXODUS 1:8–21 (NIV)

Ordinary Women of the BIBLE
✦

Ordinary Women of the BIBLE

THE
LIFE GIVER
SHIPHRAH'S STORY

CONNILYN COSSETTE

Ordinary Women of the BIBLE

THE
LIFE GIVER
SHIPHRAH'S STORY

Dedication

To Valerie, who honored the Life Giver
in her willingness to put my life
above her own and in doing so
gifted me all the beautiful moments
since that courageous decision.

PROLOGUE

Even whispers seemed too loud tonight. The whimper of a babe was quickly hushed by a mother who rocked the child, humming deep in her chest as the night grew darker outside, as the inhabitants of the little home and their guests waited. Waited. Waited.

The meal had been eaten. The bitterness of herbs still coated their tongues, and the smell of the charred remains remained heavy in the ash-laden air. But although their bellies were full of roast lamb and hastily prepared bread, the strangeness of the evening, with its blood-coated doorways and odd commands from a prince-turned-prophet, had made even the youngest of the children uneasy. As they should be.

"Why must I wear my sandals, *Imma*?" asked one girl, her wispy brows furrowed as she tugged at the new papyrus cord between her toes with a grimace.

"Hush," said her mother, smoothing a gentle palm over her child's busy hands to still them. "It is what we were told to do tonight."

"But why is tonight different than other nights?" she asked.

Her mother lifted her eyes and met those of her own mother beside her, helpless to explain to her child something she did not understand herself. The past few months of turmoil had been both frightening and hopeful, inexplicable and yet long awaited.

Blood. Frogs. Lice. Flies. Livestock deaths. Boils. Hail and fire. Locusts. Three days of night. All of it had been terrifying and yet in His divine mercy, El Shaddai had laid a palm over His people, giving them a reprieve from many of the plagues that struck their masters. But tonight…tonight something dark hung in the air. Something far blacker and weightier than the darkness that had suffocated the land and shown the Egyptians that even their exalted god of the sun had no power.

"Tonight, my little rabbit," said the grandmother, answering for her daughter as she touched the girl's lightly freckled nose with a gentle finger, "is the end of this story, and the beginning of a new one."

"Which story?" asked the girl, leaning forward, her ebony eyes gleaming with anticipation for a story from the lips of her *savta*.

"Oh, one that began so very long ago. So far back that perhaps I do not even remember the beginning," she said, her lips curling into a coy smile as she tapped her chin.

"But you must!" said the girl, sliding from her mother's lap to her grandmother's. Her small hands gripped the woman's tunic, and she seemed to have forgotten the discomfort of her new sandals. "Please, Savta, I want to hear the story. What is it about?"

"Well," said Savta, "it is about you."

"Me?" repeated the girl, those dark eyes widening in disbelief. "How could a story so old be about me?"

"But it is," said her savta. "And also you"—she pointed to the girl's older sister nearby—"and you"—she gestured to one of her cousins—"and all of you." She spread her hands wide as she met the gaze of each child in the room, ever so skillfully ensnaring them, drawing them into the tale before she even began. She was widely known for her skill at weaving words into stories, accompanied by expressive voices and gestures that not only kept the children enthralled but somehow stitched together such a vivid tapestry of words that they were rarely forgotten.

Indeed, the little girl's mother already knew which story would be told tonight. It was one she had heard many times over, one she could practically recite alongside her mother and one that she'd heard from the lips of her own savta many years before. And now it was time for her own daughter to learn the tale she would one day pass to her own granddaughter.

"There is a land called Midian, far, far away. Over desert sands and tall mountains and across a mighty stretch of water," said Savta. "And it was in this place of burning sun and fickle rains that a babe was born. Not in a home like this one, with mud-brick walls and a sturdy roof, but in a tent that shivered beneath a full moon as sandy winds tugged at its moorings with hot, insistent hands."

She paused, giving the children a few moments to follow her into the desert within their own minds. Already they were leaning forward, eyes fixed on their savta, the discomfort of sandals strapped on their feet and the eerie silence outside the little house overshadowed by the gently rising tone and soothing cadence of their grandmother's familiar voice.

"But the child was born too silent, too still, and the midwife's heart sank as she held the tiny girl in her capable hands, hands that had guided hundreds of babes into the world and seen almost as many delivered without the thrum of life within their chests."

"No," whispered one of the children, one who was well acquainted with the sorrow of losing a sibling at birth.

Savta nodded sadly. "As all midwives know, death is ever hovering at the door as a mother labors, and only the Eternal One knows which babe will be spared and which taken. But as the midwife took in the tiny features of the little one cradled in her hands, dreading the moment she would have to tell its mother—her own daughter—of its passing, something deep inside told her that this was not the end, that this child would one day stand against the flow of a mighty river and not be moved. She knew that voice. She'd heard it speak to her before during particularly difficult births and trusted it, so she took the clean cloth that had been over her shoulder and began to rub the little one's body vigorously, whispering encouragement and willing the tiny lips to part and draw breath."

"Did they?" asked the freckle-nosed girl.

"They did," said her savta with a smile, and the children cheered the good news. "A great cry burst from her mouth and the midwife placed her upon her mother's breast with eyes full of tears and the knowledge that the Eternal One had a special purpose for her. But she also knew that it was not the end of this child's sufferings, not by any stretch of the imagination."

"What happened to her?" asked one of the boys, around the thumb he'd jammed in his mouth while his father and uncles had painted the blood around the doorposts of the house and had not removed since.

"For many years the midwife thought she might have been wrong, had perhaps misheard the voice that had whispered in her soul. But even so, she told the little girl the story of her birth time and again, reminding her granddaughter that death had hovered outside the door that night but that she had been spared for a reason. And then"—she paused again, meeting each child's gaze with deliberate intensity—"in the eleventh year of the girl's life, the river overflowed its banks, winding its way across the sands and tall mountains, over the mighty stretch of water, and carried her away."

Gasps of shock rippled around the room as the savta waited, knowing that no longer were the children worried about the death that hovered at their own door tonight, but were now completely engrossed in the tale.

"But fear not," she said, with a sly grin that slowly stretched across her face as she took in the aghast expressions of her grandchildren, "that is not the end of her story, but only the beginning...."

CHAPTER ONE

The goat butted his horned head against Shiphrah, nudging her leg with a chortle and a grunt. She laughed at the plea in his luminous eyes and reached to scratch beneath his shaggy chin.

"You'd like some too?" she asked as she leaned over the edge of the spring-fed well to scoop out another dipper's worth of cool water. At least twice a year her tribe journeyed here when the rains were scarce, settling their herds and tents and families among the barren beauty and thanking the gods for providing this ancient source of life, as well as for the hands that had long ago dug deep into the earth to draw it to the surface.

Again, the goat bleated at her, insistent she not withhold another drop, so she tipped a small measure of water into a nearby trough. Then, while the little brown goat was lapping up the refreshment, she untied her own belt and looped it around his neck. Although she'd been sent by her mother for clean water, she could not just leave the animal here. He was branded on the ear with the symbol of her tribe and it was obvious he'd strayed from one of their herd.

Knowing that her mother and her grandmother would be wondering what had taken so long to complete her task, she hefted the jug of water to her hip and tugged at the belt, encouraging the goat to follow along with gentle tones and promising more water if he obeyed. She breathed a sigh of relief when he complied and ambled along behind her without so much as a bleat.

Shiphrah followed the familiar path back to the campsite, easily picking out her destination among the similar black and brown tents by the strangled sounds of pain within. After tying the goat to the well-secured tent peg so one of the men would see him upon their return later this evening, she thanked him with one more helping of water. Then she ducked in through the flap just as another loud moan emanated from the woman laboring under the expert supervision of Huldah, her mother, and Tula, her grandmother.

The story of her own birth was as familiar as tales of her ancestors Abraham and Keturah, and Tula had held nothing back in the telling. And every time her grandmother spoke of the soul-deep whisper of a mighty river, Shiphrah was glad that for the most part, this desert offered up nothing more than miserly streams and a few spring-fed oases. Only when a storm swept through did the wadis fill with crashing rivers of muddy water, a danger to man and beast alike that her people worked hard to avoid. How Tula could even entertain the idea that Shiphrah's small body could withstand such a powerful force was quite beyond her comprehension, and every time dark clouds gathered in the sky, Shiphrah prayed that Tula's prophecy was wrong.

"Where have you been?" asked her mother. The other women in the tent, relatives of the woman giving birth, turned to take in her response with raised brows.

"Forgive me, Imma," said Shiphrah, trying to ignore the stares as she placed the jug of water on the ground near her mother, who looked nearly as exhausted as the birthing woman herself. "I found one of the goats wandering about near the well and brought him back with me."

Too caught up in her task, Shiphrah's mother hummed a response as she continued rubbing circles on the back of the laboring mother, Lomah, whose face was a mess of sweat and tears. This was Lomah's first child and since she was barely more than a girl herself, narrow-hipped and the child of a woman who had herself died in childbirth, fear hung heavy in the tent. She'd been laboring heavily all night and most of the morning, and it seemed that nothing much had changed in the time Shiphrah had been at the well.

Each moan and cry seemed to soak into Shiphrah's blood, causing a knot of tears to well up at the base of her throat. But to quell the urgent emotion, she focused on each part of the process, fascinated by the ever-calm demeanors of her mother and Tula, the most skilled midwives among their clan—and indeed among many of the clans who called these desert hills and valleys home. Tula had been tending to the needs of pregnant mothers since her own mother invited her to witness a birth nearly thirty years before, and Huldah had been doing the same since she was a girl herself. And one day, Shiphrah would follow in the well-trod footsteps of these women she admired so much. In the meantime she would soak up every bit of knowledge and make herself invaluable.

Knowing her role well, Shiphrah took over for her mother, pressing on the places that might give the most relief to Lomah while Tula checked the position of the infant in the womb and her mother tended to Lomah's other needs. Tula's graying brows furrowed, concern written in the deep lines around her pursed mouth.

"Huldah," said Tula, "we must turn her. The shoulders are still lodged."

Shiphrah's heart pounded at the declaration as her mother nodded in agreement. In the past two years, she'd heard those words a number of times and knew how dangerous they were. No wonder Lomah had been laboring so long—such a condition could not only snuff out the life of the baby but the mother as well.

As she'd learned by watching these two learned midwives maintain their calm through the most harrowing of circumstances, Shiphrah smiled at Lomah while she helped her turn onto her hands and knees and brushed back her sweat-soaked hair, telling the young woman that it should not be much longer before she was holding her little one in her arms. She diligently watched her mother and grandmother work together to shift the babe, feeling a sense of rightness settle into the center of her bones and a whisper of something that told her that this was indeed what she was born to do.

But a few hours later, when Shiphrah was given the grim task of washing the lifeless child's body and wrapping him in the clean cloths that should have been his warm swaddle and as Lomah's gut-wrenching cries pierced her chest with sorrow, she wondered whether that gentle whisper had been nothing but a lie after all.

CHAPTER TWO

Reuel giggled from his perch on her back, tugging at Shiphrah's thick braids as if they were a camel's reins. Her smallest cousin had refused to be left behind this morning when the women went out to wash clothes, so she'd offered to carry him down the rocky path. Even though the stream they were heading for was far too bitter to drink from, the children still found pleasure in splashing about in the cool water as the women scrubbed and gossiped and harsh sunlight beat down on their heads.

She jostled the boy, tickling his bare toes and reveling in his laughter as she carefully navigated her way down the steep incline. His mother, Sorah—the wife of Berak, Shiphrah's uncle and the chief of the tribe—had thanked her many times for offering to watch the energetic boy, who was forever slipping off and hiding. After these past three days of mourning Lomah's babe, Reuel's unfettered joy did much to soothe the ache, and Shiphrah was grateful for the distraction.

Before Shiphrah even reached the side of the stream, Reuel was begging to be set down, desperate to join the other children who were already knee-deep in the water, splashing each other and shrieking with glee.

"Did Berak invite them to stay another night?" her mother asked Sorah, as Shiphrah set a wiggling Reuel down so he could dart off to add his own splashes to the game. Without even hearing the rest of their conversation, Shiphrah knew exactly who they were speaking of. A group of Moabite traders had arrived in camp two days before and, as tradition dictated, had been welcomed in and given food and shelter without reservation.

"He did, but they declined," said Sorah, making Shiphrah nearly sigh with relief. The traders had accepted her clan's hospitality with seeming gratitude and even gifted Berak a sack full of beads they claimed came all the way from an island across the Great Sea, but something about them had made Shiphrah deeply uneasy.

Perhaps it was only her imagination, but their eyes seemed to linger far too long on the women of her clan—especially Reuel's two eldest sisters, Sheera and Marena, who were both betrothed to sons of chiefs from neighboring tribes and were known far and wide for their beauty. The two girls were here today as well, kneeling alongside the other women, scrubbing their own clothing. Shiphrah wondered if they too had noticed the attention they'd attracted from the traders.

"I'm glad to hear it," said one of the other women. "We are already short on supplies, and their horses ate more than their share of grain."

Grain that Shiphrah knew was already a dwindling resource after a long season of wandering. But she'd overheard her father and Uncle Berak discussing the surprising expansion of the herds in the past month, as if the drought had caused the goats and sheep to multiply instead of shriveling up, so perhaps next time traders came through their camp there would be plenty of grain both for her own people and to share with travelers.

"How fares Lomah?" asked Sorah. "Has she eaten yet?"

"No," said Shiphrah's mother. "She refuses."

Sorah clucked her tongue. "Poor girl. She was not ready for a child yet, as I told her husband months ago. It is fortunate she was not lost as well after what happened to her mother."

The women murmured in agreement as they continued their rhythmic scrubbing, and the children were blissfully unaware of the heavy subject as they continued their bright-toned calls and splashing about.

"But you should have seen Shiphrah that day," said her mother, her face a mask of pride. "Throughout the girl's labor, Shiphrah kept calm, soothing her fear, anticipating her every need, and tending to the dead infant without hesitation."

The words brought back the face of the lifeless child, so tiny and well-formed, with minuscule little fingers and toes and a blue-lipped mouth that would never take a breath. Shiphrah had wrapped him in linen and handed him to his grief-stricken father before she took herself off into the outer reaches of camp and cried in the brush. "I have no doubt that under Tula's and my tutelage, she will be a great midwife someday. She was born with midwifery in her blood."

Her mother's confidence caused a swell of pride to rise up, as did the nods of the other women who seemed to agree with her assessment.

The conversation veered away from Lomah's lost child and Shiphrah's future as a midwife and into an animated discussion about the upcoming wedding celebrations of Sheera and Marena.

Although she was excited at the prospect of a gathering between friendly tribes and the new connections that would be made because of the marriages, Shiphrah's attention was drawn away from the women's chatter by the sight of a mountain nearby. The summit was barely visible from this angle, obscured as it was by other peaks, but it was one that she'd heard about for many years and which never ceased to be a source of imagination.

The mountain of El Shaddai, some called it, while others dismissed the mysterious tales of strange rumblings and inexplicable lights upon its slopes as nothing more than fancy. Or they attributed the mysteries to some of the other gods her people revered. But whenever Shiphrah saw the jagged peak that jutted high above the valley, she never failed to think of her forefather Abraham and the mountain he climbed with his son, carrying a sharp knife in his pack and grief in his heart.

The stories passed down by word of mouth varied with the telling, some saying Abraham was spared the act of killing his beloved son by the provision of a ram by El Shaddai Himself. Others said that his willingness to even bind Isaac to an altar proved that Ishmael was the true honored son. And even more popular among Shiphrah's own people was the opinion that the blessings of both Sarah's and Hagar's offspring had been replaced by Keturah's sons many years later, especially since the descendants of Isaac remained enslaved in Egypt to this day, proving their fall from favor with the Most High. But no matter what tradition might be the true one, or none at all, Shiphrah could not help but remember the story whenever they encamped in this particular area. Tula claimed that El Shaddai was the highest among the other gods, but even if the story of Abraham and his son was a fascinating one, Shiphrah could not see the difference between El Shaddai and the other household gods that graced her family's altar.

A squeal from one of the children jerked Shiphrah's attention away from the mysterious summit and back to the stream. The game of splashing and hiding behind rocks had turned into a wrestling match between two of her boy cousins and the rest goading them on with calls and cheers. But where was Reuel? Shiphrah's eyes traveled over the group of children, but her youngest cousin was not with them. With her heart pounding in her throat, she scanned the surface of the water, fearing that he'd fallen down, but then a flicker of movement off to her right caught her eye.

There he was! The slippery little lizard, always intent on exploring, had snuck away and was heading toward a wadi with a large stick in his hand. "Reuel has taken off again," she said to Sorah, before dropping the tunic she'd been scrubbing to follow after the boy, knowing her legs would eat up the distance far faster than his short ones. She would have to insist that he stay by her side after this, since Sorah had entrusted him to her keeping today.

When the distance between herself and the boy was cut in half, he turned to look over his shoulder and laughed, knowing she was pursing him, and then darted off behind one of the large boulders that filled this wadi. It was fortunate that this day was a cloudless one since any chance of rain in the sky might mean a flash flood in one of these narrow canyons.

And yet, without a hint of a storm anywhere, suddenly the sound of thunder arose at Shiphrah's back—a pounding rhythm that made all the hair on her neck stand on end. She halted in her tracks to swivel around and take another look at the sky. Just as she'd noticed before, there was nothing but an endless expanse of unbroken blue overhead.

But then the screams began.

Her stomach lurched painfully as she realized that it had not been the thunder of a storm she'd heard but the relentless beat of horse hooves on the ground. Someone had overcome the women and children gathered by the stream that was no longer in her sight. Someone was causing them to cry out in horror and agony.

With every bone in her body rattling, Shiphrah stood in horrified paralysis. Should she run back and try to help? Or run for her father and uncles back at the camp? But then she remembered that little Reuel was still off by himself and she turned to seek him out. At least she should ensure he was secure before she made any decision.

With her throat on fire and her stomach threatening to spill on the ground, Shiphrah jogged toward the place she'd last seen the boy. To her profound relief, she caught sight of his black curls behind a bush.

"Reuel," she whispered loudly, praying that somehow he would sense the urgency in her tear-glutted voice. "Reuel, stay where you are. Do not move."

She saw him shift, pulling the weeds apart so he could peer at her with curiosity. But just as she opened her mouth to repeat her commands, a shout rang out.

"It's no use trying to run, girl," said a man at her back. "You can't outrun me, and it will only go worse for you if you try."

Shaking so badly that her teeth clattered together, Shiphrah slowly turned around to find one of the traders who had sat at her father's table just last night. The man who had broken bread with their clan in supposed peace now stood with a large knife in his hand, one that Shiphrah could see was edged with blood. Whose? Her mother's blood? Sorah's? Or one of the other loved ones she'd just been laughing with at the stream? A cousin? At least her own siblings were married and gone from their tent so she knew her three older sisters were safe. But there was not one person in her clan who she did not know and love, and these evil men had already harmed at least one of them, if not many.

Her knees wobbled and the man's visage wavered as tears veiled her eyes.

"Come now," said the man, gesturing with his knife as his black eyes seemed to pierce right through her. "This can be easy or it can be difficult, but you are coming with us."

With them? The statement made little sense in her tortured mind until she realized that these men must be no ordinary traders, hawking beads and other wares to the myriad tribes that inhabited this area, but men who traded the lives of others for silver. The thought was horrifying but at the same time gave her a small amount of relief—for if they meant to trap and enslave her and the others, then surely they wouldn't kill them, would they? Perhaps together they might escape these horrors.

But again she remembered Reuel and went rigid. She had to keep the man's attention off the bushes behind her or the boy too would be trapped and enslaved, perhaps worse if they deemed him a hindrance. If there was any way she could save him from such a fate, she would do so.

The sight of the mountain peak over the trader's shoulder caught her attention, jagged against the bright blue sky and seeming to look upon this awful scene with majestic, yet detached, regard. Was it truly a place where the feet of El Shaddai touched the earth, as Tula insisted? And if so, would the God who spoke to Abraham deign to stretch His ears from such a height to hear the prayer of one insignificant girl? It was at least worth a try.

Please, Holy One, great provider who offered Abraham a way to save his son. If You are higher than the other gods as Tula says, then hide little Reuel from the evil eyes of this trader. If so, I will worship You alone.

There was no rumblings from the summit, no flashes of light or anything to tell her that her pitiful prayer had been heard, but in that moment she remembered the words Tula had spoken over her for so many years: "*She will stand against the flow of the mighty river and will not be moved."* Yet there was nothing she could do in this moment but submit for the sake of her little cousin, who thankfully had not made a sound as she faced the trader. He had remained hidden in the brush. She could only hope that he would be found quickly or find his own way back to camp.

So instead of turning around and running, as everything inside her was screaming to do, she slowly walked toward the man, keeping her eyes on his grisly knife as she did so, and let the river carry her away.

CHAPTER THREE

Eight Years Later

She had been here before. A market bartering in human flesh—prying eyes and greedy hands grasping at her arms, poking her ribs, leering eyes sampling the product before the sale. Shiphrah wrapped one arm around her middle to hold herself together. A deep shiver spiraled up from her core, and the little girl inside her wanted to scream, to chastise the men with their lustful glances.

She had been eleven the first time she was sold, with only a child's understanding of the dangers and still in shock from being stolen from her home and family and being forced to march day after endless day to Egypt. Had she not been sold to a good master back then, a master like Ankare, who sought to purchase her for his young daughter, her innocence would have been part of the transaction.

But she was no longer eleven. And her new master would not be purchasing her as a handmaid and companion for a spoiled little girl. All the servants from Master Ankare's household waited in the courtyard of his beautiful white villa and, one by one, were sold to the highest bidder. Shiphrah's master had lost everything when his crops failed during the last season of drought. Now his servants' bodies were meager payment toward his massive debts. No care was given to the intentions of the customer whose *deben* crossed the table.

One buyer grasped Shiphrah by the jaw and jerked her face back and forth, his dark eyes glittering with anticipation. Her stomach soured. He pushed his lips out, contemplation in the tilt of his head. She tried to look everywhere but at the weeping sore on the corner of his mouth.

Peti, a housemaid, stood next to her, her hand grasping Shiphrah's free one, as if her presence alone kept Peti from bolting. The man with the ugly sore on his lip caught sight of her, drawn, no doubt, by her smooth skin, shapely hips, and copper eyes. He released Shiphrah's face with a smirk and told the scribe that Peti was his choice. The rush of relief in Shiphrah that her unremarkable straight black hair and murky-brown eyes drew little attention was immediately followed with crushing guilt.

How could she wish such a thing on anyone else? Let alone Peti, who'd never been anything but kind to her?

Shiphrah squeezed the young maid's hand one more time, silently pleading with El Shaddai for mercy on the poor girl, even if she'd never heard of the God of the Mountain. Her heart ached as Peti was led away by her new master, tears streaming down her cheeks and her shoulders bowed with sorrow. Yet for as despondent as she was for Peti, she knew that soon she too would be led away to a life of misery and humiliation.

Out of twenty or more servants, only half remained now, but buyers filled the courtyard, haggling the best price over the strongest young men. The guards fetched the most, and two customers worked to outbid each other over three haggard kitchen slaves packaged together with a few items of furniture.

An older man approached Shiphrah with a limp. "How old are you, girl?"

She chanced a glance through her lashes, even as her body trembled. He did not seem to be regarding her with the same lecherous eye as many of the others, but that meant little. A man was a man and she was nothing but a slave.

"Nineteen, Master," she replied, her voice little more than a whisper.

He leaned in closer to hear her. "Nineteen?"

She nodded.

"Your name?" He focused on her lips as she spoke like it was necessary to understand whatever she might say.

"Shiphrah."

He lifted a silvered brow, cupping his hand around his ear as if to catch her words but still watching her mouth, confirming her guess that his hearing was weak. "What skills do you have?"

After clearing her throat, she lifted her voice to list the duties she'd performed as a handservant to a young mistress: bathing, cosmetics, grooming, along with other menial duties that had been assigned to her over the past few years.

The older man smiled, shocking her. "You'll have little need for those skills in our home. It is only myself and my wife now, our daughters long married off. But you seem to be a strong girl. Able to manage running a small household."

This man did not seem to be as wealthy as the others whose bodies were bathed in gold, feathers splayed as they strutted about the courtyard.

As sweat trickled down the curve of her back, she stood blinking at him, confused by his gentle tone and calm manner.

Was this the answer to her prayers? Perhaps El Shaddai had sent this very man to rescue her from the rest of the buyers that seemed more intent on abusing her body than utilizing her experience as a handmaid. Her spirits lifted higher, and she allowed herself a ghost of a smile and a nod at the man when he informed her that he would tell the scribe Shiphrah was his choice.

He hobbled off toward the bidding table, as she thanked the only God she had worshipped since the day she'd been snatched by the stream, out of gratitude for the trader never seeing Reuel hiding in the brush. She thought of the little one often, praying that as He had protected him then, El Shaddai had returned him safety to Berak's tent that day.

Her uncle had already lost his daughters and his wife, and she hated to think of Berak losing his only son as well. Sorah had died trying to fight off the men whose entire goal for visiting their tribe had been to determine which of them were the easiest to snatch away and who would fetch the highest price. Unfortunately, her daughters, Sheera and Marena, had been the answer to that question, and the two beautiful girls had been sold to rival tribes before the rest of them had even reached Egypt. But through it all, being sold to Ankare, watching her distraught cousins and friends being bartered over and led away for the last time, she clung to the promise she'd made to the God of the Mountain. That vow was all she had left.

As she watched the older man talk to the scribe and point to her, she soared on eagle's wings. What would her new mistress be like? An older woman, perhaps as kind as her husband? She would most likely be more even-tempered than Mistress Aneksi, who at times acted the pampered child and other times sulked in silence for days. Even though a giant chasm of wealth and expectation had lain between the two girls, they were similar in age and had formed a friendship of sorts. Being separated from Aneksi, especially when she did not know what would happen to her young mistress with the loss of her father's fortune, weighed heavily on Shiphrah's heart and she prayed that somehow the girl would not suffer too greatly.

Caught up in her musings, she startled when another man stood in front of her, his look appraising and his thick brows furrowed in contemplation. He was barrel chested with a hard set to his jaw and stood at least a head taller than Shiphrah. He wore his wealth in thick gold bands around his massive arms and a richly jeweled *usekh* around his neck.

"Come with me," he said and spun around, his linen kilt flapping out in his haste. Shiphrah followed him, thinking that he was leading her to the older man, but as they crossed the courtyard, she looked back. The kind man now had his back turned and was speaking with another maid, and Shiphrah was being led away by this immense and intimidating rich man.

No...El Shaddai, help me! This is wrong! she thought, even as she wondered whether she'd been wrong to place her trust in a God she could not see or hear. For why did the scribe not notice the mistake? Perhaps the God who lived atop the mountain had no jurisdiction over Egypt. Perhaps she was truly alone and without hope.

Even though her obedient feet followed, fear and instinct warred inside her, insisting that she turn around, point out the error, and run back to the older man, plead with him to take her to serve his elderly wife.

But what could she do? She was only a slave. Only a thing to be bought and sold. Accusations against this wealthy man would only see her strapped to a whipping post, or worse. She had witnessed what happened to those who stood against injustice, heard the screams of her mother, Sorah, and the other women who fought so valiantly against the traders who stole their children and left them by the stream with their lifeblood staining the sand red.

With grief burning her throat, she bowed her head, attempted to block out the voices of the past, and followed her new master to someone else's fate.

CHAPTER FOUR

The sight was like nothing she had ever seen. As the boat rounded the final bend in the Nile after almost an entire day of travel southward, the city rose up before her like a mighty heron beside the river, drawing her eyes upward to the fantastical sight. A multitude of papyrus boats jostled for position among the larger trading vessels, shouts and curses echoing across the water as everyone vied for precious space among the glutted masses.

The palace filled the horizon with splendor, its white walls and towering obelisks dazzling her eyes. New buildings were being raised near the palace, with crews of half-naked slaves streaming over the worksites like ants disturbed from their hill. The sheer number of workers needed to heft the huge stones and chisel the intricate carvings was astounding. Pharaoh had created a great city on the backs of men such as these, both slave and free working for his pleasure while the people paid hefty taxes to the king to fund such extravagant building campaigns.

After disembarking the boat, Sennofre, Shiphrah's new master, led her and the two other slaves he'd bought at the auction through town, the three of them carrying items he had acquired at the same time he'd purchased them.

One slave carried a large rolled-up rug over his shoulder, the other, a beautiful water clock that Shiphrah had passed in the front vestibule of Ankare's home every day of the past eight years. Shiphrah carried two brilliant papyrus wall hangings painted by a master artist, each costing *twice* the price Sennofre had paid for her.

The villa Sennofre led them to was similar in size to Ankare's residence but was closer to the center of the city, denoting her new master's higher status. From the regal bearing with which he moved and the richness of his garments and jewelry, she guessed he might even be a regular visitor to the court of Pharaoh himself. She wondered why he'd not sent a steward to select new slaves for his household and instead had purchased her and the two men in person.

After leaving both the two slaves and all of their burdens in the care of a tall, dark-skinned manservant named Thadeo, Sennofre ordered Shiphrah to follow him to her new mistress's quarters. Shiphrah followed his swift steps down the corridor, turning her eyes from the leering idols that stood at attention on small tables every few feet. A few of the forms she recognized from her service in Ankare's home and from the small sanctuary that stood in his courtyard, but two of the idols—a moon god and a god of storms—she remembered from the small altar in her family's tent, even if those her mother and father owned were crude wooden carvings and not overlaid with gold and electrum. Somehow though, after so many years of praying to only El Shaddai, their fixed stares made her feel uneasy and she dropped her eyes to the cool white stone beneath her bare feet as she followed her master.

Sennofre entered a room without knocking and was immediately swallowed in the darkness of the doorway. Shiphrah had no choice but to follow him into the pitch black.

"Berenice, my love. Are you awake?" His gentle tones startled her almost as much as the darkness of the room. A stifled murmur and a rustle of cloth was the only answer.

Somehow finding his way across the room, Sennofre opened the shutters and, with the dim orange light from the waning sunset, struck a flint to light an oil lamp sitting on a low table nearby. The flame sputtered and smoked for a moment before flaring to life. The woman on the bed covered her eyes and moaned, clearly disturbed by the flickering intrusion.

"Leave me alone."

The master ignored her weak demand. "This is your new body servant."

"I don't want a new body servant. Where is Reshida?"

Master Sennofre paused, and Shiphrah sensed he was weighing his words. "I sent her away."

The woman rolled over. Her pale, gaunt face made her black brows stand out like charcoal slashes across her forehead. Her eyes were deep black pools in sunken sockets and a painful-looking red rash bracketed her mouth. "Why?"

Master Sennofre did not respond, but a flicker of frustration crossed his features. "Because she did not obey my commands. She let you talk her into rising from your bed. And I

22

almost lost—" He paused, his jaw seeming to grind as he composed himself. "You know what the physician told you, Berenice. You must remain abed or you will not survive."

The woman moaned and rolled over again, turning her back to them.

As the master whisked a hand through his thick, short hair, which was sprinkled with gray, pain flashed across his face but was immediately replaced by swift anger. "Reshida has been dealt with. The wretch should not have refused her orders."

Shiphrah's master then turned to Shiphrah, his face a storm of fear and anger. "You will care for my wife, tend to her every need, but you will not let her move from that bed. Do you hear me?" He pointed his finger a feather's breadth from her face, spittle forming at the corners of his lips. Startled into meeting his gaze, Shiphrah noted that his eyes were bloodshot, as if from lack of sleep. With every bone in her body trembling, she nodded, having no desire to meet the same end as the slave who'd ignored his directives.

Master Sennofre turned and strode from the room, taking with him any further explanation of this peculiar situation. When the door closed behind him, Berenice groaned but remained with her face toward the back wall.

Unsure how to approach her mistress or ask any of the questions for which she would surely need answers, Shiphrah stood paralyzed on the cool tiles. Bereft of any idea how to proceed, she beseeched El Shaddai to give her some sort of guidance, hoping that she'd not misplaced her devotion to him after all.

Calmed by her silent prayers, she gathered the courage to speak. "Mistress. How may I help you?"

The woman did not answer, remaining still as stone on her bed, but Shiphrah sensed she was not sleeping and instead was simply ignoring the slave her husband had purchased against her will.

Shiphrah shifted her weight, bracing herself for a long wait. The room looked to be clean and tidy, so she was helpless to do anything else until her new mistress said something. As she waited, the shadows lengthened at an extreme angle across the floor until they melded with those already hiding in the corners as the last of the light faded away. A cool breeze whispered through the open window, spreading gooseflesh along her arms as she wondered whether she'd be forced to stand here all night.

The room was sparse in comparison to Aneksi's room—a bed, a low vanity table, a few baskets and wooden chests against the wall. But it was the multitude of idols that set this room apart. Every available surface was covered with them.

Isis, Hathor, Khonsu, and a multitude of foreign gods crowded the top of the vanity, the lids of chests, and vied for space on the tables. All were gods to which healing was attributed. Among them the ugly Bes made a repeated appearance, his leering features and lolling tongue credited with chasing away evil spirits. To take her mind off the distinct impression that his aggressive stance was meant for her, and assuming that Berenice had indeed fallen asleep, she looked for a place to sit down and rest her complaining legs.

Rolled up in the corner was a small bundle that she assumed would be her bed—all that was left of the unfortunate Reshida.

"Water." Her mistress's voice rasped so quietly Shiphrah considered whether it might be her imagination, but even so, she scurried to the table by the door where a pitcher stood guard.

Berenice turned on her bed to watch Shiphrah as she poured the water into a silver cup. "What is your name?" she demanded, but the challenge fell flat in her weak voice.

"Shiphrah, Mistress."

"Where did you come from?"

"Iunu, Mistress. Your husband purchased me from a household auction."

"No. Before that. Where were you born?"

In all the years she'd served in Ankare's home, no one had ever asked Shiphrah about her origins, not even Aneksi. The memories lay deep within her heart, a treasure laced with poison. But at Berenice's question, the lock rattled.

Could she speak of her home without grief seeping through the cracks? She hesitated, trying not to look at her mistress directly but afraid to look anywhere else. She feared insulting the woman by searching the face that resembled a skeleton more than a woman. But something in Berenice's expression, either desperation or perhaps just open curiosity, spurred Shiphrah to answer.

"I am from the east, Mistress. The land of Midian."

Berenice peered at her. "A prisoner of war?"

Shiphrah shook her head. "No, Mistress. I, along with a number of my cousins and other children from my tribe, were stolen by slavers and taken to Iunu."

Her mistress studied her face, her cracked lips pursed as she seemed to be weighing her next words. "I have lost three handmaids in the past few months. Two ran away after refusing to touch me, fearing the curse. And the last, as you heard, disobeyed the physician's orders by allowing me to stand and cross the room a few times."

Berenice's deep brown eyes pinned Shiphrah in place. "Help me sit up."

Shiphrah held in a gasp of confusion but could not restrain the flare of her eyes at the command, which seemed in direct opposition to what Sennofre had just told her.

"I am only barred from standing," said her mistress at Shiphrah's hesitation. "The physician said I must stay in bed until my time is complete. I can lift my torso and be propped with pillows. As if it matters anyway…"

Although she feared Sennofre might barge into the room at any moment and berate her or worse, Shiphrah sensed that what Berenice said was true. So with as much care as possible, she slipped her hands around her mistress's bony arms to give her leverage. The woman's skin was like ice and her body racked with shivers. Shiphrah flicked a glance at the brazier in the corner, wondering why it had not been lit.

Gingerly and with evident pain on her face, Berenice unwrapped her billowing dress from her body and let the cloth fall to the bed, leaving her entirely naked.

Shiphrah clamped her lips against the loud gasp that sprang up, but it came out in a strangled moan in the back of her throat.

There were a number of open sores and angry pustules on the woman's torso and arms that delivered sharp pangs of compassion in Shiphrah's chest, but it was the swell in Berenice's abdomen that was the most shocking. Not only must she be in agony over the lesions on her body and the scaly and wounded skin that ran down her legs, but she looked to be a number of months pregnant as well.

Shiphrah longed to ask questions, but she could no more open her mouth without her mistress's permission than she could unlock the chains that bound her to the woman. Although Berenice's wounds were grotesque, seeping with gore, and the stench of rot tanged against her nose, Shiphrah felt no disgust. Only pity.

The set of her mistress's chin challenged Shiphrah to wince, gag, or run out of the room. But instead, Shiphrah kept her posture still and her face blank, determined to not further the woman's distress by reacting with horror. Berenice was hurting, and both she and her babe deserved compassion. The memory of Shiphrah's mother telling the other woman of how well she'd tended to Lomah and her stillborn child welled up, but it had been a long time since she'd assisted Tula and her mother. She'd had so much left to learn back then, only just having begun absorbing their many years of knowledge. How could she possibly do this woman justice? And why would Sennofre choose *her* to do so?

Even as a hundred more questions filled her mind, spiraling into a storm of panic and doubt, a phantom whisper breezed through her mind: *This is why you are here.*

Blinking rapidly, Shiphrah looked around the room, wondering if perhaps she'd simply imagined the words. Tula had spoken of hearing such things, of deep impressions within her soul that gave insight that could not be explained, but Shiphrah herself had never experienced such a thing. But remembering that she'd asked El Shaddai for guidance, she wondered whether this *was* the answer she'd been pleading for. Could He have brought her here, not only to this home, but to Egypt for Berenice's sake? Immediately, Shiphrah was flooded with a deep sense of peace and calm that was as much a confirmation as if the Voice had spoken aloud.

Her skin prickling, she bowed her head in submission.

Berenice took it as a response to herself. "The first girl wouldn't even touch me—she covered her nose and said the gods had cursed me. She said my babe would be an abomination, if it even survives." Her voice was vacant. "I've already lost four others, anyway, so there is little hope this one will take breath."

The sight of Lomah's still infant filled Shiphrah's mind. Berenice had already lost four little ones in such a way? No wonder Sennofre was so fearful for her and the physician so adamant she remain abed. As weak as she appeared and with her skin so ravaged, it was clear that it was not only the child's life that was at stake.

Determined to help the woman who seemed resigned to such a sad fate, Shiphrah stepped forward to tuck a few more pillows behind her mistress's back, chancing her wrath by speaking out of turn. "I will light the brazier. You are chilled."

Curiosity sparked in Berenice's eyes at Shiphrah's lack of overt reaction to the sight of her sores, but she did not reprimand her audacity, instead allowing Shiphrah to wrap the filmy gown back around her body, tie the belt loosely above her swollen belly, and replace the bedclothes with gentle hands.

"Are you hungry, Mistress?" Shiphrah asked.

Berenice's cracked lips thinned. "I have not been hungry for weeks. Just the thought of food... But I am so thirsty. Bring me more water and fetch more honeyed wine so I can sleep."

Shiphrah winced. The woman must eat. Her bones jutted out everywhere, the sharp ridges like limestone thrusting up out of the desert sands. It could not be healthy for either her or the baby to go without sustenance. She remembered Tula insisting that the mothers in her care were fed extra portions of hearty fare.

"Perhaps some broth to begin with? That might help with the thirst as well."

Berenice's brows wrinkled as if she were contemplating an attempt but feared the outcome. "I have not been able to hold much of anything down."

Shiphrah poured another cup of water and held it to the woman's lips. "We can always try."

Berenice's mouth curved upward, just the hint of something breaking through. Hope, perhaps? No, it wasn't hope, not yet. But perhaps relief and a bit of gratefulness that Shiphrah was not screaming and running for the eastern horizon, like the first two heartless slaves had done.

Although Shiphrah inwardly questioned El Shaddai's wisdom in bringing her to Berenice, with her knowledge of healing so limited and her skills in midwifery mere shadowy memories of Tula's techniques, there was nothing to do but hope that she had indeed not imagined that small whisper in her soul.

CHAPTER FIVE

A lthough Master Sennofre terrified Shiphrah with his large presence and his scowls, it was more than obvious that he adored his wife. The morning after Shiphrah had been assigned to watch over Berenice, a group of priests was ushered into the room, a home visit that could only have been arranged by a large offering of silver to the temple made by a man who refused to accept that Berenice or her child would die.

Shiphrah plastered herself to the wall as the priests chanted over her mistress, the wailing sounds so eerie that gooseflesh coated her arms and legs. The leader of the holy men made a call to Set, the god of darkness and war, asking him to release the hold he had on Berenice before smearing a foul-looking concoction across her bared chest, something that smelled of blood and excrement. Shiphrah's stomach revolted, both from the tainted air and the flash of humiliation on Berenice's face. These knowledgeable physician-priests may have trained in the temple for years, but Shiphrah could not understand how any of this could be beneficial to a woman whose health was so fragile.

When incense was tossed into the brazier, Shiphrah held her breath as the sickly sweet smell of the smoke mixed together with the horrific odor of the medicine to create a putrid, eye-burning assault. Seeing that Berenice's skin had gone from sallow to deathly pale, Shiphrah wished she could fly at the priests and run them out of the room. But all she could do was clench her fists at her sides and pray it would be over soon. Before the priests left the room they encircled her mistress's bed with talismans and then gave Shiphrah instructions to continue using the medicine on Berenice's wounds until the pot was empty. She may be forced to obey their commands, but nothing could compel her to look at the many amulets of Hathor and the Eye of Horus carvings that they claimed would protect Berenice from harm. Watching the priests in their sacred work made her skin crawl as never before.

After three days of being forced to slather more of the dung and blood concoction on Berenice and burn more of the horrid incense the priests had left behind morning and night—which was so awful that it must indeed chase away evil spirits, as they claimed—Shiphrah was at a loss. It seemed that not only was her mistress not any better, but she had only become more pale and weak. When Sennofre sent his manservant to fetch Shiphrah so she could update him on his wife's health, she went to his chamber with trembling knees, wondering if she would be blamed for the lack of progress.

Instead, Sennofre asked whether there were signs that the treatment had done Berenice any good. After a long pause, in which Shiphrah wondered where he would send her to if she said no or whether she should lie to appease him, she held fast to the voice that had whispered to her and found just enough courage to shake her head.

Her master let out a long, weighty sigh, his hands mussing his dark hair and his deeply furrowed brow making his heartbreak plain. "I figured as much, but perhaps the medicine takes more time to work."

Shiphrah pressed her lips together, knowing she could do nothing but stand silent, even if she wanted to argue against such a notion.

"If she must endure it," he continued, so low she wondered whether he was speaking to himself, "then at least I can make it a small measure more pleasant for her." Then to her shock, he instructed Shiphrah to follow his manservant Thadeo into the market and purchase the most beautiful-smelling perfume she could find and entrusted her with a few precious pieces of silver to do so.

Bewildered by the request and touched by the kind considerations for his wife, Shiphrah could do nothing but silently follow Thadeo and comply with the command.

She'd not left the villa in the days since she'd begun tending to Berenice, and in fact had only left the hush of the sick room to fetch food and water, so the sights and sounds of the royal city rushed at her like a flash flood as soon as she stepped over the threshold.

Handcarts and wagons clattered by, beds overflowing with goods—bushels of barley or flax; pots of lentils, beans, or peas; rolls of linen and stacks of wool; and sealed jugs of wine and beer—making the act of following the manservant through the chaos a death-defying experience. Shiphrah did not remember such loud tumult when Sennofre had led her to his home the first time, but perhaps earlier in the day such upheaval was normal. To Shiphrah's good fortune, Thadeo was one of the tallest and most intimidating men she'd ever seen, making most of the people skitter out of the way as he approached, so she followed gratefully in his wake.

When they neared the enormous wall that separated the outer courtyards of the royal palace from the rabble, a horde of slaves was being herded toward them by a cadre of armed Egyptian overseers. Each man carried a basket of mud bricks upon his back, sweat-soaked and sun-burnished bodies gleaming in the harsh sunlight. When one of the men stumbled, his basket crashed to the ground, dusty shards of bricks spilling at the foot of one of his overlords.

Immediately the Egyptian withdrew a cane from his belt and lashed the slave, spittle flying from his mouth as he berated the man for his clumsiness. Shiphrah winced at the sound of the stick meeting flesh as the slave hunched on the ground, hands over his head in a futile attempt to protect his neck and shaven scalp.

Drawn to gawk at the public beating, a large number of passersby had halted to placate their morbid curiosity, preventing Shiphrah and Thadeo from continuing on. Some onlookers seemed unaffected by the spectacle, merely annoyed by the inconvenience, and others looked almost delighted by the punishment being meted out by one of their own. Shiphrah had witnessed discipline by her former master, usually a few lashes to lazy servants or one time the severing of a hand for a cook who dared steal a silver bowl, but the vicious glee with which the overseer was whipping the man shocked her, bringing tears of sympathy to her eyes.

"Why?" she rasped, not meaning to give voice to her question.

Thadeo, who had until now barely acknowledged her existence, surprised her with a reply. "A Hebrew," he said, before continuing on without a backward glance to ensure Shiphrah followed.

Shiphrah had only been in contact with two Hebrews back in Iunu, both servants in Ankare's home who had been sold alongside her on the day of the auction. But she had never had a conversation with either man since she'd always avoided contact with male servants whenever possible.

There was certainly an attitude of disdain by many in Midian for the descendants of Isaac, but even if her people thought the Hebrews deserved their lowly portion in Egypt for usurping the blessing of Abraham, Shiphrah could not fathom such malice as the overseer had lashed upon the unfortunate man's back for the slight grievance of a stumble and the destruction of a few easily replaced mud bricks. Even as Thadeo led Shiphrah on beneath the harsh midday sun, a shiver went up her back and her gut twisted with unease. Something deeper than mere subjugation had occurred to the Hebrews, she could feel it in her bones. She tried to put the odd sensation of knowing aside as she scurried along to keep up with the ebony-skinned slave beside her who had, to her great surprise, spoken the name of her distant relations with a faint note of compassion in his deep voice.

Thadeo led her through the bustling market, his long stride cutting through the crowd with certainty until they stood before a stall at the very end of the street laden with a variety of oils and perfumes. With nothing left of the brief hint of kindness, Sennofre's manservant told her to choose quickly before moving a few steps away and latching his intent gaze on the teeming crowd around them.

Still off-balance from what she'd witnessed, she tentatively lifted a few pots of perfume to her nose, testing which had the most pleasant smell and which were the most potent. Sennofre had only said to buy something that would please Berenice, but she could only guess at which fragrances might soothe the mistress she'd only known for a few days.

The woman behind the stall watched Shiphrah the entire time, perhaps wondering whether she was there to steal instead of purchase. She was dressed in the white linen dress of a tradeswoman, one-shouldered and well-made, but not nearly as sheer as the ones the wealthy women wore. Her skin was not as dark as most Egyptians, her face round, and her brown curls were barely contained within a white turban. Shiphrah sensed that she was of some foreign heritage but could not guess which, when there were so many tribes and tongues and nations all mixed together within this royal city.

"What can I help you find?" The woman slipped off her stool and leaned against the table, her accent making it clear that Shiphrah's assessment had been correct.

Shiphrah smiled to reassure the woman of her honest intentions. "My mistress is very ill. Her husband asked that I bring her the finest of perfumes and incense to chase away the smell of her sickroom."

The tradeswoman's expression lifted, the anticipation of a large sale brightening her eyes. "Ah. Well, you've come to the right person. I make the purest perfumes and sell the finest oils in the entire city. Even the concubines from the palace are known to wear my concoctions." An expression of pride settled on her lips.

"This one is lovely." Shiphrah took another sniff of the alabaster jar she'd been holding. "Roses?"

"Ah. I see you have a nose for flowers." She took the vessel from Shiphrah's hand and put it back on the table. "But if you really want a fine fragrance, one that is sure to endear your master to his wife, then you must smell this one."

The woman handed Shiphrah a jar in the shape of Hathor, the goddess of love. "Blue Lotus."

The sweet fragrance was indeed alluring, bringing to mind the perfumes her former mistress received from a few of her wealthy suitors before her father's future withered away.

"It is exquisite, my lady—"

The woman waved a hand at Shiphrah. "Call me Gilah. I'm no one's lady."

"Oh—well, it is lovely, but my mistress needs something with a stronger fragrance."

The woman furrowed her brow and rubbed her chin with two fingers. "Stronger than this? Hmm."

She riffled through a basket and then handed Shiphrah a short jar with a tightly fitting lid decorated with spindly trees. "Try this one."

Gilah studied Shiphrah's face as she put her nose close to the pot. The woodsy-citrus smell of frankincense was robust in the ointment, and Shiphrah felt that if she mixed a bit of the perfume in the water she washed her mistress's body with each day, it might cover the odor of her sores at the least, even if it would not block the stench of the incense.

"It is not as pleasing as the lotus perfume, but it may indeed do the job."

"And that is?"

The tradeswoman had so far been nothing but helpful, but Shiphrah wondered whether it was wise to confide in a stranger. However, Gilah did not need to know what her mistress's name was to be of help.

"My mistress is very ill and with child. The incense and the medicine the priests prescribed for her wounds are—"

"Disgusting? Revolting?" Gilah asked.

Shiphrah sighed, shaking her head. "There is not a word. Truly."

Gilah muttered something about the idiocy of the priests and then lifted her chin to pierce Shiphrah with a sharp-eyed gaze. "You do not believe in their gods, do you?"

Flinching, Shiphrah glanced around, terrified that a passerby had heard Gilah's question, a confirmation of which would be considered blasphemous to most Egyptians. Thankfully the bustle of the marketplace had camouflaged the tradeswoman's voice and not even Sennofre's manservant seemed to have noticed their quiet conversation. He remained perfectly still, arms crossed, with a scowl on his face as his dark eyes slowly moved over the crowd.

Although her heart seemed to be beating in her throat, with a small shake of her head Shiphrah confirmed Gilah's supposition.

"And what god do you serve?"

Tell her. Once again the hint of a voice lent Shiphrah courage and she stood taller, even while she kept her tone low. "I serve El Shaddai. The God of Abraham."

Gilah's eyes grew large as pomegranates. "You do? But you are not Hebrew."

"I am from one of the tribes of Midian, descendants of Abraham and Keturah. Although my people revere many gods, it is to El Shaddai I pray."

Gilah's face transformed from disbelief to joy. "Then we are cousins, for I *am* Hebrew."

"But you…" Shiphrah looked pointedly at the table before her, laden with pricey goods. The sight of the poor man huddling in the dirt beneath the lash of the overseer welled up in her mind as she attempted to make sense of it all. "How are you not enslaved like the rest of the Hebrews?"

Gilah smiled, the tilt of her lips sardonic. "My husband is an Egyptian trader. But I am from the tribe of Manasseh, even if my own lot is more fortunate than many of my people because of my marriage." She fidgeted with a stack of linens on the table, as if unsettled by her own explanation. Shiphrah wondered if perhaps she felt guilty for escaping the treatment her brethren suffered on the brick-making teams, many of which forced children as young as seven to fulfill the heavy burden Pharaoh imposed on the Hebrews and other slaves deemed the lowest of the low.

"There are a fair amount of Hebrews who've married Egyptians, you know," continued Gilah, "both male and female. And even a few who've risen above the burden Pharaoh has placed on the sons of Jacob to set themselves up as traders or artisans of notoriety." Her chin lifted as if challenging Shiphrah to contradict her. But Shiphrah was too occupied with a sudden realization to care. After all these years of wondering about El Shaddai, attempting to keep the stories Tula had told her about the God of the Mountain fresh in her mind, here was a woman who might actually have some answers!

Excitement pattered against her ribs as she finally pulled together the courage to ask. "I have so many questions—" Shiphrah began.

"We must return." Thadeo's terse interruption halted her mouth, as did the realization that not only was he looming over her, he might have even overheard the conversation between Gilah and Shiphrah.

"Oh...of course...forgive me." Pulse fluttering wildly, Shiphrah slipped her hand into the pouch at her belt and removed the three pieces of silver Sennofre had given her. "Will this be enough for the perfume?"

Not only did Gilah say it was plenty, but she handed Shiphrah the lotus perfume as well. Shiphrah stammered out a refusal for such generosity, but the woman cut off her argument with a decisive snap of her fingers. "I made this. I will charge what I like." Then she winked, leaning forward. "And I want to ensure that your master sends you here again."

Then she riffled through another basket and pulled out a clay bottle with a rolled-up leather stopper and leaned close to Shiphrah once again. "Try this on your mistress's skin as well. Perhaps if you first cover her wounds with this ointment you can prevent that awful concoction from aggravating her sores."

Shiphrah bit her lip as tears blurred her vision, gratitude for the woman's kindness warring with her disappointment. If only she could protect Berenice from the effects of the horrid salve, but if anything, Shiphrah knew her place. She shook her head. "My master would be angry if I spent his silver on something without his permission—"

Gilah stopped Shiphrah with a hand in the air. "This is a gift. If it helps, then perhaps you will find a way to come back for more, yes?"

Stunned and reeling from such unexpected generosity, Shiphrah could only pray that Sennofre would indeed send her back to this stall. She needed to know more about the God of the Mountain she'd vowed to serve, a God whom, after this surprising exchange, she'd begun to suspect had *actually* heard her lowly prayers for help with Berenice.

But if He had, then why did He not see the suffering of the Hebrews, who revered the God of Abraham just as she did? Did He not hear their cries? Or had He simply forgotten them?

CHAPTER SIX

Thankful that Berenice's eyes were closed as she lay on her hip, Shiphrah finished applying the barest skim of the awful medicine over her mistress's shoulder blade. For the past three weeks, she'd been secretly using the unguent Gilah had given her first on Berenice's skin before using only enough of the priest's concoction to keep up the pretense. And in that time, many of the sores had already disappeared and the rest seemed much less inflamed than before. The miraculous mixture from the Hebrew tradeswoman had worked better than Shiphrah could have hoped and she felt even more clearly that El Shaddai had indeed caused her to cross paths with Gilah, if only to relieve a small measure of her mistress's suffering.

"What is that new smell?" asked Berenice, as Shiphrah opened the fresh jar of perfumed oil she'd purchased from Gilah that morning and tipped a few drops into her palm.

"Jasmine and almond, I believe, my lady, and the oil from a citrus fruit brought up the Nile from the far southern lands."

Berenice inhaled deeply as Shiphrah massaged the fragrant mixture into her skin, avoiding the patches where the true medicine lay beneath the false, secretly doing the work that the priests would attribute to their own skill and not that of a lowly Hebrew woman in the marketplace.

"That is lovely," said Berenice. "Is that the fragrance my husband sent you to fetch?"

"It is," Shiphrah replied. "You seemed to enjoy the lotus and the frankincense perfumes so well that when they ran out the master told me to replace them. The woman who crafts these oils made this one specifically with you in mind."

Berenice looked back at Shiphrah over her shoulder, her brows furrowed. "For me?"

"Yes, my lady. She said she'd created it after I came the first time and had set it aside for when I returned."

Shiphrah had been thrilled when Gilah not only remembered her from before but also sent Thadeo off to help her husband carry some jugs of wine to a customer's home, in order that the two women might talk without the manservant standing by and scowling at them impatiently. In the half hour he was gone, Gilah somehow managed to answer a number of questions Shiphrah had about El Shaddai and about the sad oppression the Hebrews had suffered beneath the yoke of Pharaoh for the past few generations. Shiphrah had been loath to take her leave when Thadeo returned, feeling for the very first time since she'd been snatched from her home that she actually had a friend.

"That…" Berenice blinked at her in confusion. "That was very kind of her. Please relay my thanks next time you go to the market."

"She knew the master would expect nothing less than the best for you," said Shiphrah, allowing only the smallest of smiles before helping her mistress to lie back on her bed. At the same moment, Shiphrah's heart thrilled at the notion she would be asked to return in the future. She had so many more questions.

She refilled her palms with the perfumed oil and gently placed her hands on Berenice's ever-growing belly, both to spread the fragrance and smooth the skin, and to surreptitiously check on the position and size of the babe within. The mound had grown so much in the past couple of weeks and by the size of it, Shiphrah wondered if perhaps Berenice might have been mistaken about how long she'd been with child. She could not still be two months away from her time. Gauging the general length of a pregnancy by the feel of the mother's body had been one of the first things Tula had allowed Shiphrah to take part in all those years ago, even before she was allowed inside the birthing tent, and this infant was well past the size it should be.

"Sennofre has always indulged me," said Berenice, as if musing to herself. "A small bit of perfume is nothing to the jewels, dresses, and accoutrements he's lavished on me over the years."

She went quiet for a few moments, her eyes latched on the ceiling above as Shiphrah continued her ministrations. Along with fewer eruptions and sores on Berenice's skin, the sunken look of her cheekbones had softened since Shiphrah had come here, likely the result of the additional nourishment she'd been successful in cajoling her mistress to ingest. Apparently the last three maids had not been strong enough to convince Berenice to eat. But thankfully Shiphrah had been able to coax her by gently reminding her that even if she did not feel like eating, the babe might be affected if she did not, so Berenice had gradually moved from sipping broth to eating hearty meats and fresh vegetables from the garden in the back courtyard.

For all that Berenice talked of her own end, Shiphrah could see quite clearly that she already loved the child and wanted it to live. Otherwise, she would not have endured these long months confined to her bed with nothing more than her thoughts and careless maids to keep her company, since no one other than Sennofre ever came to visit. The poor woman had been going mad with boredom on her sickbed. But for some reason, Berenice must have decided to trust Shiphrah, because she'd begun talking more and more. And gradually, the light in the woman's eyes had begun to spark again, even if Shiphrah merely murmured various encouragements or nodded while her mistress emptied her head of all the thoughts she'd been harboring while lying in her bed.

"We loved each other from childhood, have I told you?" asked Berenice, startling Shiphrah from her thoughts. But before she could respond her mistress continued.

"We were neighbors," she said. "We spent our early years climbing over the wall between our homes to play together, and I thought him the most handsome and wonderful boy in all of Egypt. But then"—she frowned—"he reached military age and went to train with the army before there was even serious talk of a match between us. And when he was sent to a post out on the western edge of the kingdom for years and then word came that invaders had burned the outpost to the ground, I thought I might never see him again. In fact, I was nearly betrothed to another man, but I refused. I told my father I would have none but Sennofre. And it was a good thing I did, because not long after, he returned for me, telling me he could never forget me."

"He loves you very much," said Shiphrah.

"He does," her mistress replied. "And he will be heartbroken when I die. I worry for him when I am gone."

"You will not die, my lady," said Shiphrah. "You must have hope."

"Hope?" Berenice laughed, but it was a bitter, unpleasant sound. "Some evil has taken hold of me. I am cursed. And even if this babe lives, I will not, I know this full well. Even with the spell-breaking chants of the priests and the sacred medicine, the gods will not let go of me."

Shiphrah's eyes were drawn to the three amulets that remained on the bedstead near her mistress. Although the priests had left twelve of them all around the bed, little by little she'd quietly removed them, relegating them to secret places outside the room whenever she fetched Berenice's meals. With the removal of each one of the graven images, Shiphrah felt as though she could breathe freer. And perhaps it was her imagination, but since she'd removed the amulets, her mistress seemed to be sleeping deeper and awakening more rested. She'd already begun to slip a few of the smaller idols from the room as well, tucking them into soiled linens when Berenice's eyes were closed and placing them among some of the other statues that stood atop tables and altars around the villa. She could only pray that no one would notice her insubordination, for she would certainly be punished if they did. But it was worth it if the removal of such frightening images somehow afforded Berenice more rest. Shiphrah had never gotten over the idea that they were staring at her back with sightless eyes anyway.

"Tell me a story," said Berenice. "I tire of my own thoughts."

Although the words came across as a command, Shiphrah could sense the desperation beneath them. Even Shiphrah was restless after being trapped for most of the day within this suffocating room. She could not imagine being confined to a bed for every moment of every day for months. And truthfully, she was glad to have Berenice demand something of her. It showed that her strength of will was returning, and she could only hope that meant the woman might eventually fight for herself and her baby.

So Shiphrah did as she asked, telling her the same story that Gilah had told her just this morning in the market since it was fresh in her mind. The tale was about a man named Joseph who was sold by his own brothers for pieces of silver and yet who eventually rose to the right hand of Pharaoh because El Shaddai blessed him with the ability to interpret dreams of the future.

"And who is this El Shaddai?" asked Berenice. "I've never heard of such a god."

Shiphrah's skin prickled as she deliberated how much to tell her mistress. "He is the God of my ancestor Abraham and of the Hebrews. It was claimed by many in my tribe that He lives atop a mountain in my homeland, but..." She stopped and cleared her throat. "But I am not certain that is true."

After speaking more with Gilah, Shiphrah had become even more convinced that El Shaddai was not bound to a certain place. For if Joseph had been blessed by Him here in Egypt and El Shaddai had heard his prayers for guidance and rescue, then surely El Shaddai was not limited in the same ways as the Egyptian gods or those of the other nations whose influence was restricted to the regions their worshippers governed—or conquered. And yet again, she'd wondered that since the people of El Shaddai had indeed been subjugated, if He was as powerful as Gilah's stories suggested.

When she asked as much of Gilah, the tradeswoman said, *"Abraham was told by El Shaddai Himself that we would be given into Pharaoh's hand for many years, but that time is almost complete. And every day more and more of us are crying out for liberation from the heavy yoke upon our necks, calling for a Deliverer to break our chains."* She'd sighed, the sound long and weighty as she gazed over the teeming crowd of people in the marketplace, a thousand sorrows displayed in her dark eyes. *"And yet somehow I fear that the suffering of Jacob's sons may get much worse before it gets better."*

Sennofre entered the room, drawing Berenice's attention away from Shiphrah's storytelling.

"My lovely wife," said Shiphrah's master as he approached her sickbed. "You are looking well this afternoon."

She smiled up at him, the first time Shiphrah had seen a real smile on the face of her mistress. "Shiphrah has been telling me a fascinating story."

Shiphrah had scuttled to the side of the room the moment her master appeared and now stood with her back to the wall and her chin tilted downward, but she could feel Sennofre's eyes on her nonetheless.

"Indeed?"

"Yes. She spoke of a Hebrew man named Joseph who became a vizier to Pharaoh and how his God preserved him in spite of much travail."

"A slave rising to power at the side of Pharaoh?" Sennofre scoffed. "Now there is a myth if I ever heard one. What use is a god of slaves anyway? The Hebrews would be better off praying to the mud bricks they fashion from dirt and straw."

Shiphrah flinched at the mocking bark of laughter from the lips of her master but kept her head down.

It seemed Sennofre was finished ridiculing her, however, since he turned his attention back to Berenice, stroking her cheek with a gentle touch. "Your skin looks so much better, my love. I must bring an offering of thanks to the temple for such a blessing by the gods and relay my gratitude to the priests for the medicine."

Shiphrah wanted to argue, tell him that it was not that horrid mess that was healing her skin, but the salve made by one of those "worthless Hebrews" he disdained so much. But of course, she would no more speak a word out of turn to such a powerful man than she would consume the foul medicine the priests left behind. And so, as was her duty, she remained silent.

CHAPTER SEVEN

Shiphrah felt Berenice's guttural moan in her own chest as if somehow she'd taken on a measure of her mistress's pain. All those years before when she'd assisted Tula and her mother, she'd known the women giving birth and felt sympathy for their travails, but after having spent the last three months in this room with Berenice she'd somehow come to love her mistress in a way she'd never thought possible. And watching her suffer through such a long and tedious labor had been excruciating. If only she could take her place, relieve the pain that seemed to be draining the life from Berenice, hour by hour.

Muttering assurances as she rubbed her mistress's back in slow, soothing circles, Shiphrah prayed that El Shaddai would send the right midwife to help Berenice through this perilous night. Earlier in the afternoon, the royal midwife had come at the behest of Sennofre, making Shiphrah realize that her master was even more powerful and favored by Pharaoh than she'd imagined. The woman examined Berenice swiftly, declared that she was far from the end of her labor, and floated out of the room with a vague promise to return after she'd tended to one of the royal concubines who was giving birth to twins. Hours and hours passed without word, until Berenice's labor began in earnest, her pains coming one upon the other, and Sennofre sent Thadeo to the palace with a frantic message for the midwife to return. But so far neither Thadeo nor the midwife had reappeared.

Berenice let out another wrenching cry as the pains overtook her, gritting her teeth and nearly grinding Shiphrah's knuckles to dust as she gripped her hand.

"I don't want to die," she howled at Shiphrah. "I don't want my baby to die."

Her attitude was so different from that of the woman Shiphrah had met three months ago, emaciated and hopeless, with barely enough strength to drink a cup of broth as she lay listlessly on her bed. Over the last few weeks Berenice had revealed just how desperately she wanted to be a mother, something she'd dreamed of from her earliest years. She'd said that from the beginning of their marriage, both she and Sennofre had desired a large family and she felt she'd be letting her husband down if she lost the only pregnancy she'd been able to carry to fullness. It seemed to Shiphrah that Berenice mourned the inability to provide Sennofre with a child far more than she feared her own mortality.

Finally, after what seemed like an eternity, Thadeo returned from the palace, not with the royal midwife but with a very young assistant. The woman apologetically relayed that her mistress was not able to step away from the birthing room until the twins were delivered.

Sennofre fairly roared his displeasure at the young midwife, which made her large kohl-lined eyes flutter and glisten, but to her credit, she merely apologized again and then remained to tend Berenice with a gentleness that the first midwife had not.

Shiphrah continued massaging her mistress's lower back and watched as the apprentice examined a whimpering Berenice with furrowed brows. When the young woman's face went gray and the eyes that darted up to meet Shiphrah's lit with something akin to panic, Shiphrah feared for her. Whatever she had to say would not please Sennofre, who'd been pacing up and down the corridor during the examination, bellowing commands to every servant unfortunate enough to catch his eye.

The apprentice stood, took a quivering breath, and then invited the anguished father back inside.

"The babe is caught," she said, apology in her meek tone. "Its shoulders are trapped and unable to move forward."

"Then remedy the situation," snapped Sennofre. "My wife is in distress!"

"I…," the young woman stuttered, "I don't think I can. The babe is far too large to be turned. And even were I able to do so, there will be…" She fidgeted, gripping her hands together until her knuckles went white and glancing at Berenice with a look of pained compassion. "There will be tearing, and I am not trained how to fix such a thing."

"Then go fetch someone who can!" bellowed Sennofre. "Her life is at stake! And therefore, so is yours!"

The apprentice shrunk away from his fury, jaw agape. Shiphrah knew from these past months of watching her master interact with Berenice with such tender concern that it was not malice that drove his threats but fear for the woman he'd loved since he was a boy.

"I am so sorry to say that there is no one…there are no other midwives available within the guild tonight, my lord. A rash of stomach illness has four of them unable to stand from their beds and the others are spread throughout the city tending other births. It is just me."

From her bed, Berenice weakly called to her husband, a futile attempt to draw his attention away from the subject of his growing rage. But Sennofre's voice only grew louder as he ignored his wife and advanced on the young woman with menacing steps. "Then go to the temple and get a physician! A surgeon! A priest! There must be someone in this cursed city who will save her! Go, find someone! Or you will regret ever stepping foot over my threshold!"

The poor apprentice fled the room, leaving behind her leather satchel of midwife tools in her haste to escape.

Berenice let out a strangled sob, her body arching forward as another round of birth pains took hold. Shiphrah did her best to give the woman support as she suffered through the agony, but once the pain had passed they both were sweating and panting. Sennofre, for his part, stood at the side of his wife, his face a mess of terror and anguish as he looked down on her with utter helplessness.

Shiphrah had the awful sense that the apprentice would not be returning, and if one of the priests arrived they might inflict more awful remedies on Berenice like the ones they'd prescribed for her skin.

Speak, said the voice at the center of her soul.

She flinched at the strength of the silent command. She was not a royal midwife. Not a physician trained in the ways of medicine. And if something happened and Berenice died, along with Sennofre's only child, she had no doubt that her punishment would be severe. Other slaves had been whipped to death over much smaller offenses than that, and with the fury reverberating off her master, coupled with the threat he'd just leveled at the apprentice who was far above her in station, she had no doubt her life might be forfeit.

And yet she had come to care deeply for Berenice over these past weeks. Even though Sennofre had mocked the story Shiphrah had told about Joseph, her mistress had requested more stories about the Hebrews and their God. So Shiphrah had found any excuse to go to the marketplace and plead with Gilah to share more about her people so she could relay everything she learned back to her mistress, who seemed voracious for any bit of distraction during the interminable days in bed. And selfishly, Shiphrah was glad, for it gave her the opportunity to learn more herself.

Besides, along with the growing affection for her mistress, Shiphrah had seen the desperation in Berenice. Her desire to bring forth this infant into the world, especially after the loss of four of them before, grew with every hour. With the exception of the incident which caused the expulsion of Reshida and a frightening false start to labor, Berenice had obeyed the physician's instruction and remained abed without complaint. All for the sake of the life within. And Shiphrah could not turn a blind eye to either mother or child. Even if it meant she was whipped for opening her mouth. Or worse.

Berenice screamed, her limbs going rigid as she fought the pain. Shiphrah's ears rang from the awful force of it, and Sennofre let out a sound like a gutted animal as he stared helplessly at his wife who was writhing and panting on her bed. Shiphrah had little doubt that he already regretted chasing the young midwife from the house, no matter how useless she'd been in such a complicated situation.

Knowing what she had to do and that Berenice was running out of time, Shiphrah lifted her voice. "I can help," she said, her lips barely moving and the words themselves swallowed up by Berenice's panting and straining. But somehow Sennofre heard her, and his head jerked up.

"What did you say, girl?" he demanded.

Too terrified to even lift her eyes, Shiphrah sucked in a quivering breath. "My mother was a midwife. As was my grandmother." She paused, calling upon every last drop of courage she possessed. "I have seen a birth like this. I can help."

"You are a midwife?" he snapped.

"No," she replied honestly, "but I assisted at many, many births. And I remember their methods well." She did not mention that even though her grandmother had been a midwife for far more years than Shiphrah had been alive, many times she still lost mothers in the fight against death.

"No," he said, "she needs a knowledgeable midwife. Or a physician from the temple if there is truly none available, not an ignorant maid."

Although her knees shook, Shiphrah took in the agonized expression on her mistress's face, the face that had once been riddled with sores and rashes, and forced the words from her mouth that would seal her fate either way.

"The priests already nearly killed her. And if I do not step in now, both your wife and child will die, my lord." She chanced a quick glance upward and found his mouth pressed into a hard line.

"What do you mean they almost killed her?"

"The medicine they left. It was making the wounds on her body worse, not healing it."

"Of course it healed her," he growled. "Look at her. There are very few patches of inflamed skin remaining. And she has been growing in strength and in health every day. Without the priests, their medicine, and their spells and amulets, Berenice would not have made it this long."

"No, my lord," said Shiphrah. "It was not such things that healed her. They only dragged her closer to death with their amulets and their potions."

"Then how do you explain it?" he asked, his eyes narrowing, and Shiphrah knew that without revealing the truth he would never hear her. "You yourself applied the medicine that healed the sores."

"No," she said, resigned to whatever may come. "No, I did not. At least not without first treating her with a honey-herb salve to protect her from that horrific mess." She gestured to the jar the priest had left, which sat on a nearby table. "It is almost completely full of the filth they told me to smear on her."

He snatched up the jar and opened the lid. Then, having seen that she was telling the truth, bellowed, "You dared disobey my orders?"

"I did," she said. "And I would do it again."

"You will pay for your insolence." He raised a hand to strike Shiphrah, but Berenice shrieked again, the pain grabbing hold.

"She needs to be turned," shouted Shiphrah over her mistress's wails, "and certain oils applied. Please, Master. Please let me help her. I can do something. Please let me try. I cannot bear to see the priests do anything that would harm her."

Sennofre's expression was tortured, conflicted.

Shiphrah breathed out a prayer and her answer was the voice. *Your life for hers.*

She shuddered but understood what she needed to do. She looked down at her mistress, who was in so much pain Shiphrah wondered whether she'd even heard what had passed between her handmaid and her husband, and then at Berenice's belly, in which a new life struggled toward freedom.

"If she dies, may my life be in your hands, my lord," Shiphrah said, meeting her master's eyes for the first time ever, but at the same time speaking to the God of the Mountain who'd brought her to this moment. "Do with me what you will."

He flinched, likely seeing the adamancy in her countenance.

"Fine," he said, then pointed a finger at her and spoke with the force of his authority over her every breath. "But if either she or my child dies, girl, so do you."

As she guessed it would be.

"I understand," Shiphrah replied, reaching for the leather satchel the apprentice left behind, praying the Egyptian midwife might carry similar supplies to Tula. "I have need of two maids who can help support my lady, along with hot water and towels."

To her great surprise, Sennofre did not argue any further but instead went to the door to command Thadeo to fetch the two strongest maids in the house. In the meantime, Shiphrah helped her exhausted and hurting mistress turn over and shift to a better position, one which she'd seen Tula use successfully in a number of complicated births like this one.

Then although her hands were shaking and it was more than likely that Berenice and the baby along with Shiphrah herself would not see morning, she set herself to a task she was not at all certain she was capable of and prayed that El Shaddai might preserve the life of at least one of them tonight.

CHAPTER EIGHT

A tear trailed down Shiphrah's cheek as the babe in her arms gripped her finger in his tiny fist. "He is so beautiful, my lady," she said, "and strong!"

Berenice laughed, her face still puffy from the long struggle the night before, but glowing with only the sort of joy that flowed from the heart of a new mother. She brushed her hand over the newborn's soft head, adorned with a shocking amount of black hair. "And I have you to thank, Shiphrah. Without you…" She shook her head, tears glistening on cheeks that were no longer gaunt. "Without you, neither one of us would be here today."

"You did the work, my lady. I only helped guide this sweet boy along his journey to you."

Shiphrah shifted the child to his mother's arms, rejoicing at the sight of the two of them so enthralled with each other and awed that she'd had any part at all in the miracle.

All of it seemed a blur to her now after such tumultuous hours spent coaxing a very large infant from the womb, but as she'd observed when watching Tula and her mother, sometimes in the most dangerous of labors, patience and calm were the most necessary skills a midwife could have. Perhaps if the young apprentice would not have bolted and had remained in control of herself, she might not now be facing the wrath of Sennofre, who'd set out to confront the royal midwife at first light, still furious with both the woman who'd refused to come to his wife's aid and the incompetent girl she'd sent in her place.

But however joyful Sennofre had been when she announced his firstborn had arrived safely and that his wife lived as well, Shiphrah knew without a doubt that she would be called on to answer for her actions before the birth. Her insubordination would not go without punishment, for certain.

As if in answer to her thoughts, Thadeo knocked on the door and then entered the room, his eyes turned away from their mistress as he instructed Shiphrah to follow him to Sennofre's chambers.

Berenice gave her an encouraging smile that she did not in the least believe, but Shiphrah squared her shoulders nonetheless and followed the manservant with her knees trembling and a hundred pleas to El Shaddai circling through her mind. She hoped that her success in saving the lives of his wife and child might mitigate his fury in some small measure, but she knew in all likelihood that it would do little more than spare her life. She may very well end this night in chains, just like Joseph had at Potiphar's hand. However, there would be no rise to power once her sentence was finished, only a life in the mud pits alongside the rest of the lowest slaves in Egypt.

Thadeo led her through the house without comment and wordlessly ushered her through the door to Sennofre's rooms with nothing more than a silent tip of his chin, but just as she passed over the threshold, he whispered, "Well done." Before she could blink away her profound surprise at his encouragement, he spun and strode away, leaving her to face her master all alone.

Sennofre was seated at a small table, reading some sort of document. She shuffled into the room, eyes on the floor, and waited patiently for him to acknowledge her. The sound of papyrus being folded whispered in the quiet room before Sennofre stood from his chair, came around the front of his table, and perched on the edge of it, arms folded in front of him.

Shiphrah's hands were clasped tightly before her, but there was nothing she could do about their violent trembling. This man owned her. By law and tradition he could do with her what he liked. She had insulted his gods and his priests and undermined his authority time and again. He could have her flogged publicly, naked and tied to a pole, and she could do nothing but endure it, for no one would come to the rescue of a Midianite slave woman. She only had one friend in the world anyway, and she'd never see Gilah again.

"You came into my home to do one job. To tend my wife's needs. You were expected to obey my orders without question. And that included applying the medicine that the priests directed. And yet not only did you willfully disobey such commands, you used my trust to sneak around in the market and used my silver to purchase additional salve without my leave."

Shiphrah was tempted to argue the point, inform him that Gilah had given her the honey-herb balm without any payment, but knew it would be unwise to provoke him further.

"And then," said Sennofre, his voice rising, "atop your defiant actions, you stripped my wife's chambers of most of our gods, didn't you? I did not notice until this morning, but few of the amulets the priests left remain, and only a few token idols are still standing on a table in a corner, all of them facing away from my wife's bed."

She let out a shaky breath but did not respond. What could she say? It was the truth.

"Who is your god, young woman?" he demanded.

Her lids dropped closed as she spoke, her voice barely louder than the squeak of a mouse. "El Shaddai, Master."

"The god of the Hebrews?" he asked. "The slave god?"

She nodded her head.

"And for this god whose people are subjugated to Pharaoh, who spend their days knee-deep in muck and straw at his behest, you would dare disrespect the gods of Egypt?"

How could she make him understand something as incomprehensible as a voice that spoke to her spirit? A whisper that sometimes visited her dreams? And the stories of a God who provided a way of escape for a young man tied to an altar as his grief-stricken father held a knife to his throat?

She couldn't. Not unless she wanted to suffer further. And so she kept her mouth closed and her eyes on the ground.

"And does this god of yours have a sanctuary? A place I can go to give my thanks?"

Shiphrah's head jerked up in confusion. "My lord?"

"I have loved Berenice since I was nine years old, Shiphrah. She is my sun, my moon, my stars, the breath in my lungs. I watched her endure the loss of four infants, all nearly halfway through her pregnancies. I watched her curl in upon herself, becoming more and more desperate to be a mother with each loss, even though I tried to convince her that we could adopt a child—or ten—like other people we know instead of placing her in more danger. For a time I even refused to enter her chambers at night. But she was adamant in her desire. She begged me with such heartbreaking pleas...." He stopped, swallowing hard. "It was nearly impossible to deny her. When she became with child and grew sicker and sicker, I was furious with myself for giving in. But she endured, in spite of a ravaged body and worthless maids. But then, when I heard my old friend Ankare had lost his fortune and was concerned that his servants would be sold to harsh masters, I made the trip up the river to the auction. Do you know why, out of the dozen or so maidservants there that day, I chose you, Shiphrah?"

She shook her head, still dazed from all he'd revealed.

"Because when the young maid next to you was sold to a man whose intentions were in no way honorable, the compassion on your face was as bright as the sun. Although you were helpless to do anything, you reached out a hand to comfort her, to impart her with a small measure of peace, no matter how futile."

He had seen her small action with Peti before she was led away?

Another wave of guilt crashed over her at the reminder of her brief moment of callous relief that it had not been she who was walking away with that horrible master.

"If only I could have saved her. Or taken her place," she murmured, then immediately regretted opening her mouth without being given leave to do so.

"I am grateful you did not," Sennofre replied with an adamant tone. "For if you had, then my wife and child would be dead right now. I know nothing of your slave god, Shiphrah, but if it was he who brought you here, as my wife insists, then I will ever be beholden to him as well."

Her mouth went dry at the sincerity in his voice.

"Last night when you told me that you had disobeyed my orders to give Berenice the medicine that the priests gave her, I nearly called for Thadeo to drag you from the room and take you to be flogged. But then you offered your own life up to me...." He exhaled a shuddering breath that did not fit with the strong and powerful man who stood before her. "I have never seen such courage, Shiphrah."

"It was not courage, my lord. It was desperation to save her and the little one. And resignation to my fate, since I knew my life would be forfeit if I did not succeed."

"But you did succeed."

She nodded. "I did, yes, but I did not expect to."

His brows flew upward. "You did not?"

"No, my lord." She took a deep breath and then because she had nothing more to lose, she told him the truth. "I only observed such methods during births attended by my mother and grandmother."

His expression was pure shock. "But you seemed so certain, so knowledgeable."

She remembered the way she'd willed her hands to stop shaking, the barrage of doubts as she manipulated the infant's body inside his mother's, and the constant fear that she was doing more harm than good.

"No. I was terrified, second-guessing my every decision. It was only certainty in the provision of El Shaddai that kept me from running from the room the way that apprentice midwife did."

"You were *that* sure of your god?"

Her voice was small since even with his talk of courage earlier, she still could not determine whether he was testing her. "I am learning to be."

He was silent for a long while, so long that she ached to lift her eyes and gauge his expression but she resisted.

"You are free to go," he said.

"My lord?" Shiphrah blinked up at him in bewilderment. Was he withholding his punishment for now? Or had he decided to grant her mercy?

"You are free, Shiphrah. I release you from the contract that binds you to me as a slave. You will leave this house as a free woman because you not only saved my family but were fearless enough to go against me—even though I held the power of life and death over you—in order to heal Berenice. Without your disobedience in this matter, she would likely have died even before last night, and my firstborn son with her. I can never fully repay you for what you've given to me, but I *can* give you freedom."

Shiphrah's knees wobbled and she reached to brace herself, finding nothing but air. "You are letting me go?"

"I am. I have already employed another maid for Berenice and a wet nurse for the child, and they will arrive shortly, but I suspect it will not be long before my wife returns to full health after all that you did for her."

"But…where do I go?"

"Anywhere you please. You can return to your homeland if you so wish. This"—he handed her a leather satchel that jingled in a familiar way but had an altogether unfamiliar weight—"will likely sustain you for many years. Perhaps you can use it as a dowry. Or to purchase a home. Whatever you wish."

There were so many thoughts and questions floating around inside her head that she could keep none of them straight. She was no longer a slave? Her master—former master—had given her a bag full of what she suspected were silver pieces? She could go back *home*?

"As I said, I do not know anything about your god, Shiphrah. Perhaps it was he who saved my wife through you, or perhaps it was only your skill, but I vow to you that I will not rely on the priests again to treat Berenice. I should never have put my poor wife through such horrors. I was just desperate to find a solution. Desperate not to lose my love to the life beyond, just yet. I did not dare even hope that my child would take breath in this one. But you have given me the gift of both of them and for that, I will be eternally grateful."

She was relieved to hear that no one would be smearing foul substances on her mistress again but still so astonished by the revelation that Berenice wasn't actually her mistress anymore that she barely heard the effusive thanks Sennofre offered, nor when he called for Thadeo to escort her back to Berenice's room to say her goodbyes.

Just before she followed his manservant out of the room, Sennofre put out a hand to stop her, causing her to shrink back out of habit. He held up both palms to show he meant no harm.

"I know that we do not serve the same gods, Shiphrah, but I will offer sacrifices in your name to my own, out of gratitude, and I hope that you will bring the name of my wife and child before yours. Perhaps between the two of us, we can ensure they both live a long life." A smile grew on Sennofre's face, one with a hint of mischief that astounded her. Never in her wildest imaginings had she guessed that the enormous and powerful man who'd glowered at her during the auction and purchased her out from beneath the kindly older man would smile at her with something akin to affection in his eyes.

"If I can ever be of service to you, Shiphrah," he said, a sincere note of humility in his tone, "please, come to me. I will ever be in your debt."

She walked from the room, still entirely dazed as she followed Thadeo through the house and back to Berenice's chamber, where both she and her mistress wept as she said her goodbyes. But as Sennofre had done, Berenice insisted that Shiphrah accept the gift of freedom without argument, reminding her that thousands of slaves would give anything for such an opportunity. Then she insisted that Shiphrah dress in one of her own soft linen dresses, one that would set her apart from slaves but not cause others to assume she was a wealthy woman, and then gave her a pair of sandals made from the finest of kid leather.

After a final kiss to the forehead of Berenice's son, who was yet to be named by parents that Shiphrah knew would pamper and adore him every moment of his life, she asked Thadeo to accompany her one last time through the city and to the marketplace, heading for the only place she knew to go with her newfound freedom.

As they neared the market, Shiphrah caught a glimpse of the Nile between two tall buildings, the sun glimmering off its mirrored surface while boats of all shapes and sizes were carried along to destinations she could only imagine.

She paused, the sight of it reminding her of Tula's prophecy. How could her grandmother ever have thought she could stand firm against something with so much power? As she had been since she was eleven years old, she was helpless against such currents, hopelessly buffeted about by whatever twists and turns the river took. Even now when she should be rejoicing at her new freedom, she had nowhere to place her feet and no solid ground upon which to stand, and she certainly had no strength to hold her ground against the flood.

No matter how much silver Sennofre had given her, she was still alone. Even as she considered how she might possibly find someone who was traveling east, toward Midian and the land of her birth, she could almost feel the water rising, pressing against her chest, and sweeping her up at its capricious whims. How could she even find her tribe, as mobile as they were, always searching out the best pastures for their flocks and never staying in one place for too long? One thing she did know for certain, she needed to be as far away from this river as possible.

"This is where I will take my leave of you," said Thadeo, startling her from her overwhelming thoughts as they entered the market. "You will be fine to go on from here."

She dragged in a shuddering breath, fighting her instinct to beg him to take her back to the villa, where she could plead with Sennofre to rescind his far-too-generous offer.

But just before she opened her mouth to do so, Thadeo bowed to her, with the same deference he did Berenice. "May peace go with you, my lady," he said, with obvious sincerity, "wherever El Shaddai leads you."

She stood paralyzed in shock as he spun around and walked away, her eyes pinned on his tall form until he melded into the crowd and disappeared. As she turned to find her own way through the swirling gathering of customers haggling over prices and inspecting the merchandise, her mind whirled with questions. What did Thadeo know of the God of the Mountain? Did he too believe in the One who spoke to Abraham and provided a way of escape for his son? And if so, how had she not known that she was not the only one within Sennofre's home to eschew worship of the gods of Egypt?

Knowing that she would likely never have answers, she thrust the thoughts aside and headed for the very last stall, one which she now suspected had been specially selected by

Thadeo not only for the quality of the perfumes but for the woman who made them.

When finally she stood before Gilah's market table, her Hebrew friend's mouth gaped open as she took in the sight of Shiphrah's new clothing.

"What has happened?" she asked, her brown eyes as large as full moons. "Where did you get that dress?"

Tears pricked Shiphrah's eyes as she brushed her hand over the whisper-soft fabric. "Berenice gave it to me. Right after Sennofre set me free."

"He what?" gasped Gilah. "I've never heard of such a thing. How did this happen?"

Shiphrah explained about the birth, the way she'd felt compelled to help, and how afterward Sennofre had been so grateful he'd removed her shackles for good.

"But what...? Where? How will you live?" Gilah sputtered.

Knowing it would be beyond foolish to bring attention to the leather satchel tied at her waist, Shiphrah only smiled and dropped her voice. "My former master ensured that I would not have cause to want for anything. Not for a long, long while."

The usually talkative Gilah was stricken mute by such a statement, but there was little Shiphrah could do to help her absorb such astonishing news since she herself had not even begun to understand it all.

"There is one thing I do have need of," Shiphrah said, fidgeting with the well-crafted leather belt Berenice had insisted she wrap about her waist. "I have no one else to ask. You are the only person I know in this entire city outside of Sennofre's villa."

"Of course," said Gilah, "anything."

"Perhaps I will return to my people as Sennofre suggested. But for now, I need someplace to sleep."

Gilah gazed at her for a few long moments, her brows furrowed in concentration. But then her wide lips tilted upward and her laughing eyes sparkled. "I believe I know just the place for you."

CHAPTER NINE

After asking a fellow tradeswoman to watch her market stall, Gilah led Shiphrah on a winding path through the city to the southern outskirts, where instead of white villas and soaring temples and palaces, the narrow streets were lined with ramshackle mud-brick homes, one next to the other, without a crack of light between them. But where the streets of the royal city were bustling with life and commerce, this quarter was fairly quiet, only a few unsmiling women making their way up and down the road with baskets or jugs of water on their heads and a few very young children quietly playing games in the dirt with rocks and sticks. She nearly asked Gilah where all the men were before remembering the team of slaves trudging along with armloads of mud bricks and the man cowering beneath the lash of the overseer. This must be the Hebrew quarter. Anyone who was able to tread mud and straw in the pits, form bricks to bake under the sun, heft them to work sites all over the city, and stack them one after another after another into monuments to Pharaoh's greatness was likely occupied with those tasks.

When Gilah stopped in front of one of the largest of the crumbling homes, Shiphrah put a hand on her arm before the tradeswoman could knock.

"Why have you brought me here?" she asked, her gaze sweeping back over the barren street.

"Because since the first day I met you I have felt that there was a reason you appeared at my market stall. And when you told me how you came to be freed, I finally knew why."

Without expounding on her cryptic statement, Gilah knocked on the door, which was opened by a small Hebrew woman with lines around her eyes that seemed to tell a story of both deep sadness and fathomless wisdom.

"Marva," said Gilah, "this is my friend Shiphrah. She is in need of a place to rest her head tonight. Might we come in?"

To Shiphrah's surprise, Marva not only smiled broadly, but she also ushered the two of them inside without hesitation. "Of course!" she said. "You will both eat with us, and then we will make plans for where you will stay."

The words were delivered with a softly lilting tone, but the authority behind them was clear. Shiphrah felt certain that it was rare anyone would cross the woman, no matter how diminutive she might be.

Although the home was larger than most others on this street, it still contained only the main room in which they were standing and two small sleeping rooms with fabric for doors. The entire house might fit within Berenice's chamber and was only sparsely furnished. A few threadbare cushions surrounded a wool blanket on the well-packed dirt floor, and on it sat a large steaming pot of stew, a jug, and a number of empty bowls and cups. Marva insisted that the two women sit down while she bustled about plucking more bowls from the shelf, then filled them from the large pot of stew before pressing them into their hands.

"Go on, eat. The boys will be home any moment and will lick that stewpot clean, so you'd best get your fill before they descend like a swarm of locusts."

Although Shiphrah was tempted to argue, feeling as though she was taking food from the mouths of Marva's children, she knew better than to refuse such hospitality. A spear of memory slammed into her at the thought, for it had been her father's own magnanimous hospitality that had led to her kidnapping and slavery, along with the deaths of her mother, aunts, and the other women who fought so valiantly to save their children at the stream that day.

She swallowed hard against the reminder and thanked Marva for the food, which smelled so delicious her stomach squeezed with anticipation.

"Now, my friend," said Marva, folding herself down onto a cushion with surprising ease for a woman with silvering hair. "Tell me what brought you to my doorstep."

As Shiphrah brought the bowl to her lips, Gilah told Marva of how the two of them had met and how in the ensuing weeks they'd formed a friendship whenever Shiphrah managed to find her way to the market as she tended to Berenice's needs.

"And how long have you been enslaved in Egypt?" asked Marva.

"Since I was eleven," Shiphrah replied.

Marva's gaze traveled over Shiphrah's face with such a searching scrutiny that Shiphrah shifted in her seat.

"And where are you from?" Marva asked.

"Midian. I belong to a tribe descended from Abraham and Keturah."

Marva's brows lifted. "Do you indeed?"

She nodded. "I intend to find my way back home."

Marva made an indecipherable noise in the back of her throat, then turned back to Gilah. "Tell me why you brought her to me."

Gilah began to tell the story of the night before and how Shiphrah had stepped in to deliver Berenice's baby when the royal midwife's apprentice had fled. Hearing the story told again brought back all the fear and doubt but also stirred up the feelings of elation Shiphrah had experienced when Berenice's son made his entrance into the world.

"Ah," said Marva, when Gilah had finished explaining Sennofre's decision to set Shiphrah free in gratitude for saving his family, "now I understand."

Profoundly confused, Shiphrah looked back and forth between the two women, whose lips were curled into knowing smiles. "What is it?"

"Marva is a midwife, Shiphrah. But not just any midwife. She is the most skilled woman among those who oversee all Hebrew births in this region. I brought you to her because I believe there is no better place for you."

"But I am not a midwife," said Shiphrah. "I only did what I watched my mother and grandmother do, and somehow El Shaddai protected Berenice and her babe from my bumbling efforts."

"What is a midwife?" asked Marva.

Shiphrah blinked in confusion. "What do you mean?"

"Tell me what a midwife does."

"Helps a woman through childbirth."

"And did you do that for your mistress?"

"I did, but I don't know enough—"

"You have much to learn, this is true. But I would guess that you watched a good number of births with your mother and grandmother?"

Shiphrah nodded.

"And from the way it sounds, your natural instincts are excellent." Her mother and grandmother had said much the same thing when she was a girl, speaking of her being a born midwife, saying that one day she would outshine them both.

"Do you want to learn to be a midwife?" asked Marva. "Because if you do, I would be happy to teach you."

Shiphrah stared in bewilderment at this woman whom she'd only just met but who now offered to change her life in a way she'd never expected.

Before she could respond to the surprising gift, the door swung open and a tall, wet-headed man strode across the threshold, his tunic stained the color of mud and his black-eyed gaze immediately colliding with Shiphrah's across the room. Instinctively, Shiphrah shifted closer to Gilah, a frisson of unease passing across her shoulders as the newcomer strode over the threshold followed by three other young men.

"Avi! Boys!" said Marva as she bounded to her feet with surprising agility. "You are home! Come, sit. I have your meal ready. Let me get you all something to drink, and then I'll introduce you to our guests."

The four young men complied, folding their long legs down around the wool blanket, all of them giving Shiphrah a smile of acknowledgment, except for the first one, Avi, who looked to be the eldest. He merely nodded his bearded chin, his eyes narrowing slightly before he looked away. Between his cold reception and the large male presence in the room, Shiphrah fought the instinct to bolt from the house. Only ingrained respect for Marva's authority and hospitality kept her seated on the floor.

However, when Gilah suddenly announced that she needed to return to the market and break down her stall for the evening, she nearly changed her mind. Thankfully, Gilah assured Shiphrah that she would return tomorrow to see that she was settled, before darting out the door and into the waning sunlight, leaving Shiphrah feeling unmoored.

After Marva doled out cups of beer and a kiss to each young man's cheek, she seated herself next to Shiphrah on the floor and patted her knee, a soothing gesture that Shiphrah hadn't realized she needed and one that brought the sting of tears to the back of her eyes at the unexpected affection from a stranger, especially one who reminded her in a small measure of her own mother. Shiphrah noticed that the woman's fingers were bent in a slightly odd way, and she wondered if they pained her.

"These are my sons: Avi, Oren, Micah, and Yaniv." Marva pointed a gnarled finger at each in turn, pride undergirding every word as she introduced them. "And this, boys, is Shiphrah.

She is from the land of Midian but has been living here in Egypt for the past few years."

Although she called them boys, even the youngest among them looked to be around seventeen years of age. Shiphrah wondered where Marva's husband was but dared not ask. She suspected the answer would not be a happy one.

"Shiphrah will be staying with us for a while," she announced, then turned to Shiphrah with a glimmer of amusement in her dark eyes. "Or perhaps a long while, if I have my way."

Shiphrah flushed. Even with the attention of four strange men in the room causing her pulse to quicken, she'd not felt so welcome since the last time she'd walked out of her tent back in Midian. There was something about Marva that drew her in, and she found herself wondering what the harm would be in staying, if only long enough to learn midwifery from this kind woman. Perhaps she could spend a few months beneath her instruction and *then* return to her home.

"Imma," said Avi, lowering his voice as if that somehow prevented Shiphrah from hearing him, "perhaps we should discuss this before we make any decisions?"

Marva's brows flew upward. "Your father may be gone, and you may the eldest, but I am still your mother. And if I want to invite someone into my home, I will do so."

Avi's lips pressed together tightly, but he did not argue the point with his mother. However, his obvious annoyance at her invitation caused the discomfort Shiphrah had felt at his entrance to multiply tenfold.

"I do not want to cause any problems," she said, rising to her feet. She had no desire to be the cause for division within this family. "I will find someplace else to go."

"You will do nothing of the sort," insisted Marva, leveling a glare at her oldest son. To his credit, Avi did appear a small measure chastened by his mother's scowl.

A knock sliced through the thick tension in the room, followed by a second before Marva could even reach the handle. When the midwife opened the door, a young woman stood at the threshold, perhaps three or four years younger than Shiphrah, with her chest heaving from running and her long black braid nearly undone.

"Puah!" exclaimed Marva. "What is it?"

"You must come, Marva, Dobah's twins are coming."

"I thought that might be the case. I'm glad I asked you to stay and watch over her these last couple of days." Marva was already in motion, scooping up a leather satchel and wrapping her hair up in a tightly wound turban. "Shiphrah, the bricks are there in the far corner. Please fetch them."

Bewildered by the command and yet her curiosity piqued by the mention of a double birth, Shiphrah ignored the feeling that Avi was glaring at her back and obeyed Marva. The ornate birthing stool that Berenice had labored upon had been decorated with all manner of flowers and goddesses and scrolling vines, but these birthing bricks were plain and unadorned, only the deep outline of a foot pressed into the surface so a mother could keep her balance as she crouched atop them in the age-old posture of labor.

When Shiphrah tried to hand the bricks over to Puah, Marva waved her away. "No, she needs to run back to Dobah's home and keep her comfortable until we arrive. She'll be much faster unburdened."

Her heartbeat stuttered and then sped as she understood Marva's meaning. "You want me to come with you?"

"Of course! There's no better time to begin your training than now, and I'll have need of both you girls tonight. Puah," she said, with a fluttering gesture toward Shiphrah, "this is Shiphrah. My newest apprentice."

Puah grinned at Shiphrah, the small gap between her two front teeth giving her sweetly rounded face a unique and endearing quality and making Shiphrah realize that Puah was likely younger than she'd realized, perhaps only thirteen or so. "Shalom, I am pleased to meet you."

"Go," said Marva to Puah as she ushered Shiphrah out the door. "Use those swift little feet of yours and fly back to Dobah's side and keep her calm. We'll be along shortly."

Still reeling from the presumptive declaration Marva had made, Shiphrah watched Puah's lithe figure dart off and melt into the twilight.

She'd been moments away from walking out the door and either trying to catch up with Gilah at the market, using some of Sennofre's silver to find a place to spend the night, or perhaps even securing passage on a boat that would take her northward on the Nile—even though the thought of going near that terrifying river made her insides go cold. But the mere mention of witnessing a double birth had all but pushed that idea from her mind, regardless of what Marva's eldest son thought of her. And by the smug little smile on Marva's face as she pulled the door closed behind her, the midwife knew exactly what Shiphrah was thinking. For now at least, it seemed as though she had someone who might help her keep afloat as she navigated these new waters.

CHAPTER TEN

Three Months Later

Climbing the narrow steps that led to the roof to retrieve the laundry that she'd hung there to dry a few hours ago, Shiphrah adjusted the empty basket on her hip, as usual skipping the final stair, which she'd learned the hard way was loose and unsteady.

Greeted by the sound of the dry linen cloth flapping in the breeze, alongside a couple of tunics worn by the men on rare days when they were given a break from their eternal labors at the brick pits and construction projects, Shiphrah gave herself a few moments to pause and take in the view from the roof, where the slightly superior height of Marva's home gave her a glimpse over the surrounding multitude of mud-brick homes and toward the sparkling Nile off to the east.

She could never have imagined that, while living here in the Hebrew quarter among a people who'd been enslaved to Pharaoh for hundreds of years, she would feel so much freedom. Perhaps it was simply because Marva had taken her under her wing and no one dared question the respected midwife, but she was glad for it, just the same.

The only person who seemed to resent her presence from the beginning was Avi, who did his very best to avoid her at all times, barely looking her way when he returned with his brothers at night, avoiding her eye at mealtimes, and brushing past her swiftly in the small house as if the thought of even touching her made him ill. She could not understand what she'd done to offend him, and none of his brothers treated her with anything but respect, all of them quick to thank her for her part in the meal preparation and other household duties, which made Avi's obvious disdain for her all that much more pronounced. But inasmuch as she enjoyed learning from his mother, she'd forced herself to ignore his slights and serve him cheerfully. What good would it do to return his coldness with hostility of her own? She'd endured much worse living as a lowly servant in both Ankare's and Sennofre's homes anyway.

Perhaps, like Sennofre, there were reasons for his behavior that went far deeper than the presence of a Midianite woman intruding in his home. So she kept clear of him when she could, feeling a small bit of the same gut-churning fear she had when the slave trader found her in the wadi whenever Avi's piercing black-eyed gaze happened to briefly meet hers. Even if he was Marva's son, he was still a man, whose broad-shouldered build and large hands could easily overpower her, just as the slaver had done when she was a girl. Something about Avi made her feel unmoored, as if the river were tugging at her again and spinning her about like she was caught in an eddy.

But regardless of Avi's disdain for her, from that very first night three months ago, Shiphrah had been swept into his mother's current without complaint. The learned woman had guided that frightened young mother through the treacherous double birth with surprising ease, even allowing Shiphrah to deliver the second one under her watchful eye. By the time they returned to Marva's home, such excitement pulsed in Shiphrah's blood that she'd not been able to control the smile that remained on her lips until she fell into dreamless sleep.

Marva had deftly enfolded her into the household, sharing her tiny room, showing Shiphrah how to prepare the simple but flavorful meals her sons looked forward to every evening when they returned from their heavy labors, and of course including her in every birth, every meeting with expectant mothers, and even the postbirth visits, where she aided the women with nursing and tended their exhausted and sore bodies as they recovered.

The breadth of knowledge that Marva possessed was astounding to Shiphrah. She'd thought her grandmother Tula had been a wise woman, having benefitted from the knowledge passed from generation to generation among their tribeswomen, but Marva also had formed friendships with all the midwives in the city, including those who were educated by temple physicians and tended to the royal family's needs. Therefore Marva was steeped in not only the traditional Hebrew ways of childbirth but also those considered superior by the Egyptians as well. And Shiphrah could not get enough of any of it. It seemed as though there was always something new to learn, some new technique, some new herb or oil to apply, some new mother and child to attend. And through it all, that buzz of anticipation she'd felt on that first night never seemed to abate. Indeed the only thing that did fade was the pull to return to Midian, until soon it was only a very quiet hum in her bones.

As she stared out at the glitter of waning sunlight on the mighty river that she'd been told cut its way through the entire length of Egypt with unstoppable strength, a shiver moved across her shoulders just as a deep voice startled her from her musings.

"I thought I might find you up here."

She whirled, shocked to see Avi a few paces away, arms folded over his chest and those unnerving midnight eyes locked on her. "Your meal is prepared. It's all laid out for you down there," she said, feeling a pulse of alarm at the uncharacteristic way he was speaking directly to her. "I was just collecting the laundry before nightfall."

"Where is my mother?" he asked, his gaze never wavering.

"Sleeping," she replied. "We attended a difficult birth that lasted all day yesterday and throughout the night. She needed rest."

Shiphrah, Marva, and Puah had barely been able to keep their eyes open by the time the tiny girl slid into the world, unmoving and beyond help. Shiphrah had slept for a few hours when they returned home with heavy limbs and heavy hearts, but she'd still been so burdened for the poor mother that she'd not been able to close her eyes again once she woke. Instead, she rose from her bed to tend to the meal and the chores just after the sun had parted ways with the jagged limestone cliffs in the distance, determined to finish it all before her mentor awoke. Although she rarely complained, Marva's hands had been giving her so much pain lately, the knuckles locking up and fingers curling into rigid angles that made even Shiphrah gasp in sympathetic agony, so she gladly took on whatever chores she could.

"And you do not?" Avi asked.

She blinked at such a question coming from his lips—as if he cared whether she was overtired. "I am fine. You all needed a meal and there were household chores to tend to. I do apologize that there was nothing warm for you last night when you came home."

He shrugged one shoulder. "Imma had a neighbor bring us something to eat, as she always does whenever she is long tending a birth."

Of course Marva would do such a thing. The woman was an expert at considering all possible outcomes with laboring mothers and preparing for each eventuality so that nothing seemed to surprise her, not even the most difficult of situations. And since her sons were the most important things in the world to her, there would be no question of her considering their needs before all others.

Unnerved by Avi's persistent stare, Shiphrah turned to set about removing the linens from the ropes strung across the rooftop and hoped that the ensuing silence meant he'd gone downstairs and left her to her task. But as she struggled to slide a heavy woolen blanket from a line strung too high, two large hands reached over her head and tugged it free.

She spun around, heart thrashing about in her chest as she found a man looming over her, blocking out the sun and leaving her in deep shadow. A cry burst free as a flash of memory from that day by the wadi reared up, invoking the smell of blood soaking into the sand, the sound of the mothers' cries as they fought against their murderers, and the feel of the trader's hands yanking her hair as he dragged her to his horse. Her knees wobbled as helplessness crashed over her like a torrent, blocking everything out but the horrors of that day. But instead of the harsh rasp of a kidnapper's voice giving her no choice but to leave little Reuel to fend for himself, someone said her name gently, repeating it along with an assurance that she was safe, that he would let no harm come to her. The terrifying vision began to splinter, leaving her cowering and trembling on the rooftop of Marva's home, with Avi's long fingers wrapped around her arms, keeping her from tumbling into a pitiful heap.

"Shiphrah," he repeated, a wreck of dismay and regret in his expression. "Shiphrah, are you well?"

She blinked up at him, the threads of memory still clinging to her as she considered whether to jerk away from his grip and run down the stairs or spin around to cover her burning face with both hands. But instead of releasing her, his hands tightened ever so slightly and he began to speak in a low and soothing tone.

"I remember the first day I went to work alongside my *abba*," he said, the strangeness of the statement pulling her further out of her terror-stricken state. "I was only seven and thought myself such a man to be allowed to be included with the others who made bricks and built Pharaoh's kingdom. I'd heard the stories of what our people endured, of course, and saw the weariness of my father's body each day, but I could not have understood."

Shiphrah could almost picture young Avi, dark eyes sparkling with the prospect of being given such a responsibility, so innocent, so trusting. Her heart ached with the knowledge of what was surely to come.

"Of course, my excitement lasted as far as the worksite," he said, his tone smooth as a river stone and his hands still keeping her steady, "when the truth was laid before me. The countless groups of men treading mud and straw, the backs bent under the vicious sun, the whips and canes meeting those same exhausted backs whenever the pace was too slow. I grew up that day, in a matter of hours, and when my abba was trampled to death beneath the hooves of an overseer's steed only three years later in front of my eyes, what shards were left of my innocence were stripped from me in an instant."

There was no more trembling in Shiphrah's knees now. Her entire attention was focused solely on Avi as he went silent and his eyes drifted over her head where twilight would be creeping over the eastern hills. Just as she opened her mouth to express her regret for his loss, both of his childhood and his father, he dropped his gaze to meet hers.

"And for months, no…years, I too was plagued with visions of that day. Both my days and my nights were filled with sounds and smells and sights I could not fight away, no matter how loud I screamed and how much my imma soothed me and prayed over me."

She caught her breath, remembering how she too had fought nightmares for so long. But after terrifying her young mistress with shouts a couple of times in the middle of the night, she'd learned to keep her mouth locked as she lay on her pallet in the corner, shaking violently as the awful images faded away. If only she'd had her own mother to brush tears from her cheeks and whisper reassurances in her ears. All she'd been able to do was silently plead for El Shaddai to chase away the evil spirits that had followed her all the way from Midian.

And now that she was listening to Avi talk about his own horrifying memories, she realized that those dreams had indeed faded away. In fact, until today, when she was taken off guard by Avi's proximity, she'd not been assailed by visions of the trader in years. Perhaps El Shaddai *had* heard her lonesome prayers in the night.

"Where did you go? When I surprised you?" he asked, his voice even softer, kinder than Shiphrah would have ever guessed from the man who'd spent the last few weeks glaring at her. But somehow, in the telling of his own past, his presence had transformed from unnerving to comforting.

All reticence undone by the way he'd so freely bared his heart to her, she took a long slow breath and then told him about her home, her family, and how it all was stolen away in a moment of terror. He listened without speaking, his large hands still curved around her shoulders, no longer keeping her upright but holding her steady just the same. When she finished by telling him of the long weeks spent walking through the desert tied to cousins she'd not seen in over eight years and had no idea what their fate might be, he lifted one of those steadying hands to wipe a tear from her cheek.

Flushed with embarrassment, Shiphrah stepped backward and breathed a sigh of relief when he let her go freely. This sudden change in his attitude was far too confusing, as was the warmth that had flooded her bones when his skin touched hers.

He sighed, his expression pained. "I have been unfair to you. I've known this for a few weeks and should have said something long before now. But you must understand..." He paused and searched the dimming horizon. "I did not want you to stay."

Hurt flared in her chest. "I can find somewhere else to go. I have imposed on you far too long."

She'd made an attempt to pay for her food and lodging, knowing that an extra mouth was a burden upon the family, but Marva had adamantly refused to accept even one of the silver coins Sennofre had given Shiphrah, insisting that as the head midwife she was well compensated for her work and that Shiphrah should keep her fortune secreted away in a safe place for when it would be truly needed. Perhaps she should offer it to Avi now.

"No," he said, palms upraised. "No, you will not go any-where. I was wrong. This is where you belong. I know that now."

Her brows furrowed as she searched his face for clarity.

"When you arrived," he said, "I admit I was suspicious of you. A Midianite woman, claiming to have been freed by an Egyptian master? It all seemed far too remarkable to be true. And I have heard of spies among us, people reporting to the overseers at any perceived hint of rebellion or too-loud calls for deliverance. But now I know that you were sent here not as a spy but as a gift."

"A gift?" she echoed.

"For as spry as my mother is," he said, "she is slowing down. The long nights alongside laboring mothers are wearing on her and her hands are getting worse, not better. And perhaps I am wrong, but it seems lately as though there are more Hebrew babies being born than ever before. There are far too few knowledgeable midwives in this city who can shoulder the burden, and I know your presence here has been a relief to her. She has nothing but wonderful things to say about what a help you are and what natural skill you possess. So even if you are a spy"—his mouth curved into a small grin and the sight nearly made Shiphrah gasp in surprise—"at least you are lessening her load somewhat."

She laughed. "I can assure you I am no spy and am only too happy to learn from your mother. It is she who is the gift to me. I wanted so badly to walk in the footsteps of my mother and grandmother and never thought I would have the opportunity to do so after what happened to them. In just these short weeks she has taught me far more than I could have ever dreamed to know. I can only imagine what I could learn in a year, or five."

"You have changed your mind then, about returning to Midian? You will stay?" he asked, brows lifted, as if the thought of such a thing was no longer abhorrent but welcome.

Her eyelids fluttered as she considered the question, one she'd asked herself many times over the last weeks but had not firmly answered, even in her own mind. She could not help but wonder what it might be like to return to her tribe, to search out their familiar black wool tents among the sandy hills and see the faces of the people she'd known as a child, but she also knew that the chances of finding them were very small, especially alone.

And it was likely that her father would not even see her return as a blessing after all these years. By now he had certainly replaced her mother with another woman and had more children. She would only be one more mouth to feed. One more dowry to provide.

Here she was needed. Useful. Welcomed. She'd already made a number of friends among those who worked with Marva and among the women she ministered to. In fact, even though she was very young, Puah had become one of Shiphrah's favorite people in the world thanks to her bright spirit, willing hands, and inquisitive mind. The girl's tendency to ask constant questions had done nothing but add to Shiphrah's training. She had no doubt that one day Puah would make an excellent midwife and it would be a privilege to see her grow into that role. It would be a privilege to stay among these people and offer her own hands in service to Marva and the Hebrews.

"I will stay," she said, making her commitment firm as she did so. "But I do not want to be an intrusion on your family. When you and your brothers marry, you'll bring your wives to live with you, and I will only be in the way. I will seek out somewhere else to live when that happens."

Avi did not respond, only stared at her with some indefinable expression on his face. The silence had a strange edge to it, one that made her wonder if she'd been wrong about the shift in his perspective of her. The longer he took to speak, the heavier the weight in her stomach sank. Perhaps she wasn't welcome after all.

"When my father died," he said, "my imma was all alone, with four boys to raise. I watched her grieve him. Watched her struggle through the pain and carry twice the load. She cried at night when she thought I did not hear her, begged Yahweh for answers as to why he'd stolen her husband and left four boys without a father to teach them to be men."

The abrupt change in subject confused her, but she could not help but bleed for Marva as he spoke. She knew the agony of loss, but she could only imagine how frightening and painful those early years must have been for a woman who'd not only lost the man she loved but was now solely responsible to provide for and protect four little boys who were grieving as well.

"It was in that time I determined never to marry," said Avi. "I worked in the brickfields, and my father was far from the only casualty in the mud. I've seen men whipped to death. Men fall from precarious perches on building projects. Men expire in the vicious heat after being denied shade and water by cruel overseers. We are but numbers to them. Nameless, faceless animals that are easily replaced by little boys who should be giggling, playing chase, and kicking balls without fear of receiving stripes on their tiny backs."

Tears in her eyes, Shiphrah's gut clenched tight as he described such horrors.

"How can I justify marriage, Shiphrah, knowing the chances are that I would leave my wife to suffer such burdens without me? And how can I justify bringing new lives into this world if those lives are born into slavery?"

At first she thought he was only voicing his pain, not expecting an answer from her, but the silence stretched long between them, giving her time to collect her thoughts and offer one.

"There were times," she finally said, "when I wished to die as the traders marched us through the desert, knowing that my life would never again be my own. I knew that only torment and slavery were at the end of the trek. But even though I begged El Shaddai to end my life, especially when the traders told me what was likely to happen to my body once I was sold to an Egyptian master, and even though two of my cousins perished along the way, I was spared."

She took a deep breath, willing her voice to remain steady even if the memories tore new pieces from her heart as she spoke them aloud. "And though I was a slave, my every heartbeat owned by a master who had the power of life and death over me, there were moments of joy. Times when my first young mistress laughed and called me her closest friend, sharing treats with me in secret and inviting me into her play. Times I was allowed to enjoy the coolness of the lovely gardens near the pool, breathing in the sweetness of the exquisite flowers there and listening to birdsong in the shade of the palms. And after I went to Sennofre's home I found joy in my friendship with Gilah at the market, with Berenice as I shared new stories of El Shaddai, and in my unexpected part in the birth of her firstborn son. Not to mention all the miraculous births I've witnessed alongside your mother in these past weeks. And somehow through it all, I've come to understand just how precious this one life I have been given truly is. That the sparkling moments of love and kindness and beauty are worth all the pain. My life is precious—all life is precious—and I will fight for it and for every bit of joy I can experience along the way until El Shaddai determines which heartbeat is my last."

Avi's gaze was locked on her face, and another rush of embarrassment came over her at the looseness of her tongue. "Perhaps that is not an answer to your question—"

"No," he cut her off, stepping closer, "no, that is *exactly* the answer to my question. I think I have been looking at everything upside down and backward. Egypt wants to strip us Hebrews of our joy. To steal those moments of beauty and love by pushing our faces into the dirt. To make us believe that our lives are worth nothing more than the mindless animals they expect us to be."

His voice strengthened with conviction as he continued. "But what better revenge to take on those who mean to grind us down than to thrive? To obey Adonai's command to be fruitful and multiply? To steal back those moments by being grateful for each of those allotted heartbeats and looking for joy among the ashes?"

His dark eyes glittering with intensity, he stepped even closer. It took everything she had to keep from shying away, from bolting from the transformed man before her and the furious pounding behind her ribs.

Then he reached for her, placing his palms on either side of her face, and everything seemed to go still.

"I lied earlier," he said, his voice dropped to a whisper. "I didn't think you were a spy when you came."

"What do you mean?" she replied, matching his quiet tone.

"When the door opened and I saw you sitting there with my mother—a mystery wrapped in such beauty that I could not breathe—I immediately knew you were a threat. Not to our household or my people but to my resolve. And every day since then you have undone that wall, brick by brick. Every time you smiled this sweet smile…" He brushed a thumb over the curve of her mouth, causing her heartbeat to stutter and her mind to swirl with doubts about why he was saying such impossible, beautiful things. "Every time you insisted that my imma sit down and rest her feet and hands while you bustled about lightening her load. Every time you served me cheerfully in spite of my scowls, you destroyed my reasons for doing so in the first place."

He pulled a playful frown, and it startled another laugh out of her. But just as quickly it dissipated as he leaned impossibly close, so close she could feel his quickened breath on her lips. "You are right," he murmured, "this life is precious. And we should fight for joy. Shouldn't we?"

The challenge hung in the air for only a moment before Shiphrah smiled and nodded, all doubts overcome by the sincerity in his eyes and the feel of his large, warm hands holding her face as if it was something to be cherished.

And then he kissed her, and she knew that these moments would be among those she treasured most in this beautiful life given to her by El Shaddai, one in which new ripples of hope had begun to spread on the surface of the waters that she'd once thought were meant to pull her under. As she reveled in the feel of his strong arms around her and the beginnings of their story together was being written, she was under no illusions. There would be times when the current would threaten to overtake them, but somehow she knew that if they held on to each other, they could find the strength to keep their heads above water, one breath at a time.

CHAPTER ELEVEN

The newly married couple entered the courtyard, the bride bedecked with flowers on her crown and the groom with a smile that could, on its own, illuminate the evening's festivities. Hand in hand they greeted their guests, accepting blessings from all their neighbors and small but generous gifts of precious dry goods, salted fish, and wool that would be used to start their lives together from a place of relative plenty.

Shiphrah leaned back against Avi from their place beneath a shadowy eave, watching the couple weave through the crowd, the light of joy on their faces highlighting the beauty of two becoming one.

"That was us not so long ago," said Avi, his rich voice rumbling against her back and his warm breath on her ear.

"I barely remember," she replied. "It was such a whirl of celebration and dancing and so many new things all at once." And indeed that lovely evening she married her Avi five months before had been so full of heady euphoria that it had seemed days before her feet touched the ground.

"I remember." Her husband slipped a well-muscled arm about her waist, tugging her back against his body. His lips skimmed the side of her neck, causing a delightful shiver to slide over her skin. "I remember every moment of the perfect day I finally was allowed to make you mine."

She released a breathy laugh, feigning a struggle against his hold. "*Avi*. People will see us. Your *mother* will see us."

"And what of it?" he asked, tightening his hold and brushing another kiss to the hollow behind her ear. "They will see nothing more than the most blessed man in all of Egypt delighting in his bride."

For as cold as he'd been when Shiphrah had arrived at Marva's doorstep and the weeks that followed, once he'd given in to the draw between them on the rooftop, he'd treated her as nothing less than a treasure. She'd thought he'd saved his warmest smiles and tightest embraces for his mother, but they were nothing compared to the affection he lavished on her now. When Avi loved, he loved fiercely, and she was the fortunate recipient of adoration that she'd never even dreamed possible.

Even Marva had remarked on the shift in him the very night they'd announced their betrothal, telling Shiphrah with a sheen of tears in her eyes that her own husband had been the same: a man of passionate emotion and deep loyalty.

Then the woman she'd come to revere, both as a midwife and a bosom friend, took Shiphrah's face in her gnarled hands, kissed her on the forehead, and told her to call her Imma from that day on. She said she had considered Shiphrah a daughter from nearly the moment she crossed her threshold and refused to even wait until their wedding day to label her as such—an honor that Shiphrah still could not fully wrap her mind around.

How had El Shaddai blessed her so mightily when her faith in Him was sometimes little more than a flickering shadow?

Overcome with gratitude for everything she had been gifted by a God she was only just beginning to understand, she turned in Avi's arms, grateful for the deepening shadows around them. "It is I who have been given far more than I could have ever dreamed possible, my love."

His dark eyes reflected the glow of a torch across the courtyard that connected their home with seven other wind-battered mud-brick houses. "If only you did not have to leave your hard-won freedom behind to be joined to me." The regret that filled his voice left her chest aching. Was this something he'd been worrying over all these months?

"You could have taken that silver—" he began.

She placed two fingers on his lips to halt his words, shaking her head. "You have given me a home and a family that I would not trade for every piece of silver in all of Egypt, nor for one hour outside the long reach of Pharaoh's grip. Freedom would be nothing but a prison of loneliness without you. I am where I am meant to be."

"The two of you will draw all the attention away from the bride and groom," came a teasing voice at Shiphrah's side. Puah's gap-toothed grin peeked up at her, the girl's deep green eyes sparkling with mirth.

"Ah," said Avi, looking down at Shiphrah with unabashed admiration, "but you see, my bride outshines them all. It can't be helped."

A warm flush came to Shiphrah's cheeks.

Puah sighed, the sound conveying girlish longing as she grinned at the two of them. "If only someone might someday look at me the way Avi looks at you."

Avi laughed and released Shiphrah. "My mother is beckoning me," he said, then placed a kiss on his wife's cheek. "I'm certain the two of you have babies to discuss. I'll leave you to it."

Her husband knew them well. Usually when she and Puah were together they talked of little more than the work they both adored so much.

In the past months since Shiphrah arrived in the Hebrew quarter, the two had worked together as Marva's apprentices nearly every day. Shiphrah's experiences with midwifery had been much broader than Puah's since she'd watched her own mother and grandmother deliver babies for years, but her young friend was eager to learn, keenly intelligent, and had a knack for speaking plainly whenever the situation warranted. In fact, Shiphrah envied Puah's bluntness, since Shiphrah struggled to push past the knots of deep emotion that clogged her throat whenever she was forced to deliver heartbreaking news to a mother or father.

But as Marva had said, when Shiphrah had grumbled over her hesitant words, not only did Puah make up for that lack in Shiphrah, but it was the deep vein of empathy and the almost preternatural ability to sense a mother's needs during delivery that made Shiphrah an excellent midwife. Marva made no pretense of hiding her goal to pair the two young woman as a team that she hoped would once day rise among the midwifery guild to a place of joint authority, just as she had done herself many years ago with her friend Hodayah, who'd passed into the world to come after a short illness only a few months before Shiphrah had arrived.

Shiphrah could only hope that Marva's confidence in their pairing and their joint talents was not misplaced. But no matter what, she would be ever grateful for her friendship with Puah, whose own mother had died during Puah's birth. The girl looked to both Marva and Shiphrah for the maternal guidance Puah's father could never replace, no matter how much he cherished his only daughter.

"Has Aviva sent for us yet?" Puah asked.

"No," said Shiphrah. "She should have at least three or four more weeks. And all five of her former deliveries were slow and easy. Marva doesn't anticipate she will even need us unless there is a surprise complication. The woman is strong as an ox."

Puah nodded, her attention traveling over the wedding guests as the dancing began. "Well, that is a relief, as there seems to be nearly as many women expecting babies as those of age to conceive."

Shiphrah followed the direction of her gaze to Jochebed, a woman who lived four houses down. The woman was swaying gently to the music with a tender smile on her face as she watched her husband, Amram, play a pipe with inordinate skill for a man who spent seven days out of seven making bricks. They had been married a number of years but it was still just the two of them inside their little home. It was a circumstance Shiphrah knew Jochebed mourned, especially when so many

Hebrew babies were being born in the past few years and the poor woman was forced to continue watching all her friends grow round with child.

As Jochebed continued watching her husband while a flock of the bride's young friends performed a lively dance, her hand brushed over her belly—only once—and with a subtlety that would make it detectable to only the most observant. It seemed that perhaps Amram's home might not be so empty within a few months. Shiphrah anticipated that Jochebed would be visiting Marva very soon to confirm what she seemed to have already guessed: a new life was being formed within her womb. A new life that would hopefully take breath in this world, laugh, cry, sing, play, one day marry, and create progeny of its own. And the cycle would, if El Shaddai willed, go on and on and on, perhaps spreading like the branches of a tree into a thousand generations.

"...think that Marva will let me?" Puah asked.

Shiphrah blinked, her attention slipping away from the future written in the secretive curve of Jochebed's lips and back to Puah. "Let you...?"

Her young friend furrowed her brows, tilting her chin as she searched Shiphrah's face. "Are you well?"

"I am. Now what is it that you want Marva to give you permission to do?"

"Never mind," Puah said. Then she grinned, her charming tooth gap on full display. "Right now, I think the two of us should dance."

"Dance?"

Puah nodded, then tugged at Shiphrah's hand. "Come. Dance with me."

Shiphrah dragged her sandals as Puah urged her forward. "I don't know how,"

"You danced at your own wedding," she said, ignoring Shiphrah's resistance.

"No," Shiphrah said, "I did not. I told Avi that if I had one request at my own marriage celebration, it was that my feet remained untangled."

"I'll help you," Puah said, undeterred by Shiphrah's argument.

Having learned these past few months that Puah was one of the most determined and strongheaded young women she'd ever met, Shiphrah resigned the fight and allowed herself to be drawn into a circle of revelers clapping, bouncing, and twirling with such joy that one would never know they were enslaved to the mighty king of Egypt. After a while, Shiphrah forgot that she hadn't danced this way since she was a girl and that the reminder made her heart ache. She shouted and spun with the rest of the women until she ran out of breath and sweat ran down her back in rivulets.

When she finally retreated and made her way back to her shadowed corner, she leaned against the wall and watched Puah frolic with the other young women, looking much more like a thirteen-year-old than she normally did while working alongside Marva and Shiphrah, where her youth was far overshadowed by her intense desire to know everything about midwifery. She also noticed that she was not the only person watching her young friend. Across the courtyard Micah, Avi's youngest brother, had his attention latched to Puah as well, his dark eyes following her as she lifted her arms into the air and twirled with her head thrown back in laughter. Shiphrah felt certain Micah was not yet ready to take a bride, and, shy as he was, it might take him a long while to even nail together the courage to make his interest known. But it seemed as though Puah already had her wish and didn't even know it.

So much had changed since Shiphrah had been released from Sennofre's home. She wondered where the river might take her next, no longer dreading the bends in its path as much as before because it had taken her to beautiful places she never could have anticipated. Secure in the knowledge that she was deeply in the shadows where not even Avi would see her, she dropped her hand to her belly, her own secret smile curving her lips.

CHAPTER TWELVE

Hold tight to Puah," said Shiphrah to the laboring mother, "and push with your feet against the bricks as you squat."

The woman obeyed, gripping Puah's wrist in what looked to be a painful hold. But Puah did not wince. She only wrapped her other arm around the woman's back and continued to speak calming assurances as the woman gritted her teeth and bore down.

Shiphrah and Puah had done everything they could to ease her through this painful process, using all the herbs and oils in their arsenal, until nothing more could be done but pray that El Shaddai would grant a swift and safe delivery. Marva adamantly refused to attend any Hebrew woman who displayed images of Hathor and Tawaret within their homes and Shiphrah was grateful for it. She was determined to follow Marva's good example, even if some women might choose to call other, more lenient midwives to attend them rather than give up their childbirth goddesses.

Shiphrah gestured for the woman's sister to come on the other side, giving her another arm to hold on to, and together the four women fought hard for the child whose delivery had begun easily but devolved into one which Shiphrah desperately wished Marva had not chosen to leave. There had been another laboring mother two streets over who was delivering twins and needed her expertise, so she'd left Shiphrah and Puah with nothing more than plenty of assurances that they were ready to handle this birth on their own and that someone could fetch her easily if there were complications.

Not only was Shiphrah determined not to let Marva down, she refused to let this mother or child suffer. She knew what to do. Her mother and grandmother had assured her from the beginning that this occupation was in her blood, and Marva had only confirmed it. She was under no illusion that every child would survive under her care, but this one would not die. Not tonight. Not her first unsupervised delivery since Berenice's, which had been more prayerful guesses than training.

When the cry of a newborn finally filled the little room, everything inside Shiphrah danced for joy including, for the very first time, the tiny flutter of life within her own womb. It was as if her own child was just as delighted for the victory as she was in that moment.

Through every birth she'd witnessed since the first one, a knot of emotions lived at the base of her throat, and she was forced to battle against it until each babe was delivered safely and it released its searing hold. But this time, she relinquished the fight. She let the tears roll down her cheeks as she laid the little boy on his mother's breast.

Then with a trembling hand she caressed the burgeoning swell of her own abdomen and remembered the moment

Marva had confirmed her greatest hope and told her that she would be a mother. It had never truly seemed real until this very moment, and she wished she could cling to the indescribable joy she felt right now for the rest of her days. She could not wait until Avi would be able to feel the little one's movements beneath his great big palms. Knowing her husband, he'd likely be nearly as tearful as he had been when she gave him the news of her pregnancy a few weeks ago.

Once the new mother and her son were clean and comfortable, and Shiphrah was satisfied that the tiny boy was suckling well, she and Puah left the house. They'd been there since early this morning and the sun was well past the noon hour now, so the two headed toward their homes, needing a few hours of rest before the men returned from their hard labors in need of sustenance.

When they came to the tiny two-room home Puah shared with her father, Puah stopped to face Shiphrah. "That was…" She shook her head, an expression of awe on her round face. "That was wonderful. Can you believe you and I did that on our own?"

Shiphrah smiled. "I can, because Marva trained us well."

"I am so tired," said Puah, rubbing at her forehead with a little sigh. "But I do not think I could even force myself to take a midday rest." Her dark green eyes sparkled with a soft sheen of tears. "I cannot remember a time that I did not want to be a midwife, Shiphrah. One of my earliest memories is of my father telling me about my birth and how my mother died because no midwives were available to help that night. And today, for the very first time, I truly felt as though I have accomplished that goal."

Shiphrah took Puah's face in her hands and placed a kiss to her forehead. "I am honored to work alongside you, my sister."

"And I, you," said Puah.

"Go now," said Shiphrah. "Your father will be home before too long. And whether you can force those eyes to close or not, you should at least lie down. He'll be famished when he returns."

The two parted ways, Shiphrah passing by Jochebed and Amram's home and lifting up a prayer for protection over the woman whose child was due only a few weeks before her own. Amram was delighted with his wife's pregnancy, telling anyone who might care to listen that the life within her womb was inordinately blessed. Although most dismissed his predictions as the boasts of a proud father, Shiphrah knew Amram to be a humble sort of man and not prone to outlandish outbursts. Perhaps his claims might prove to have some merit after all. Only time would reveal the truth.

The house was empty when she entered. The men would not come home for at least a couple of hours and Marva was likely still with the mother of the twins. So Shiphrah went to the tiny chamber she shared with Avi, the one Marva had insisted on giving up for the sake of their privacy, and lay down on the bed. For a few moments she simply breathed in the quiet, eyes closed, waiting for the ripple of sensation she'd felt earlier to reappear. After a while she tugged her tunic upward until her belly was exposed, then placed her hand where she'd felt that little flutter of life before and waited.

Who would this child be? Would it look more like Avi with his deep mahogany eyes and black curls, or would it favor her? If it was a girl, would she follow in her mother's footsteps and become a midwife herself? Or would it be a son who would one day be forced to follow in the footsteps of his father, like Avi dreaded so much?

When finally she felt that strange sensation deep inside her womb, she wrapped her arms around her abdomen, longing for the moment she would hold her baby in her arms and yet at the same time wishing her body could always shelter the life within her from every hurt it would encounter in this world.

Suddenly, a great commotion came from the main room. Shiphrah bounded off the bed and tugged down her tunic, then pushed past the fabric door to her chamber to find Avi and Yaniv coming over the threshold with Oren, the second oldest of Marva's brood, propped between the two of them, his head lolling to the side.

"Avi!" said Shiphrah, surging forward. "What is wrong?"

"He collapsed," said her husband. "He insisted that he only needed some water and rest in the shade, but his skin is a furnace and when he fell again, the overseer gave us leave to bring him home."

"Provided, of course," muttered Yaniv, "that we fill his brick quota as well before the sun goes down."

Oren moaned, his eyes bright with fever and his cheeks flushed with color. "Imma?"

Shiphrah passed her palm over his forehead, nearly hissing with shock at just how hot he was. No wonder he was delirious.

"Lay him down on his bed," she told Avi. "I'll see what Marva has for the fever."

The men did as she asked while she checked the herb jars. They were low on willow leaves. She'd have to send someone to collect some from one of the trees that grew near the canal, but they had a few other things that might help ease Oren's discomfort.

Avi came to her, a deep furrow between his brows. "We must go back. I hate to leave him when you have no help."

"I'm fine," she said, pressing her hand to his bearded cheek. "I'll fetch Puah if I need someone and your mother will be home soon. You and Yaniv should get back to the worksite before the overseer adds even more to your workload."

He took a deep breath. "We will be fine. The other men will pitch in. That is what we do when others can't fulfill their quotas. I am more concerned about Oren."

"He'll be fine," she said, praying that she would not be proven a liar with such a certain statement. She kissed him. "Go. I have work to do."

Reluctantly he complied, leaving her alone to tend his brother, who spent the next few hours alternating between violent shivers, panting, moaning, calling out for his imma and abba, and twice spilling the cups of cool water she attempted to get him to drink in his semiconscious flailing about. As the afternoon passed, a rash quickly spread on his arms and chest, confirming what she'd already guessed—whatever this fever was, it had little to do with being out too long in the sun. And when Marva returned and saw her second son so afflicted, she immediately sent Shiphrah from the room so she alone could tend to him, making it clear that Oren was far sicker than she'd even guessed.

Avi, Yaniv, and Micah did not return home until well after dark and all three were far beyond exhausted. It seemed Oren had not been the only man to fall ill today, and those who remained standing had been forced to make up the difference in workload or face the lash. Pharaoh cared nothing for his laborers, only for what they could do to further his legacy, brick by brick.

All night Marva sat beside Oren's bed, mopping his brow with cool water, encouraging him to drink the weak willow-bark tea Shiphrah had prepared. By the time the sun rose and the men were forced to return to their labors, their brother was no better and Marva had to finally give in and allow Shiphrah to help so she could sleep for a couple of hours. But as soon as Marva awoke, she insisted that her daughter-in-law leave the room so she could care for her son.

By that afternoon the fever had swept through the entire Hebrew quarter. Few homes were left untouched and Marva and Shiphrah were forced to send away two different anxious fathers-to-be when they appeared at the door.

Just after the second man left with directions to the home of Chaya, the closest of the local midwives, Shiphrah realized that her throat felt raw and her body had begun to ache. She drank some cool water, grateful for the relief, and went into the courtyard to begin meal preparations for the men, who would soon be home and would undoubtedly be famished after the extra workload they'd endured today.

But just as she knelt to slap a few loaves of dough on the inside wall of the oven, her head went light and a chill swept over her skin. She wavered, having to place a hand on the ground so she would not fall forward into the flames. Her eyes went bleary and the ache in her throat swelled from bothersome to painful. Leaving her task unfinished, she pushed to standing and headed for the back door of the house. But just as she neared the threshold her knees wobbled, a black wave of exhaustion rolled over her, and she knew no more.

Everything hurt. She tried to peel her eyes open but the room was dark. Someone shifted on the bed beside her and then an icy hand tracked down her cheek. She moaned, the touch a relief and an irritant at the same time. She shivered, her teeth chattering.

"Hush," came Avi's voice, raspy and weighted with concern. "Rest, my love."

She obeyed, letting her eyes close and sinking into the cold, cold water that carried her away.

A cry reached down into the abyss and pulled her to awareness. It was as dark as the depths of the Nile within the room but she sensed that she was alone.

"No! Adonai!" came a stark plea from the next room. "Not my son! Not my precious son!"

Shiphrah tried to make sense of the mournful wail as another heavy current of fatigue and coldness lapped at her body. When yet another brokenhearted plea echoed through the house and she finally recognized the voice to be Marva's, she felt the anguish of it deep in her own abdomen—a pain that refused to ebb until Shiphrah relinquished her hold on consciousness.

A soft glow awoke Shiphrah, the diffuse light filtering through her eyelids. A warm breeze caressed her skin, bringing with it the fragrance of the jasmine vine in the courtyard that Marva tended like one of her own children. It was the fragrance of contentment to Shiphrah, of peace, because she associated it with her mother-in-law, who somehow smelled of the essence of that plant at all times.

She took a deep breath, her body aching from the unfamiliar movement, and opened her eyes.

The room was empty and still but for the flutter of a linen cloth hanging from a nearby stool. A bird chirruped outside, the delighted melody seeming almost too cheerful to bounce off the mud-brick walls of the tiny chamber she shared with Avi. From the slant of the light she could see through the high window, Shiphrah decided it must be just past sunrise.

Unable to restrain the urge, she stretched, her muscles protesting as she did so. A groan came from behind her and she startled to find Avi in the bed next to her. She turned to face him and found him looking at her with a bleary-eyed expression of relief.

"You are awake!" he said, the sound of his voice raspy. He placed a warm hand on her cheek. "I worried you might not…"

The strangely distorted images from her time in this room rushed at her suddenly. The blackness. The cold. The pain. The cries of mourning. Marva and Oren.

Her breath caught in her throat. "Avi. What happened? With your brother?"

His eyelids dropped closed and when they opened again, his dark eyes were watery. "The fever took him. There was nothing any of us could do—" His words halted and he shook his head.

"Oh, Avi. No," Shiphrah said, her mind racing through memories of her brother-in-law, a man who had only just been betrothed to a neighbor's daughter and whose booming laughter was as infectious as it was full of joy. She could not believe he was gone.

"There have been so many lost to this illness," he said. "The overseers finally gave in and told us all to go home for a few days, hoping to keep the lot of us from perishing. Wouldn't do to lose their entire labor force to a fever, now would it?"

Remembering how warm Avi's hand had been on her face, she touched her cheek to his forehead. "You are sick too?"

He sighed. "Yes, but it seems as though I escaped the worst of it. I'm already feeling much better. Micah and Yaniv only had a small fever and my mother is fine. She says she remembers an illness like this when she was young and many died then as well."

"She will need my help," said Shiphrah, shifting in order to rise from the bed. "And you'll need some fresh water." As she swung her legs onto the floor, a dull ache suddenly throbbed deep in her abdomen. Her hand went to her belly as another memory assaulted her from sometime during the hazy, disconnected hours she'd been wracked with fever.

Blood.

Pain.

Marva's red-rimmed eyes overflowing with tears as she gently wrapped something in linen.

A guttural sob came from her lips as realization slammed into her. Her abdomen was no longer sweetly rounded. No life fluttered with promise beneath her hand.

Avi's arms were suddenly around Shiphrah, holding her tight to himself as he rocked her back and forth. "Oh my sweet wife," he said, the words coming out on a painful rasp as his own tears fell on her neck, "my love."

"It can't be," Shiphrah sobbed. "I felt the baby move. It moved, Avi!"

How many times had she seen mothers go through this same grief? How many women had she consoled? And yet nothing could have prepared her for this soul-shattering moment.

"I know," he said, a shudder going through his body. "Perhaps the fever caused it, or perhaps she was not meant for this world—"

Her body went rigid. "It was a girl?"

The only answer was a strangled sob from Avi's mouth that vibrated against her back.

A daughter. A little girl who would never grow to become a midwife. Or run and play and laugh. One who would never give birth to her own children someday.

Trembling with anguish, Avi pulled her back down with him on the bed. They wept, tangled together as they mourned the precious life that had been ripped from their arms.

CHAPTER THIRTEEN

Two Years Later

A knock rattled the door, the sound so familiar in their household that when she opened the door, her hands still sticky with bread dough, she was unsurprised to find an agitated young man on the threshold. Most likely an expectant father.

He barely waited for the door to finish opening before he began speaking. "Is this the house of the midwife?"

Knowing he was speaking of Marva, whose name was equated with midwifery in this quarter, she nodded and directed him to come inside.

"Please," he said without moving from the threshold, "my sister is in labor. Her...the waters have broken. She is so very young. And so small."

"How young?" asked Shiphrah, bracing for the answer, since the man standing before her was likely no more than sixteen years himself.

He let out a shuddering breath. "Barely twelve. My father and my brothers, we didn't even know. Our mother died from the fever and my sister must have hidden it." His eyes filled with tears. "It wasn't until she began crying out in pain that she revealed the truth. I don't know how…" He placed his hand over his mouth, shaking his head. "How did we not see?"

Shiphrah placed a comforting hand on his shoulder. "Some women barely show and can hide behind an unbelted tunic. Do not blame yourself."

He nodded but seemed unassuaged by her words. The poor young man must love his sister very much to be so distraught. She hated to ask the next question, but as Marva had taught her, it was best to gather all the facts she could before walking into an unknown situation.

She kept her voice low and even. "Do you know who the father might be?"

He bit his lip, and a tear slipped from his eye. "An Egyptian. One of the guards who patrol this quarter. She said he noticed she was home alone much of the time while we are out in the fields and one day—" He choked to a halt, his face replete with anguish.

She squeezed his shoulder. The poor young man looked as though he might vomit on the floor if forced to retell his sister's story. "I can guess the rest. Please," she said gently, "come inside, have a mug of beer while Marva and I gather our supplies."

Reluctantly he complied, accepting a cup from Marva, but eschewed the stool she offered him, saying he preferred to stand.

Shiphrah went to collect her midwifery bag, glad that she'd learned from Marva that she must always be prepared. The two of them would collect Puah as they followed the young man to his home.

"You and Puah go," said Marva, lowering her voice so the young man pacing across the room would not hear. "I'll make certain the boys are taken care of."

Shiphrah's brows went high. "But we need you. It sounds as though this young woman might be in some distress."

Marva shook her head. "No, daughter. You do not. It is time."

A flash of panic came over Shiphrah. "Time?"

Marva raised her palms. Her fingers had almost completely curled in on themselves now, and more than once Shiphrah had heard her gasp from the pain of trying to stretch those tortured hands while going about her daily tasks. "I am finished, Shiphrah. My time as a midwife is over."

"No." Shiphrah shook her head, the blood seeming to drain from her head in a rush. "No, we need you, Marva. We need your wisdom. We cannot do this on our own."

"A lie if I've ever heard one," Marva chastised. "The two of you could have been on your own for many months. I've only held on because I am a stubborn old woman."

"But—"

"This is not the moment to argue with me, daughter. Go fetch your partner and get to the girl. I have taught you everything you need to know and the rest you must trust Adonai to provide."

Shiphrah's stomach lurched as she stood blinking at Marva in shock and confusion. Now was the moment she had decided to step away? When the life of a young girl and her babe were in danger?

Marva stepped close to Shiphrah, eyes the same color as her husband's pinning her with intensity. "This is why you are here, Shiphrah. El Shaddai brought you to me, for this moment. To step into my role. Adonai has made that very clear to me. I will disobey no longer. Please go to the girl. She needs you. *I* need you."

From the first day she'd arrived here, Marva had been the one constant in her life, a woman of vast wisdom whose counsel she valued above all others. She had no other choice but to trust it now.

Left without an argument, Shiphrah closed her eyes for a moment, bowing her head in submission, then slipped her bag over her head and, gesturing for the restless and pale young man to follow her, went to fetch her partner.

Shiphrah was surprised at the distance the young man had come for their help. His family lived on the opposite side of the Hebrew quarter from hers. Usually women in labor chose to call one of the midwives who lived close by instead of crossing to the other side, but perhaps with the dangerous situation, her father felt Marva's expertise was required. Little did he know they would only have Shiphrah and Puah today.

"Will she be all right?" asked the young man, just as they reached the threshold of his home. He still looked just as shaken as he had the moment Shiphrah had opened the door to him.

"We will fight for her. And for the babe." Then she placed her hand on his cheek, hoping to give him any small measure of reassurance. "The rest is in the hands of the Giver of Life Himself—the One who made your sister *and* the life within her womb. We will trust Him. Yes?"

Repeating Marva's words to the distraught young man was as much for herself as it was for him, and she prayed that she might keep those truths at the forefront of her thoughts today. To her relief, the assurance seemed to calm him, but it did little for the roiling in her stomach. She drew in a deep breath as she and Puah followed the young man inside, hoping that she would not embarrass herself, and Marva, by letting her nerves get the best of her.

As they entered, the girl's agony rang through the narrow home, her youthful voice pleading for relief as she sobbed. Shiphrah felt a jerk of pain in the center of her chest, a reaction she always had whenever a laboring mother was suffering. But as had become her habit these last two years, she pressed her reaction down, reminding herself to remain calm so she could do her job without making a perilous situation worse.

"Who are they?" A large man with a mud-stained tunic stood in front of the curtained doorway, behind which the girl keened a horrific sound and a female voice murmured a soft command to breathe. The strong odor of incense wafted through the room, turning Shiphrah's stomach.

"The midwives," said the young man. "I asked someone to direct me to the most skilled ones in the Hebrew quarter. And here they are."

Shiphrah wanted to argue with him, explain that it was Marva he'd meant to seek out, but the thunderous expression on the man's face halted her tongue.

"We already have midwives, Ram. I told Yehudah to run for Chaya as soon as I realized what was happening to Lili."

Ram dug his fingers into his thick curls, his lips trembling. "I didn't know, Abba. I just wanted to help. I'm sorry. I could not think. Lili was yelling so loudly. I just wanted to help." The poor young man was so distraught Shiphrah wanted to throw her arms around him.

His father's features softened. "I know, son."

A woman came through the fabric doorway, wiping her hands on a linen cloth tucked into her belt. "Baruch, we need more fresh water." Then she caught sight of Shiphrah and Puah, her gaze dropping to the leather satchels at their sides. "What are you doing here?"

A year ago, Marva had been charged to deliver the news to all the Hebrew midwives that every birth must now be reported to the Egyptians, without fail. Therefore, Shiphrah and Puah had tagged along, eager to meet some of the other women in the city who delivered babies. This woman and her partner, Zippor, had been among the midwives they'd visited that day. Although she'd been nothing but cordial as Marva introduced them, Chaya's bold perusal of Shiphrah, from head to toe, made her feel like she was some mysterious scroll the woman was attempting to decipher. That same pointed scrutiny was directed at her now.

"There was some confusion," said Baruch. "One of my sons misunderstood my directions and retrieved other midwives."

Chaya's lips flattened as she turned her attention back to Shiphrah. "Where's Marva?"

"She is no longer attending births," Shiphrah said and saw Puah flinch at the revelation. In their swift journey across the Hebrew quarter with Ram, she'd not had a moment to tell her what Marva had said.

"Is that so?" asked Chaya.

Shiphrah nodded. "She sent us to take her place."

Chaya's brow furrowed as she let her gaze travel from Shiphrah's face to Puah's and back again. "This girl needs experienced midwives."

"Marva sent us with full confidence in our abilities," said Puah, never one to back down from a challenge. "So that is all you need know about our experience."

Chaya huffed a derisive laugh at Puah. "You are barely older than that girl in there. What do you know of midwifery? In fact," she said with a sneer, "I would wager my entire month's earnings that neither one of you has even given birth."

The truth of her barb was like a spear to Shiphrah's gut. Without forethought, her hand went to her belly, over the womb that had remained so very empty since the fever had swept her tiny daughter away while Shiphrah lay insensible. Month after month she mourned the arrival of her flow, and even Avi had stopped reassuring her that they would have another child.

Shiphrah could practically feel Puah stirring herself into a tempest beside her, so she reached out to wrap a gentle hand around her friend's wrist, a silent command to remain calm.

Thankfully Puah obeyed and kept her mouth closed. It was clear from the triumphant look on Chaya's face that she would welcome a conflict.

Both Baruch and Ram looked horrified by the exchange between the midwives. But when the girl in the other room screamed so loud that Shiphrah winced from the anguish in her voice, Zippor stuck her head out of the fabric door, her own dismissive glance skimming past Shiphrah and Puah. "I need you, Chaya, the feet are coming first."

Shiphrah's heart dropped to her feet at the pronouncement. Not only was a young girl giving birth, a girl whom her brother described as very small, but a breech delivery was an added complication. The urge to press past these two midwives and insist on taking charge was strong, but it would not help the poor girl for a battle to be waged as she crouched on the bricks. And from Chaya's combative glare, Shiphrah knew that's what would happen if she did not retreat now.

"We will take our leave," said Shiphrah, managing a small smile for Baruch. "I am certain Chaya and Zippor will take good care of your daughter."

With a condescending smirk, Chaya turned and held the striped fabric aside as she swept back into the room. In that brief moment Shiphrah caught sight of two things—the white face of a girl who looked beyond terrified, her pupils swimming in blood from the strain, and a house altar complete with the cow-headed Hathor and the hippo-goddess Tawaret. No wonder Chaya harbored such malice toward Marva. Avi's mother was not shy about decrying the use of Egyptian gods and charms in the birthing room, so it was more than likely that Chaya's and Zippor's insistence on using such things had been a point of contention before.

But of course there was nothing Shiphrah could do. She could only pray that the poor girl lying in the other room would survive, for judging by the blue tinge of the tiny legs protruding from her womb, the babe had already passed. Her heart ached to know that the girl's mother would not be there to comfort her. For all she knew, Baruch's daughter had not even understood all that had been happening to her body after such a heinous act done to her.

Before she turned to leave, Shiphrah lowered her voice, hoping that Baruch would hear her over the tumult in the next room. "If there is anything you need. Or your daughter needs, afterward..." She glanced at the curtain to ensure Chaya was not peering out. "Ram knows how to find us."

Baruch's eyes were full of tears. He may have seemed abrasive when she and Puah arrived, but it was clear he was distraught over his child. He simply nodded and then slumped down onto a stool, head down as his little girl screamed as though her body were being torn in half. Ram went to stand next to him, putting his hand on his father's shoulder.

A deep and gut-wrenching sob followed Shiphrah and Puah out the door, the anguish of a helpless father reverberating in Shiphrah's chest. Even though she knew she could do nothing since Chaya was so determined to keep her away, she couldn't help but feel as though she had failed in some way.

Perhaps Marva would have ignored Chaya, pushed past the awful woman and insisted on doing what was best for Baruch's daughter, perhaps even demanding that the room be cleansed of the horrid idols, but Shiphrah wasn't strong enough. She knew her job and was more than content doing what was necessary, and in that respect she could step into Marva's sandals. But she was no inspiring leader of others like her mother-in-law. In some ways, she still felt like that little girl standing in a wadi helplessly listening to the sounds of her loved ones being slaughtered by the stream.

And from the way Chaya had sneered at Puah's youth, no matter how gifted she was and how much knowledge she'd absorbed during their extensive training, her young friend might not be taken seriously as a midwife for years to come. Perhaps Marva had made a mistake in even pairing the two of them in the first place.

Perhaps Shiphrah had made a mistake by accepting the apprenticeship at all.

"Well," said Puah, once the two of them were far enough away that they could no longer hear the bone-chilling screams they'd left behind, "*that* was awful. If only Ram's brother hadn't found those two first."

Shiphrah sighed. "But Chaya and Zippor have been doing this much longer than we have. Perhaps it was best that they tend to the girl."

Puah halted in the road, spinning to face Shiphrah with a determined scowl. "Do not let those terrible women make you doubt yourself. You and I have been trained by the best midwife in this city, perhaps in all of Egypt. They may not have any faith in us, but Marva does. The opinions of her and Adonai, who brought you here in the first place, are the *only* two that count." Then she grinned with a wink. "And mine counts too, of course, and I know that someday you'll even outshine your teacher."

Shiphrah studied the face of the young woman who'd become as close as a sister to her in these past two years. Even at fifteen, she was wise beyond her years, her mind a vast reservoir of knowledge she'd gleaned from Marva that she was able to spout off without a beat of hesitation, and was exceedingly compassionate to the women in their charge. If anyone outshone Marva in the future, it would be Puah.

"Marva has decided to no longer attend births?" asked Puah, in a gentle voice. She, of all people, would understand just how shocking such an announcement would be to Shiphrah.

"She insisted that it was time. That Adonai had made it clear to her that she was being disobedient by continuing to work as a midwife. But that makes no sense to me. How could she be disobeying by doing what she loves to do? By serving women in need?"

Puah paused, her chin tilted as she considered. "I don't know, but I trust Marva's judgment, and if she says it is her time to step away, then we must submit to her wisdom."

And yet the first time Shiphrah made an attempt to replace her, she'd been rebuffed and sent away. Her chest constricted tightly, worry wrapping its many-fingered vines around her heart. Would she let both Marva *and* Puah down?

"Enough with the frowning," said Puah, tugging at Shiphrah's hand. "I have an idea!"

"And what is that?" asked Shiphrah, familiar with Puah's exuberant outbursts and quick shifts in mood.

"Since we aren't needed for now, let's visit Gilah! I'm almost out of that hyssop and rose ointment she made for me. And I know it's been weeks since you've seen her."

With a huff of amusement, Shiphrah shook her head at Puah. "Why do I have the feeling that you will not accept an answer of no?"

Puah grinned, that charming gap between her front teeth making its appearance and her dark green eyes glittering with mischief. Assuming rightly that her partner would give in, Puah slipped her arm into Shiphrah's and the two headed toward the market.

CHAPTER FOURTEEN

The two women made their way toward the city, following the well-trod path past green pastures teeming with cattle, across narrow wood-plank bridges over the canals that networked through the city, and through fields of blue-flowered flax being harvested by bent-backed slaves. As they walked, Puah told her about how Miriam, the two-year-old daughter of their neighbor Jochebed, had found an injured cat in an irrigation ditch and talked her smitten father into bringing the thing home, where it promptly gave birth to six kittens.

"She's a precocious little thing," said Shiphrah, "and she knows she has Amram in the palm of her chubby little hand."

It had been difficult at first to see Jochebed with her tiny daughter, who'd been born just two weeks after Shiphrah had lost her own, and Shiphrah had struggled against the instinct to be angry that out of all the women who were pregnant during the fever that plagued the Hebrew quarter, *she* had been one of the few to lose a baby.

But although the wound never seemed to fully heal, always throbbing dully at the center of her soul, within only days she'd been back to her work as a midwife. And by the time Miriam had been old enough to walk, Shiphrah was just as enchanted as everyone else by her willful and vibrant little nature and felt certain that Amram's prophecy that she would be a child of inordinate blessing would indeed prove truthful.

Puah's lighthearted chatter did its intended work of pulling Shiphrah's mind away from the sad situation they'd left behind, along with the muddle of confusion Marva's announcement had stirred. So, by the time she and Puah had reached the marketplace, the pressure on her chest had lightened considerably and she was instead anticipating her visit with Gilah.

It had been weeks since Shiphrah had seen her merchant friend who—although she crafted perfumes and ointments that the entire city coveted—still faithfully tended her husband's market stall every day. Her husband had tried to talk her out of doing so many times, but she insisted, saying that nothing gave her more pleasure than the bustle of the market and bartering with the many people who sought out her creations. Shiphrah wondered if it might be loneliness that drove such a choice, since Gilah and her husband did not have children of their own.

The bright cacophony of the market reached Shiphrah's ears long before the teeming square was in sight. A swarm of customers buzzed around the stalls, wagons, and storefronts that lined the road into the main marketplace, so Puah and Shiphrah held hands while they pushed their way through the glut of bodies. Here, where everyone in the city congregated to purchase the goods that came by boat from both ends of the Nile, there was little delineation between slave and free, rich and poor. They all stood shoulder to shoulder bartering for goods, gossiping with friends, and complaining over the recent rise in taxes due to Pharaoh's coffers. A rise that was, according to some of the conversations she passed by, purely for the sake of constructing a new and more glorious tomb for the queen. Shiphrah wondered how the addition of yet another building project would affect Avi's workload. Her husband had never once complained of his heavy burden during their marriage, and he still was as strong and capable as ever, but Oren's death had been a blow to her Avi. One that, coupled with the loss of their daughter, had dulled a small measure of the joy they'd found in the early days of their marriage. Joy that Shiphrah diligently prayed would be restored. Although she knew in her mind that it was the fault of the fever that their child had been taken, she could not help but feel as though her body had betrayed both her and the husband she loved so much.

When they finally wound their way through the crowd and made it to Gilah's stall, Shiphrah was surprised to see her friend engaged in an intense conversation with a silver-haired Egyptian man off to the side while a number of customers perused the goods on her table. However, as engaged as she was in whatever she was arguing about with the Egyptian, one of Gilah's eyes was on her merchandise and suddenly she darted over to grab the tunic of a young man who'd just turned away from the table.

"Put it back," she snapped, a hard edge of warning in her usually sweet voice.

The young man's eyes went as round as full moons for a moment before a belligerent expression crossed his face. "Put what back?"

"The alabaster jar of perfume you just stole," said Gilah. "The one made from the most costly ingredients I've ever mixed together. A fact I suspect you were well aware of by the calculated look on your face while you slipped it into your satchel."

The young man sneered at her. "You cannot prove anything," he said, unaware that the Egyptian man Gilah had been arguing with before had come around behind him.

"If my wife says you stole from her table, then you did so," said the Egyptian in a deep, resonant voice. "Which means you've also stolen from *me*."

The wide-eyed thief turned to take in the sight of Gilah's husband, who stood at least two hands taller than he. Then his eyes darted toward the crowd as if he were considering how fast he could melt into their numbers.

"I would not bother trying to run," said Gilah's husband. "My men are already closing in on you and have been since the moment my wife grabbed you. You will not get away. But"—the Egyptian leaned close—"if you will hand over the jar now and vow to never again come near this stall, I will let you go."

Shiphrah was surprised at the offer of mercy. The law against thievery was very clear, and Gilah's husband would be well within his rights to have the young man thrown in prison or flogged.

After only a short pause in which the young man surveyed the crowd, no doubt searching out which among the multitude were the men poised to grab him, he reached into his woven satchel and retrieved the stolen jar. Even though his jaw was set with defiance, he placed the perfume in Gilah's outstretched hand.

"Now go," said her husband, his voice sharp with danger. "And do not show your face here again."

The young man complied, spinning away and brushing past Shiphrah and Puah to plunge into the crowd. Catching sight of his expression, which now looked more shaken than defiant, Shiphrah wondered if his knees were wobbly after such a fraught exchange. Hers certainly would have been if she'd endured the scrutiny of Gilah's tall and forbidding husband.

"Shiphrah! Puah!" Gilah's exuberant greeting was free of any hint of the tension that had reigned over this stall for the past few minutes. She placed kisses on their cheeks and dragged them both by the hand into the shade of her awning. "I guess you witnessed the excitement."

Nodding, Shiphrah released a breath. "Does that happen often?"

Gilah shrugged both shoulders. "From time to time." Then she leaned closer. "Usually if it's someone who looks like they have need of whatever article they've stolen, I let it go. But that boy's clothing gave him away as the son of someone with plenty of means. It's likely he wanted that perfume to impress a girl, not to sell to feed his family."

Her husband, who'd followed them into the shade, slipped his arm around Gilah's shoulders. "If you had your way you'd give all our profits to those in need."

"As would you, my love." Gilah grinned up at him, adoration evident in the way she gazed at the Egyptian she'd married.

"Thankfully your trading business is thriving, so we *can* be generous with those less fortunate." Then she turned back to Shiphrah and Puah with her proud smile still in place. "Nedjem, these are Shiphrah and Puah, friends of mine who are mid-wives among the Hebrews."

"Indeed?" Nedjem's brows rose high. "This is the Shiphrah you've spoken of before?"

His wife nodded and the Egyptian's dark brown eyes took in Shiphrah's face with a pointed but not unkind scrutiny.

"Tell me," said Gilah, "what brings the two of you here today?"

Puah launched into a conversation about the ointment she'd been in search of. Never satisfied with mixing the same ingredients, Gilah was always experimenting with any new herbs, spices, and oils she could get ahold of in the market, a skill she'd become famous for over these past couple of years, fame that Shiphrah suspected might be due to her former mistress's fondness for Gilah's creations. According to Gilah, Berenice regularly sent Thadeo to purchase various oils and cosmetics, and more than a few wealthy patrons had been sent to her stall on the recommendation of Sennofre's wife.

As Gilah and Puah discussed all manner of medicinal herbs and ingredients, something Shiphrah knew Puah was nearly as fascinated with as midwifery, Shiphrah surveyed the barely controlled chaos in the market, remembering the first day she'd come to this stall with Thadeo. So much had changed since then. She could have never guessed that El Shaddai would provide her not only with a home, a husband, and a family, but friends like Puah and Gilah, who almost seemed more like sisters than the ones she barely remembered from Midian. A flash of guilt skittered through her at that thought.

"I am well acquainted with Ankare," Nedjem said. As she'd been musing about her past, he'd come to stand beside her. "Gilah tells me you served in his household."

Shiphrah blinked in surprise for a moment. However, a trader with the sort of extensive connections Nedjem had could certainly have come into contact with her first master, so she should not be surprised at the revelation.

Shiphrah cleared her throat of the nervous warble that threatened when she responded. The man might be Gilah's husband, but he was still Egyptian—and a fairly wealthy one at that. "Is his family well?"

Nedjem smiled as if pleased by her question. "That they are. It has taken a few years for him to repay the extensive debts he incurred when his crops failed, but I have little doubt that in years to come he will thrive again. He is a shrewd man with a strong head for business."

Indeed, Shiphrah remembered Ankare to be so, which was why it was so shocking that he'd lost everything during those two desperate years of drought.

"And his daughter? Aneksi?" she asked, hoping Nedjem would not think it odd that she inquired after the girl she'd served as a handservant.

But Nedjem only smiled wider. "Doing well. She is married and has two little ones."

"I am glad to hear it," she replied.

It seemed so odd to be conversing cordially with this older Egyptian man in the middle of the marketplace. Each of her encounters with Sennofre had been replete with tension and she'd been acutely aware of the vast chasm between their positions each time, but Gilah's husband acted as if she were equal to his level. Regardless of the way he'd asserted his authority over the thief before, it seemed as though Gilah's insistence that her husband was a man of boundless kindness was not an exaggeration. Sennofre's generosity had been born from his gratitude for Shiphrah saving Berenice's life, but this Egyptian was just a good and caring man by nature. No wonder Gilah risked censure by her fellow Hebrews to marry him. It was plain that there was deep affection between them.

"I wish I could talk her out of coming here every day," said Nedjem, glancing over at her with a rueful look. "It's what we were arguing over when you arrived."

Her cheeks flushed as she realized he'd seen them watching their exchange.

"Things are changing," he said, pressing on without concern for her obvious unease. "A new vizier has the ear of the king, and he has a distinct distaste for Hebrews. I don't even know where it stems from. But I do not foresee the burden on my wife's people diminishing in any way. In fact, it may be the opposite." He frowned. "There have been rumblings that they are growing far too numerous and that more restrictions should be placed on their movements in the city."

Gilah must have told Nedjem of her heritage since he spoke of the Hebrews as if she were not one of them now, bound by her marriage covenant.

"Is that why you have men here?" she asked, her eyes gliding over the crowd again.

He nodded. "What I said to the thief is true. She is being watched by men in my employ. But I haven't told her who they are or what they look like. I fear she might try to send them away."

She laughed as he shook his head in consternation. "She likely would. Your wife is nothing if not courageous."

"One of the many things I love about her." He turned solemn eyes on her. "She is my heart and I will not lose her to baseless hatred. I would do anything for her. Anything."

His fervent statement reminded her so much of Sennofre that for a moment she thought she might be imagining Thadeo approaching. But but when she blinked and the tall, dark-skinned man was only a few paces from Gilah's stall, she realized that he was really there, with a very small little boy clinging to his back like a monkey and her former mistress at his elbow.

Berenice stumbled to a stop in front of her, her mouth gaping. "*Shiphrah?*"

Tears stung Shiphrah's eyes as she took in the sight of the woman. It had only been a little more than two years since she'd seen her, but she almost seemed like a different person entirely. Gone was the hollow look in her cheeks and the sallow skin tone of a person cooped up inside her chamber for months on end. The Berenice who stood before her was breathtaking. Her kohl-lined eyes sparkled with life, her cheeks and lips were tinted with a natural rose color that no cosmetic could mimic, and in place of the skeletal and ravaged form that had lain on that bed in agony, she was the very portrait of the curvaceous figure the Egyptians lifted up as the definition of beauty.

"I cannot believe you are here!" said Berenice, surging forward to clasp Shiphrah's hands. "Thadeo told me you were still in the city somewhere, but I never thought our paths would cross."

Stunned by the joy in the eyes of her former mistress, Shiphrah could barely get the words out. "I...live in the Hebrew quarter...with my husband's family."

"You are married?" Berenice's smile grew even wider and she squeezed Shiphrah's hands tighter. "I am so glad to hear it. And you are well?"

"I am. I am a midwife now."

"Now that is not a surprise to me at all." She looked up at the little boy whose hands were wrapped around Thadeo's long neck, all the love in the world swimming in her eyes as she gestured to her son. "Without you, I would not have my sweet Kafele."

"This is Shiphrah, my son," said Berenice, with a hand on her shoulder. "It is she who first placed you in my arms."

The rush of memories from that night came over Shiphrah so swiftly in that moment that she nearly gasped from the force of it. It was as if she were back in that room now feeling Berenice's cries in the center of her bones, smelling the blood and sweat, her belly aching from the desperate urge to run and tell Sennofre she'd made a mistake and had misrepresented her experience. But she also remembered how, in spite of the fear that splintered through her each time she gave Berenice instruction to shift or push or breathe, she'd lifted constant prayer to El Shaddai and somehow her grandmother's instructions came to her out of her shadowy childhood recollections. It had almost felt as if Tula was standing by her side, whispering in her ear, and she knew it was a gift from the God of the Mountain, the Great Provider.

Blinking away the overwhelming onslaught of latent sensations from the night he was born, Shiphrah looked up at the child perched on Thadeo's back. He was the very portrait of his mother but his eyes were Sennofre's, solemn and piercing, and she wondered if Kafele would be just as unwaveringly loyal to his loved ones as his father.

This is why you are here.

The assurance moved through her like a gentle caress, reminding her that it was for children such as Kafele that she was a midwife. It was for every spark of life that flickered into being within a mother's womb. For every first breath. For every tiny soul created by the One who breathed that first breath into Adam in the Garden.

It had nothing to do with Chaya. Nothing to do with those who might question Shiphrah's experience, her heritage, or Puah's youth. It was for the sake of life that she served the women of the Hebrew quarter, and she would fight for them, and their children, as long as Adonai gave her the strength to do so. And as Marva had admonished her to do earlier, she would trust Adonai for the rest.

Shiphrah was quiet on the way home from the market, mulling over the day's revelations. They'd spent a long while talking with Berenice, who'd just happened to come to Gilah's stall that day in person to select a fragrance to gift to a friend—a happenstance that Shiphrah firmly felt was not coincidental at all. Her former mistress told her that Sennofre practically worshipped their son and never let him out of sight without Thadeo as his personal guard, something Shiphrah had no problem believing. The fact that Berenice had not fallen pregnant again had likely been both a blessing and a curse to the woman, for although her body did not tolerate pregnancy well and another might very well kill her, Shiphrah knew just how ardently she'd desired to be a mother—a yearning that she too felt in the marrow of her own bones.

Somehow Puah must have sensed Shiphrah was in need of solitude as they walked and so remained silent as well. But just before they parted, Puah placed a hand on Shiphrah's arm to stop her.

"Thank you," she said.

"For what?"

"For never looking down on me because I am young. For trusting me to be your partner." She leaned over to kiss Shiphrah on the cheek, making Shiphrah realize that somehow in the last two years Puah had outgrown her by at least three fingers.

No longer was Puah a precocious and exuberant child but a lovely young woman who would soon marry and have children of her own. Shiphrah's heart overflowed with love for her friend as she walked back to her own home, and she vowed that she would never again let anyone minimize Puah's skill and knowledge based on her short years.

The moment Shiphrah stepped over the threshold, Marva flew to her with a thousand questions about the birth she'd been sent to tend. Shiphrah relayed the sad outcome of their visit to Baruch's home and the run-in with Chaya, but even as she did a wave of fatigue crashed over her. The events of the day and the long walk to the market and back must have taken more out of her than she'd guessed.

"You are pale, daughter," said Marva, taking her by the hand and leading her to the bedchamber. "Lie down for a bit. I'll take care of the boys when they arrive."

"I am fine," said Shiphrah. "I just need a few moments to sit down and perhaps some food." Her stomach loudly agreed with this assertion, but Marva did not capitulate.

"You *will* close your eyes," she said, pressing Shiphrah to lie back on the bed. "You must be well rested in case anyone else goes into labor this evening. Let me care for you and our family while you rest." She brushed a gentle hand back and forth over Shiphrah's forehead, which made her eyes flutter closed. "I told you, daughter, Adonai said it is time."

"Time?" Shiphrah murmured.

"Yes. You have waited so long. And you have so much to do now. El Shaddai brought you to me when I needed you most, sweet girl, and now it is I who can serve you as you have done for me. I will help carry your load so you can do the job He wants you to do."

Shiphrah felt Marva's gnarled hands on her abdomen then, and her eyes flew open to find tears on the woman's cheeks and a smile on her lips as her mother-in-law pressed down gently, her knowledgeable fingers searching out confirmation of what Shiphrah had not dared to even speak in her own mind for fear of what an answer might do both to her own heart and to Avi's.

Then Marva's deep brown eyes met hers with a flash of pure, radiant joy and there was no more question in her mind.

CHAPTER FIFTEEN

With tears of joy on her cheeks, Puah kissed the baby's forehead before placing him in Shiphrah's arms. The tiny boy immediately curled into the warmth of his mother's body, his mouth searching for sustenance.

No matter how many births Shiphrah witnessed, each time she was struck by the breathtaking miracle of life. But this... this was far beyond anything she could have ever imagined. The deep river of love that flowed through her body was all consuming.

"He is beautiful," said Puah as she began cleaning up from the delivery. Although Marva had been here in the room as Shiphrah gave birth, her strong and steady presence a balm throughout the long hours her daughter-in-law labored, it was Puah's capable hands that had guided Shiphrah's child into the world.

These past months had been fraught with tension, the fear that something would go wrong an ever-present burden on Shiphrah's shoulders, but every day that she grew larger with child and every time she felt the little one move within gave her more hope. And now, here he was, the culmination of everything she had prayed for and finally—*finally*—she felt she could breathe fully.

"That he is," Shiphrah said, trailing her finger across his downy head, already dark with wisps of black hair that she knew would look just like Avi's, and across the curve of his silken cheek as he suckled. So far he'd made very little noise. When he'd made his entrance he'd barely protested. Instead, his eyes had popped open almost immediately and his tiny mouth gaped open as he took in the new world around him with solemn curiosity. Shiphrah wondered if that would always be the case with him, that he—like his father—would be a man whose emotions ran quiet but deep.

It had been so difficult for Avi to walk away from the house this morning, knowing that Shiphrah was already in labor, but the Egyptian overseers cared little for the anxiety of new fathers, even ones who'd spent the last few months with their ears held to their wives' burgeoning bellies every night, desperate to feel and hear every move within. To know that he would be returning to a son—a firstborn son—thrilled Shiphrah to no end, and she was grateful that the sun would soon be sinking into the west.

Marva had not been content to wait to tell Avi about her grandchild's birth and had left to search him out and share the good news before the afterbirth was even delivered, but not before laying a hand on her grandson's sweet head and speaking a heartfelt word of blessing and then lifting a song of prayer to the Most High in gratitude for his precious life. All three women had been overcome with emotion by the time she finished, their tears of joy flowing freely.

"I can never thank you enough for tending his birth, my friend," Shiphrah said. "There is nothing more fitting than his *doda* being the one to catch him."

Puah's gap-toothed smile grew even wider, her green eyes glistening yet again. "You consider me his aunt?"

"Of course," said Shiphrah. "You are the sister-of-my-heart. He will look to you as nothing less than his doda Puah. Besides, it may not be long before…" She let her words melt away, realizing what she'd nearly revealed.

But Puah was nothing if not perceptive. Her brows rose in question. "Before—?"

Shiphrah squeezed her eyes shut for a moment, wondering if she should speak or continue to let things unfold naturally. However, it had been over three years now since she'd first noticed Micah's eyes on her midwifery partner, and the young man had yet to even make his interest known. Perhaps a small measure of external pressure might be necessary to move things along….

"Before Avi's brother asks for your hand," Shiphrah said, the words coming out in a rush.

Puah's nose wrinkled. "Yaniv?"

Shiphrah released a huff of startled laughter at the confusion on her friend's face. "No. Yaniv insists he would rather sleep on the roof alone for the rest of his life than marry."

A look of intrigue replaced the confusion on Puah's face. "You mean Micah?"

A smile quivered on Shiphrah's lips. At her breast her son yawned and squirmed, his full belly drawing him into a milk-induced nap. "I do. Don't you know that boy watches you constantly?"

Puah's mouth gaped open and she shook her head. "I…I never thought…. He hasn't said anything or expressed interest. I simply thought he considered me a nuisance when I come here. He's always frowning at me."

Shiphrah laughed. "I think perhaps he is frowning at himself, Puah. He is shy and you are anything but. He is likely frustrated by his inability to conquer his fear of approaching you."

Her lashes fluttered with confusion. "He's told you this?"

"Oh, by no means! I think he might hide up on the roof with Yaniv if he even knew that I suspected how he feels about you."

"How long have you guessed this?" Puah asked, still looking like she'd been stricken with a boulder from the heavens.

Shiphrah sighed. "Since Liat and Asher's wedding."

"That was over three years ago! They have two children, Shiphrah!"

"That they do. But I'd hoped that by now he would have made an attempt to speak to you."

Puah's lips pressed tightly together, and she stared out the high window at the dimming sky.

"Are you angry?" asked Shiphrah hesitantly. "Should I not have said anything?"

"Of course I am angry! But not at you." She turned to begin replacing her now-clean tools in her satchel with such vigor that Shiphrah feared for their integrity.

Shiphrah chuckled beneath her breath, then was distracted by the sensation of her precious son sighing in his sleep and cuddling closer to her skin, content in his absolute trust in his imma. How strange it was to think that she was a *mother* now!

Mumbling quietly to herself, Puah slipped her satchel strap over her head and headed for the door.

"Where you are going?" asked Shiphrah.

"To do what needs to be done," said Puah, firm determination in her voice.

"And what is that?"

"If he won't speak, I will."

Shiphrah's eyes flared wide. "You will confront him?"

Puah nodded once, folding her arms over her chest. "I've waited long enough, and all this time I thought he had no interest in me. We could have already been betrothed if he'd not been such a coward. What if someone else had offered for me?"

A bubble of amusement mixed with sympathy for Micah. "Go gentle on him, my friend. Remember it took Avi a long while to gather the courage to speak to me as well."

"Three months! Not three *years!*"

"True. But still, remember that he is the quiet sort. Much more so than Avi. And from the way he watches you, his feelings run very deep. He likely is afraid you will reject him."

Puah's expression softened. "Of course I won't reject him. There is no one else for me. There never has been. Honestly, I'd given up hope and thought perhaps it was my lot to simply do my duty as a midwife and never have little ones of my own." Her eyes glittered like emeralds in the sunlight. "And although I'd vowed to do just that if that is what Adonai wished…I could not help but dream…"

"Then go," said Shiphrah. "Find that young man and give my son here an aunt in truth."

With a mischievous smile, Puah bent to lay a kiss on the baby's soft black curls. "Can I get you anything else before I go?"

Shiphrah shook her head. She had everything she could possibly ever want right here in her arms, and when her husband returned her cup would be full to overflowing.

With a wink, Puah stretched to her full height, and then she walked from the room with a determined stride.

Poor Micah! For as long as he'd been watching Puah from the shadows, he'd never seen this side of her partner. The one who, when faced with any sort of challenge during a birth, became so focused on finding the solution that she refused to give up until either the battle was won or there was no longer any hope of victory.

However, something made her think that Micah would be more than happy to surrender without a fight.

A soft kiss on her lips woke Shiphrah. Her eyes fluttered open to find her husband bent over the bed, his brown eyes alight with joy. The warm bundle in her arms had not moved while she dozed, both of them too wrapped up in exhaustion from their ordeal to notice that they were no longer alone.

"My strong wife." Avi kissed her again, then let his lips brush over her brow before coming to rest at her ear. "My beautiful and brave wife whom I adore." The warm whisper made her shiver, her husband's attentions still just as affecting to her now as they had been the very first day he'd made his heart known to her. "Look what you have done."

He gazed down at their son with the look she'd seen on the faces of many a new father in the past two years—immense pride mixed with unabashed awe. "Is he well?"

"He is," she replied with a sleepy smile. "Ten fingers. Ten toes. And looks just like his abba."

An enormous grin broke out on her husband's face. "Then it is as I suspected and he is the most handsome baby ever created."

Unable to help herself, Shiphrah laughed and in response, the baby's hand flexed against her chest and then one foot, which had somehow escaped his swaddle, stretched its tiny toes as his eyes blinked open to take in the sight of his father above him.

Avi caught his breath as the two regarded each other with matching expressions of curiosity. "Can I...can I hold him?"

Her gut clenched with the strange instinct to pull the infant closer to her, like the act of relinquishing him might somehow allow him to disappear, as if he'd been nothing more than a complete figment of her hopeful imagination. Pushing aside the irrational thought, she carefully lifted the little one into his father's waiting arms, making certain that Avi knew just how to hold his neck steady.

And then she fell in love with her husband all over again as she watched him fall desperately and irrevocably in love with his firstborn child.

He looked down at her, his eyes shimmering with emotion. "What shall we call him?"

"Benjamin, of course. After your father."

He nodded, turning his attention back to the face of his son. Then he cleared his throat, twice, before speaking again. "Benjamin. I can think of no better name."

Shiphrah scooted herself up on the bed, wincing at the tenderness of her body, but grateful for every twinge because out of that pain had come the greatest joy she'd ever known. Avi sat down beside her and slipped his hand around her back, pulling his little family into her very favorite place in all the world, the circle of her husband's strong arms. Then they sat in silence, simply taking in the perfect moment and the sight of the child they'd waited so long for.

"How will I ever let him go?" asked Avi in a raw whisper. She knew that he was thinking of that awful day seven years from now when Benjamin would be forced to follow his father to the brickfields.

Shiphrah placed her hand on her husband's wet cheek. "We will never let him go. Only entrust him to the One who gave him to us in the first place. The Giver of Life Himself."

He nodded but she felt his chest shudder as he took a deep breath. Leaning into him, she watched as Benjamin lost the fight against his heavy eyelids and the comforting warmth of his father's hold.

"Shiphrah?" came Avi's soft voice near her ear, a note of concern in his tone.

She hummed a response, curious, but just as relaxed by his reassuring nearness as their child.

"Why did Puah just march past me on the road as if she were heading off to war?"

Thankfully little Benjamin proved to be a sound sleeper, because Shiphrah could not control the laugh that burst from her lips.

CHAPTER SIXTEEN

Six Years Later

While Shiphrah dealt with the afterbirth and swept up the soiled straw from the floor where the new mother had labored, Puah applied salt and oil to the newborn babe, gently rubbing the mixture into the tiny girl's skin before rinsing her with warm water and then swaddling her.

The two of them had become such a well-organized team over these past years that they barely needed to discuss which techniques to use or what tool was required. It was just assumed between them and then accomplished easily. And into their capable hands countless babies had been born, both those who were handed to teary-eyed mothers to nurse and coo over and those whom the two midwives carried away to be buried outside town.

The tiny girl let out a shriek just as Puah laid her in her mother's arms, and everyone in the room laughed at the angry sound.

"She'll be a strong-willed one," said her grandmother with a knowing grin. "No soft-petaled flower shrinking away from voicing her opinions."

One of the mother's three sisters—all of whom had stayed the entire length of her travail and did nothing to keep their own opinions quiet—leaned over to brush a finger down the baby's soft cheek with a smile. "She'll keep us all in line, I would wager."

"We'll find her a good, strong husband," said the mother, smiling down at her little daughter with pride as she suckled, "one who will view her strong mind as a blessing and not a curse."

A man like Avi, thought Shiphrah, the reminder of her husband flooding her with tenderness. Never once had he complained about her duties or grumbled that as a highly skilled midwife she received far more respect than a man whose feet were ever encased in mud and whose hands had been forced to build many homes and buildings that he was considered too lowly to even enter.

Shiphrah could not imagine her life without her kind, handsome, and generous husband by her side, and from that first day on the rooftop, when he revealed his heart to her, she'd never once regretted staying in Egypt and leaving Midian in her past. This was where she was meant to be, where El Shaddai had led her, and she was far too grateful for all the beautiful moments in these past nine years to wallow in the painful ones along the way.

Although she would never forget that tiny life that had lived within her for only a few brief months, the births of her four precious children had overshadowed that grief with boundless joy. And when Avi held their youngest—a tiny little girl with black curls just like her abba—in his arms for the first time, with tears streaming into his beard, Shiphrah thought her chest might burst from the exultation pulsing in her heart.

After ensuring that mother and child were comfortable, Shiphrah and Puah left the two in the care of the women of their family, knowing they would be watched over diligently. They would visit again in a day or two, to make sure that all was well and that the baby was thriving in her new world.

"Do you think perhaps we could convince the women of this city to hold off their labor pains for a couple more days?" asked Puah, rubbing at her bleary eyes. "I need sleep."

Shiphrah chuckled. "As do I, my friend. But with the number of babies expected over the next few months, I have a suspicion that there will be little rest for us."

Indeed the number of pregnant women had seemed to multiply in the past couple of years, as if El Shaddai suddenly felt the need to bless the Hebrews with more children to make up for the many they'd lost during their time in chains. But as the city grew and the birth rate expanded, there were times when Shiphrah and Puah went from one labor to the next without time for a meal or to catch their breath. There simply were not enough midwives in the city to meet all the needs, and Shiphrah was grateful that the Hebrew women in general were a strong lot, some only calling them to births when complications arose.

Shiphrah could not ask for a better partner than Puah, who had just as much energy and vivacity as she had when she was Marva's thirteen-year-old apprentice. The young woman might be slender but she was strong, able to support a laboring mother with ease, and with her slim arms and nimble hands had turned many a stubborn infant within the birth canal and saved lives doing so. That, along with her impressive knowledge of herbal medicines, had melted away any trepidations people once had over calling such a young midwife to their homes. Together they were known as two halves of the same whole, their names linked together so frequently that it was practically one word. And neither would have it any other way.

"Let's both of us hurry home and take what rest we can," said Shiphrah. "There are at least three women nearing their time that I'm aware of, including Jochebed, who has already been having a few scattered pains. We must be ready."

Puah lifted a hand to shade her eyes from the afternoon sunlight. "Please, El Shaddai," she moaned, "keep Jochebed's little one so comfortable that he remains tucked away within her womb for at least a day or two more!"

On a shared laugh, the two of them parted ways. When they'd married nearly five years before, Micah had moved into the tiny home Puah shared with her father, but they had yet to be blessed with children, so two rooms were plenty for now. However, Shiphrah hoped it would not be much longer before Adonai would open Puah's womb and cause the house to be overfull, for the sake of her friend, who struggled greatly over her childlessness.

The moment Shiphrah opened the door, the voices of her children greeted her.

"Imma!" cried Ayla, as the two-year-old barreled across the main room to throw her arms around Shiphrah's thigh. Eyes the same midnight color as her father's pleaded for justice as she immediately delved into a half-coherent story that seemed to be about Nathanael and Yared taking her favorite doll and hiding it in the bottom of a pot of beans.

Dodging her gaze with guilty smiles, her second- and third-born boys looked far from contrite from their place in the corner, where they were playing a game with animals Avi had carved for them out of a large bone he'd found near the river. At four and five, the two of them were difficult to manage and full of energy that never seemed to wane, but somehow Marva—in the infinite wisdom of one who'd raised four strong-headed boys of her own—kept Shiphrah's brood in line.

"But Beni found it," said Ayla, smiling over at her oldest brother, Benjamin, who was seated nearby, grinding spices with a mortar alongside Marva—as usual helping his grandmother with the daily meal. Where Nathanael and Yared were whirlwinds, Benjamin was more like a deep well. Quiet and serious, he preferred aiding Marva with tasks or sitting at his abba's feet learning about Adam and Isaac and Joseph to running or wrestling. The rest of the time he carried Ayla about as if she were a doll herself. He was in all things her champion, and she worshipped him with nearly the same fervor as the Egyptians did the sun.

"Then it sounds as if all was made right," said Shiphrah, then bent to place a kiss on her daughter's forehead before handing the girl her midwife's satchel. It gave the little one no end of delight to have the responsibility of placing the small bag of tools on the stool by the door each day, where it would be easily snatched up the moment Shiphrah was called to a pregnant woman's side. Perhaps one day Ayla herself would use the very same bag to attend labors. As fascinated as she was with any and all infants, Shiphrah guessed her daughter might very well follow in her own footsteps, as she had done with her mother and grandmother.

How delighted both of them would be to see Shiphrah's work now. It made her heart glad to imagine that wherever El Shaddai had given rest to their souls, her mother and Tula might be able to see how much their influence had shaped her path.

"You look half asleep on your feet, daughter," said Marva, one twisted hand waving toward the chamber Shiphrah and Avi shared. "Go lie down."

Shiphrah could not argue with her assessment. She seemed to have suddenly crashed into the wall of fatigue that she'd been avoiding all night long. "I'll wait until the men come home," she said. "I'm nearly as hungry as I am tired."

Marva nodded her head, even as she silently corrected the way Benjamin was holding the pestle in his hand, ever patient with his sweet determination to be a help to her.

At times Shiphrah almost felt guilty for being able to do the work Marva loved so much, as if she had stolen something precious from her mother-in-law. But as she'd said from the first day she'd revealed Shiphrah was pregnant with Benjamin, Marva insisted that it was her time to step back and serve her family by caring for the children whenever Shiphrah was called away. And truly, Marva delighted in her role as grandmother, caring for the children with such open joy that any pang of guilt quickly melted into gratitude for how El Shaddai had placed such a generous and kind woman in her life.

As Shiphrah was removing her sandals, preparing to wash her dusty feet, the door opened and Avi came in. Any peace that had reigned under Marva's authority flew directly out the window as Nathanael and Yared promptly forgot their bone animals and ran to their father, eager to be snatched up by the waist and lifted into the air. Familiar with his role in this daily tradition, Avi complied until the two were breathless with giggles, heedless of the bone-deep exhaustion Shiphrah knew he carried home with him every day.

As soon as the boys' squirming feet hit the floor, Ayla was at her father's knee, bouncing on her toes as she pleaded for her own turn to be swung up onto her father's shoulder. With an enormous grin, Avi surprised his daughter by not only lifting her into the air but turning her upside down and swinging her gently back and forth by the ankles while she shrieked with glee. By the time he lowered his delighted daughter to the ground, Ayla's black curls were a tangled cloud about her head and her little face was red from laughter, but she immediately begged him to do it again.

Shiphrah's overflowing heart gave a squeeze of pure contentment as Avi laughingly ignored his daughter's repeated pleas in order to greet his mother with a kiss to her cheek and Benjamin with a gentle tousle of his black curls, which was repaid with an uplifted smile of adoration from his eldest son. The two of them were so much alike—focused, serious minded, and with hearts larger than their entire bodies. Shiphrah knew for certain that Benjamin would one day also be a husband and father of unerring steadfastness and abiding love.

As was his custom once Avi had greeted the rest of the family, he crossed the room to Shiphrah and unabashedly took her into his arms.

"How are the mother and child?" he asked.

For as many nights as Shiphrah was summoned well before first light, she was grateful that Avi slept like the dead and rarely woke when she slipped from their bed to attend a birth.

"They are well," she said, glad to report a successful labor when there were countless times she'd sought comfort in his embrace after those that did not end with a healthy mother and child being united in joy.

"Glad to hear it, my love," he said, before placing a kiss on her lips and one on the edge of her jaw. His warm skin smelled of sunshine, hard work, and the canal he'd bathed in on his way home, scents that reminded her of his heavy burdens imposed by Pharaoh as well as his strength of both body and mind that enabled him to endure such a load for so long. Over the past few years, he'd found favor with the overseers and had recently been chosen to lead a group of fifty men on a new project—a sanctuary that would be dedicated to yet another Egyptian god.

Although her own people had worshipped more than just El Shaddai, the sheer number of deities Pharaoh's people revered never ceased to amaze her. And with every nation

Pharaoh conquered or made a treaty with, another foreign god was added to the number, creating a strange mixing and melding of divine powers and jurisdictions that Shiphrah could not possibly follow. She was glad that she'd chosen only one God to bend her knee to. A God who somehow had led her all the way to this very doorstep. A God who'd given her far more blessings than she could have ever fathomed as she took those eternal steps toward this land of slavery and torment.

"Where is Yaniv?" asked Shiphrah, realizing that Avi's younger brother had not entered the house behind him. Yaniv was as yet unmarried, so he slept blissfully alone on their rooftop. Shiphrah teased him regularly that he'd need to find a bride who did not mind sleeping under the stars since he much preferred the snug woolen tent he'd rigged in one corner to abiding beneath a roof.

Avi's dark eyes glittered with mischief. "He'll be along shortly. He saw Rehuvi down the street."

"Ah." Shiphrah returned his knowing smile. "I knew once he found the right woman all those insistences about never marrying would cease. If, that is, he can persuade Avner and Leah to allow him to ask for her hand."

Avi shook his head, grinning. "Oh, Avner and I have already discussed it. They are willing, so it is Rehuvi he needs to convince. The girl is making him practically chase after his own tail to win her."

Shiphrah laughed. "Well, he gave your mother plenty of grief as a boy, from what I've been told, so perhaps it is time someone paid him back in kind."

"I am certain my imma would agree," said Avi, but his mirth seemed to melt away as his eyes went to his mother and eldest across the room. "Rahotep asked after Benjamin today."

All the sweet contentment Shiphrah had been basking in drained from her body with just five words. "It is not yet time," she said, her voice strangled. "He has a few more months before his seventh birthday."

"That is what I told him," he said, his voice rough, "and he did not push the matter further. But he reminded me that no exceptions are given. That all Hebrew boys seven and up are obligated to pay tribute to the king with the work of their hands."

As if any son of Jacob would forget such a thing over the past two hundred years of bondage to Egypt's every demand. They'd entered the Black Land of their own free will, taking refuge from famine here under the benevolence of the Pharaoh beside whom the great Joseph ruled, and within a few generations found themselves completely enslaved to the very people who'd offered them respite.

And now, as Avi had dreaded all those years ago, his first-born would all too soon be obligated to labor at his side. Shiphrah could feel her heart tearing into pieces already just imagining the day when the two of them would walk out that door together. No more would their little boy be sheltered beneath their roof with his doting grandmother to watch over him while Shiphrah tended her duties. Even Avi would have little to no say in what burdens Benjamin would be forced to carry. She could only pray that the favor Avi had garnered over the past few years with Rahotep would carry over to his son.

"He is a hard worker, Shiphrah. Sober and never complaining about any task he's given. As much as it makes me sick to think of him laboring out in the sun, I have little concern that he will be ill-treated by Rahotep." He sighed, indicating Nathanael and Yared with a tip of his chin. "I have far more concerns about those two trouble makers keeping on task when they reach seven years."

"They will certainly have plenty of energy," said Shiphrah with a grim smile, although her eyes began to burn at the thought of all three of her sweet boys laboring under fear of an overseer's whip or bearing burdens that young backs should never carry. Even Avi groaned in his sleep from the effects of hauling too-heavy loads of bricks and stones for years.

Avi took her face in his hands, forcing her to turn her eyes on him. "My brothers and I survived, Shiphrah," he said, "and our sons will too. Day by day, moment by moment, we will place them in the hands of El Shaddai, who provides. And who knows?" The corner of his mouth turned up. "Perhaps the Deliverer will come and they'll never be forced to serve Pharaoh at all. Our time here is nearly up, after all."

One of the most surprising things that Shiphrah learned about the God she served was the prophecy given to Abraham. Adonai had told her forefather that his descendants would sojourn in a country that would mistreat and enslave them for over four hundred years but that when the time was complete they would come out of that nation as victors. The heavier their oppression before, the more the whispers about their coming liberation multiplied. Many believed that a man would soon be lifted up from among them who would rise up against Pharaoh—a Deliverer who would lead them with great and glorious fanfare back to the land of Canaan.

But for as much as Shiphrah hoped that such things might happen within her lifetime, she could not help but wonder how, even if El Shaddai prepared a military leader of such skill and power, an army of broken-back slaves could ever hope to defeat the most powerful man on earth—along with hordes of his rigorously trained soldiers, who had chariots and horses and every sort of weapon known to man at their fingertips.

However, as she'd learned during her years in Egypt, it was El Shaddai who was in control, not she. She would leave such incomprehensible things up to the Eternal One and thank Him for each breath and for those of the children He had blessed her with.

"Perhaps you are right," she said, laying her head on her husband's shoulder with a sigh, the exhaustion of her long night washing over her again, "but in the meantime, *these* are the moments. The ones we agreed we would not let our enemies steal from us. This is our revenge."

He pulled her close and they watched four pieces of their hearts play and laugh and live blissfully ignorant of the storm clouds that were building on the horizon.

CHAPTER SEVENTEEN

S quinting against the glare of sunrise invading the crack between door hinges, Shiphrah rolled a length of clean linen into a ball and pushed it into her midwifery satchel. Needing to be ever ready in case she was called to a mother's bedside, she checked every morning and evening to ensure that her stock of oils, medicines, and tools was complete. It had been many years since Shiphrah had forgotten any necessary item, such was the consistency of her routine, but she would not take any chances. She'd been thrilled to have gotten a full night's sleep, since neither Jochebed's family, nor that of any of the other expecting mothers, had knocked on her door last night, but that could change at any moment.

The back door opened and Marva entered the room from the shared courtyard behind their home.

"Where have you been?" asked Shiphrah, surprised that her mother-in-law was awake already, although Avi had left nearly an hour ago.

"On the roof," she said, with a shrug. "Praying. Enjoying the sunrise."

"I love this time of morning," said Shiphrah, "before the birds are even awake."

"As do I. For some reason El Shaddai seems nearer in such stillness."

For as many years as she'd known Marva now, she never failed to marvel at the faith of the woman. Her mother-in-law had endured more grief than any one person should have to bear, and yet she did not display even a hint of bitterness—not for the loss of her husband, her son, the use of her fingers and therefore the work she loved, or even for the debilitating pain she experienced on a daily basis. Watching Marva praise El Shaddai for His provision, even in the midst of slavery and heartache, had taught Shiphrah more than anything about who the God of the Hebrews was and caused her to thirst for more understanding of the mysterious divinity who'd brought them to Egypt in the first place.

Having spied a new pot of ointment on the shelf where Shiphrah stored her tools, Marva removed its lid and lifted it to her nose. "When did Gilah come by?"

"When you were resting yesterday afternoon," said Shiphrah. The strong scent of sage and mint wafted from the unguent, undergirded by some exotic herb that Shiphrah could not place. Over the years Shiphrah had benefitted greatly from Gilah's creations, some of which had become integral to her midwifery practices.

"How is her husband?" asked Marva, knowing that the Egyptian trader had been suffering from a deep pain in his lower back for the past few weeks, keeping him from traveling on his ship up the Nile to Avaris where he traded his wife's highly sought-after unguents and perfumes with men from across the Great Sea.

"Better," said Shiphrah. "She thinks that before the new moon he'll be back to traveling."

A loud knock at the door startled her from thoughts of her friend's kind Egyptian husband. Perhaps Jochebed's time had come after all. She snatched up her satchel and her headscarf and opened the door, expecting Amram, Jochebed's husband, or perhaps Miriam, Jochebed's sweet daughter, to be at the threshold.

Instead, Puah stood in the doorway, her face pale and her eyes wide.

"What is the matter?" asked Shiphrah, confused as to why she had not simply walked inside without knocking, as had been her custom for many years.

"We have been summoned," she replied, her voice warbling with something that sounded like fear.

"Summoned?"

Puah nodded and then pointed with a trembling finger to something out of sight.

Shiphrah took a step forward to see and nearly gasped aloud at the confusing picture before her. A chariot was in the middle of the narrow street between mud-brick houses, its highly polished six-spoked wheels shining in the early light. One of Pharaoh's *Medjay* stood beside it, fully armed, with his kohl-lined eyes latched to the two of them. With the stoicism inherent to the fearsome royal guard, the man remained motionless as he held firm to the bridle of one of the enormous brown horses that twitched and nickered with impatience.

Puah's voice was barely above a whisper. "We are to go with him, Shiphrah. He will not tell me why. Just that we have no choice."

Of course they had no choice. If one of the royal guard was sent to collect you, the only option besides obedience was death. But that did not keep Shiphrah's mind from whirling with questions about why two lowly midwives would be summoned from the Hebrew quarter. She remembered well the haughtiness of the royal midwife who told Sennofre she could be of no help to his dying wife, but surely the woman would not know who Shiphrah was. Could it be Marva who was being called to Pharaoh's palace instead?

"Perhaps there is an issue with a birth? Do they want Marva?"

Puah shook her head. "He asked for us by name, Shiphrah."

For as strong as she usually was, the poor young woman looked as if she might crumble into a thousand pieces right there on the doorstep, so this was not the time for Shiphrah to do so as well. Instead, she took a deep breath and nodded.

As she turned to close the door behind her, she glanced over her shoulder. As she'd expected, Marva was standing a few paces behind her, having heard everything, with her face as pale as death. Without words, Shiphrah pleaded with her mother-in-law to watch over her family. The woman who knew her nearly as well as she knew herself nodded and placed a hand over her heart, a gesture that Shiphrah took as a silent promise. Marva would be on her knees the moment the door shut.

And somehow after all these years of feeling like her grand-mother's predications were nothing more than the ramblings of an old, confused woman, she wondered if perhaps the river was rising again after all.

In all the many times she'd seen chariots fly through the streets of the city, Shiphrah had never in her wildest imagination thought she would one day ride in one. She and Puah clung to the wood railing as the conveyance bounced and rattled out of the Hebrew quarter, their bodies pressed close to both stabilize and reassure one another.

People in the streets stared as they rolled by, likely as baf-fled as the two of them were by the sight of Hebrew women being escorted by one of Pharaoh's specialized guardsmen through the enormous palace gates. To add to Shiphrah's con-fusion, their chariot was joined by three others, all carrying women she recognized, including Chaya and Zippor, the women who'd so rudely dismissed Shiphrah and Puah all those years before. Every one was a local midwife of either Hebrew or other foreign origin. Surely *eight* midwives were not needed to assist the royal midwife with a birth! But for what other reason would all of them be called to the royal abode?

When the chariot finally jolted to a stop, Shiphrah and Puah were ordered to climb down and join the other bewil-dered women. Two of the younger midwives already had tears streaming down their cheeks, and even though the rest remained silently stoic as the group was ushered forward into the palace itself, Shiphrah guessed that every single one of their knees was trembling just as badly as her own—including Chaya, who looked on the edge of vomiting from fear. Yet no matter that terror was flowing through the deep rivers of Shiphrah's body, Marva's training in calm during difficult deliveries served her well now. She refused to capitulate to her instincts and hoped that Puah and the other midwives would take heart from her example.

Even in a state of near panic, Shiphrah could not help but be enthralled by the glories of Pharaoh's residence. With ceilings that towered above them, the hallway was decorated with brightly painted scenes: a plethora of birds and fearsome crocodiles nestling among the reeds in the Nile, lotus blooms and frothy papyrus dancing upon an invisible breeze, and depictions of Pharaoh and his family consorting with the gods in the paradise etched upon the walls. One could not help but see these murals for what they were—boasts from Egypt's king about the superior fertility under his rule and a reminder to all guests, be they unwilling or not, that he and his progeny were counted among the divine.

The awestruck midwives were led past column after enormous column, all decorated with vibrant designs, and most so large that two of the Medjay might not be able to touch each other's fingers should they attempt to encircle them with their arms. When they reached the end of the hallway, the guards herded them through the gaping doorway of a long chamber lined with even more colorful columns, murals depicting

Pharaoh's grand victories, and high windows to let in fresh air and light that set all the gold, silver, and electrum in the room to sparkling. At the far end of the room a dais was situated, the stairs leading to its raised surface decorated with figures of Egypt's enemies for the king's feet to tread upon as he took his place. And seated upon the golden, lion-headed throne was none other than the Lord of the Two Lands himself.

Shiphrah's knees went from trembling to liquid, but somehow she willed herself to not heave the contents of her stomach on the gleaming tile floors. She had only seen the exalted Pharaoh one time before, during a parade celebrating the Wepet-Renpet Festival at the head of the year, but there was no mistaking the double red and white crown upon his head, nor the regal set of his jaw as he looked down upon the midwives he'd called into his presence.

A command was given for the women to prostrate themselves before the manifestation of Horus and the Priest of All Temples. Knowing it would mean death to defy the order, all of them complied. When finally they were allowed to stand, Shiphrah and the rest kept their chins down, none willing to risk meeting the eye of the man who held their lives, and those of their families, in his powerful hand. But even though she kept her gaze turned down, Shiphrah could see a well-decorated older man standing at right flank to the throne, holding a staff that made clear his elevated role. Shiphrah guessed he must be the vizier that Gilah's husband had once spoken of, a man who answered to no one but the king himself and hated the Hebrews for some unknown reason.

From beneath her lashes, Shiphrah saw the same man lean forward, an expression of haughty disdain on his face as he kept his eyes trained on the terrified women before him and whispered words meant only for the ears of the man on the throne. And then, after a few excruciating moments of silence that seemed to echo off the vivid walls of the chamber, Pharaoh spoke and the flood crashed over Shiphrah so swiftly that the very breath was knocked from her lungs.

CHAPTER EIGHTEEN

Shiphrah felt as though she were dragging a boulder behind her sandals as she made her way home from Jochebed's house. All during the birth of her neighbor's infant, Shiphrah had been able to push aside the horror she'd carried back with her from the palace—along with the question over what she would do if the babe was born male—as she focused on merely guiding Jochebed through each movement, each breath, and each push as smoothly as possible.

But when the child had emerged and his gender was clear, everything that had happened that morning rushed back in a moment, nearly blinding her with panic.

With her heart pounding like a signal drum, Shiphrah had looked down at the tiny boy in her hands and remembered the words of Pharaoh from his high seat above her.

"You will kill every male child born to a Hebrew woman. There will be no exceptions. I am the Lord of the Two Lands and you will obey my commands."

The tiny boy had been perfectly formed, his thick black curls glistening, arms and legs flailing, and his little mouth pursed in frustration that he'd been thrust into such a cold and inhospitable world. Before the infant even uttered a sound,

Shiphrah had been forced to contemplate whether or not to snuff out his breath.

If she'd disobeyed the king of Egypt and allowed the child to live, she knew that her own life might be forfeit. Pharaoh did not suffer rebellion, and the simple act of handing the little boy to his mother, allowing him to take sustenance from her body and grow past the hour of his first breath, was the ultimate act of defiance.

But then his dark eyes opened, seeking the unknown frantically for a brief moment, before landing on her. And in the space of only three heartbeats—as the boy whom Jochebed would name Tovyah searched Shiphrah's face, unaware of his utter vulnerability, and the images of all the infants she'd delivered both dead and alive seemed to hover behind her eyes—she knew her answer.

No.

No, she would not end the life of this precious child.

No, she would not steal even one breath that had been gifted to the boy by the *Ruach HaKodesh*.

No, she would not obey this command from a king who was obviously being advised by evil men to commit evil deeds.

And yet even as she smiled at Jochebed, announced the sex of her child, and watched the mother's face go pale with the knowledge, Shiphrah had so many things to consider.

If she did continue to defy these orders from Pharaoh, then it was not only her own life she was endangering. Puah, too, would be taken to account for disobedience, and Shiphrah could not make that decision for her. And knowing the Egyptians as she did, Shiphrah assumed that even her own family might be at risk as well.

Her sons and daughter. Her husband. Marva. All of them might suffer for her choice.

But what else could she do? She was a midwife. Committed to helping women give birth to their children. Committed to helping infants take their first breath in safety and placing them in the arms of their mothers so they could grow and thrive and go on to be fruitful and multiply themselves.

She herself had been the victim of a horrific crime. Had seen the aftermath of the deaths of her mother, aunts, siblings, and cousins by the stream, and she carried the weight of such devastation wherever she went. She could not perpetrate such a heinous act against anyone else.

She was not a murderer. And she would not allow Pharaoh to turn her into one, regardless of the cost. No matter how much power he claimed to have, he was not El Shaddai, not the Eternal One who breathed life into existence. And if the God she'd turned to for protection and provision in the desert had brought her here, kept her from violation, helped her heal Berenice, and offered her freedom through Sennofre, then surely He could provide a way of escape now.

Yet no matter the conviction that pulsed through every part of her, she dreaded telling Avi.

This had been his fear from the beginning. That death would tear their family apart. That his children's lives would be offered upon the altar of Pharaoh's greed. Although, instead of it being Avi leaving behind a grieving family,

it looked now as though Shiphrah might be the one to
do so.

With the sun now going down at her back, she paused at
the threshold of her home, one hand gripping the doorpost as
she called up the images of her beautiful children. Her sweet
little Ayla with her wayward curls and lisping voice. Her bright-
eyed Nathanael and her always-smiling Yared. And of course
her soft-hearted and generous Benjamin. She loved them with
every fiber of her being and was putting them in danger with
this decision. But how would she have faced them now if she
had obeyed Pharaoh and killed Jochebed's son?

The door flew open and Avi was there, his chest heaving
and his eyes wild. He'd been out in the brickfields all day, so he
must have only just discovered that she'd been taken by the
Medjay this morning.

He stepped over the threshold and yanked her to himself
and crushed her in an embrace, but he was trembling, making
clear just how terrified he had been. She melted into him,
wishing that she could just stay here in the circle of his strong
arms and block out the rest of the world forever.

When finally Avi allowed her to pull back, he kissed her
face, both cheeks, and then her lips as he rasped her name.

"Where have you been?" he asked. "My mother said you
were taken in a chariot and no one has seen you since."

Poor Marva. Since she and Puah had been summoned by
Jochebed's daughter, Miriam, the very moment they returned
to the Hebrew quarter, her mother-in-law must have been
beside herself for all this time.

"I will tell you everything," Shiphrah said. "But I do not want to frighten the children, so let's eat our meal and put them into bed before I say what I need to."

Her husband's dark eyes bored into her, a thousand questions brewing in their depths, but he nodded and then kissed her one more time before allowing her to pass him. And then those precious faces she'd been dwelling on before greeted her with unbridled joy that made her heart squeeze so tightly that it hurt. To them she'd only been off tending to another mother and baby, the hours she'd been missing nothing more than routine. But in those hours everything had changed and she wanted them to remain in their innocent ignorance for as long as possible.

"This cannot be," said Marva, tears tracking down her face. "How can anyone command such a cruel thing?"

After the children had finally settled beneath their warm blankets, Shiphrah laid out the terrible demand Pharaoh had made of the midwives to the Hebrews in detail to her husband and mother-in-law, even describing the way the king's vizier hovered at his elbow, whispering into his ear as if fomenting whatever notions had driven Pharaoh to such extreme measures.

"But why?" asked Avi. "What good will killing his workforce do? Why slaughter the boys who will one day make bricks and build his monuments?"

"All he said was that there were too many Hebrews," said Shiphrah. "But I guess from the suddenness of the command

and the strange look in the eyes of both Pharaoh and his vizier, they fear the future. They fear the Hebrews."

"What do you mean?" asked Marva.

"Think of it," Shiphrah replied, "El Shaddai told Abraham that after four hundred years your people—"

"*Our* people," interrupted her husband.

She smiled gently. Even after all these years of being joined in marriage to the descendants of Jacob, there were times she still forgot she was one of them. "*Our* people would leave the land that had enslaved them in great victory. This is not knowledge that is hidden. It has been spoken of from generation to generation. It has no doubt reached the ears of Pharaoh and his vizier from the Egyptians that live and work among us."

"You think they believe our prophets?" asked Marva.

"I think that not all memory of Joseph has faded completely from the house of Pharaoh," said Shiphrah. "If Joseph's interpretation of that king's dreams saved Egypt from famine, an interpretation that was attributed to El Shaddai, then perhaps the priests have taken other Hebrew prophecies seriously as well. But there is no way to know what their reasons are. They certainly would not tell a group of midwives."

"Regardless of the reason," said Avi, "something must be done. Perhaps it is time to rise up and throw off Pharaoh's yoke. Surely this will light a fire beneath us, wake us from our slumber!"

"Do you think this will spark a rebellion against our slavery?" Marva asked her son, a quaver in her voice. "That this will mean war?"

Avi's brow furrowed. "If there was any time for a Deliverer to rise up, surely it is now, when innocent lives are at stake. When our midwives are being commanded to murder. And the call for El Shaddai has never been louder than it is now. Even out in the brickfield and while we are stacking those bricks into walls, the whispers are there."

"It may be," said Marva, "that the time is nigh for such things to happen, son. Although I heard those same whispers when I was your age and nothing ever came of it. But what about in the meantime? We need to get Shiphrah away from here."

"What?" Shiphrah exclaimed.

Her mother-in-law grasped her hand. "My dear girl, I have known you for nine years now, and you would no more kill someone else's child than slaughter one of your own. And since you will not comply with Pharaoh's orders, you will be imprisoned, or put to death. You must flee this city."

"No! I won't leave my family." Shiphrah shook her head vehemently, a sick feeling clutching at her insides.

"But you must," argued Marva, "or we will lose you forever. You still have the silver your former master gave you, along with your manumission documents. You can travel somewhere that no one will know you, at least until this horror is over."

In all the time she'd lived in Marva's home, she'd never seen the woman so rattled, so uncertain. But should she really run from this city and hide?

The more she considered her mother-in-law's suggestion the clearer the answer became. For as much as Shiphrah loved and respected her, Marva was wrong. Not only could she not abandon her husband and children in such a dangerous time, but there were a number of expectant mothers in the Hebrew quarter who were nearing their time and needed her to walk beside them—to fight alongside them for the lives of their children—just as she had done for Berenice and vowed to do so for all of her days.

Besides, she'd seen the faces of the other midwives this morning at the palace and knew that some of them would capitulate out of fear. If she left, who was to say that another frightened woman might not finish the job that Shiphrah refused to do? The memory of the blasphemous altar Chaya and Zippor had put in the room of that young girl was a stark reminder that not all the midwives who aided Hebrew births looked to El Shaddai for guidance.

"I will not be going anywhere," she said to Marva. Then Shiphrah turned to her husband. "A decade ago you and I vowed to not let the enemy steal our moments of joy from us. That we would take revenge by thriving, which we have done with every one of the days we've had together." She straightened her shoulders, thinking of little Reuel hiding in the wadi and how she'd known even then that her choice to protect him by sacrificing herself was the right one. "If there is anything that I have learned since those traders snatched me from my homeland, it's that life is precious and we should fight for it with everything we have. If we believe that a Deliverer will be raised up who will lead us out from Egypt in great victory and back to the land of Abraham's promise, then what better weapon can we wield in the meantime than the salvation of the many sons of Israel who will one day leave their chains behind and plunder Egypt as El Shaddai foretold?"

Both Avi and Marva stared at her incredulously, their eyes wide and mouths slightly agape, and she wondered if perhaps they thought her sick in the mind for even considering such things.

But then Marva sighed heavily and bowed her head for a moment before raising a watery gaze to her daughter-in-law. "You are right, Shiphrah. Forgive me for allowing fear to rule me. I have known since you walked in that door that El Shaddai brought you here for a purpose. I thought it was to give me relief and take my place as one of the head midwives in our city." She lifted her gnarled hands, a glint of sardonic humor in the lift of her silver brows. "But perhaps it had nothing to do with me at all."

Shiphrah turned to Avi, hoping that he too understood her reasons, but he'd turned away, his gaze latched on the doorway to the room where all four of their children slept, unfettered in their dreams.

"And how will you save these boys, wife?" he asked, his expression somehow conveying equal measures of both pride and fear. "What happens when the Medjay comes to ensure that Pharaoh's command has been carried out?"

She thought of Jochebed and the sight of sweet, defenseless little Tovyah looking up at her while she held his life in her hands. "I don't know," she replied, the truth springing easily to her lips. "But I will trust El Shaddai to give me the answers."

CHAPTER NINETEEN

Sweat ran in great rivulets down Degana's reddened face as she groaned through gritted teeth. The poor woman had been laboring for hours upon hours, and from the way her legs were shaking and she was pleading for it all to be over, it seemed her strength was nearing its end. But Shiphrah had seen women at this point of exhaustion many times before. She knew Degana would dredge up something from whatever reserve was deep within her bones for these last critical moments.

"Another breath, Degana," commanded Shiphrah, "and then another hard push. You have done so well. Your little one will be in your arms soon."

Degana shook her head. "I cannot. It is too hard."

"Of course you can, my friend," said Puah, smoothing the woman's wet hair off her forehead and out of her eyes. "You already have three children. You know how difficult this is but also that this pain will pass."

Another contraction hit Degana and a loud cry slipped free from her lips as she struggled against the natural instinct to bear down.

With a panicked glance at the window, Puah shushed her. "There could be Medjay about. You must stay quiet."

"They will take it," Degana wailed. "They will take it and then kill us all. I cannot do this."

Shiphrah's gut roiled. Degana had heard the rumors then. It had only been three weeks since Pharaoh had ordered the midwives to end the lives of all Hebrew sons at birth, and not only had the command become common knowledge, but fearful tales were running rampant.

As was her fear, some of the midwives had indeed followed Pharaoh's directive, snuffing out the very lives they'd committed to protect in order to save their own. And in one instance a Medjay had spotted a newborn, which had then been snatched from its mother's arms, only to be dropped in the Nile, and the midwife who'd attended that birth taken away in chains. Although these stories were rare, Shiphrah feared that things in the Hebrew quarter would only get worse.

Thankfully over the past weeks Shiphrah and Puah had only been called to five births, and, blessedly, four of those had been girls. The one male child had not lived an hour past his birth anyway, his far-too-small body unable to sustain breath, so it was El Shaddai who'd determined his end, not Shiphrah.

She suspected that more than one expectant mother had forgone even calling a midwife to attend labor, and she was glad of it. It was one less decision she would have to make with regard to her defiance of the king. She could only pray that somehow any boys born in secret would be kept hidden by those brave mothers, just as Jochebed had done with her Tovyah these past weeks. It helped that the boy was inordinately quiet, not prone to hours of pained crying like some infants, but Shiphrah knew fear was weighing heavily on her neighbor and she wished there was something more than prayer she could offer in help.

Puah, of course, had not thought twice about rebelling. She'd told Shiphrah that even if he personally held a sword to her throat, she would never obey Pharaoh. Shiphrah admired her spirit, but also could not help but envy the fact that her decision to thwart the king affected little more than herself. Puah's barren womb gave her the freedom to disobey without having to consider the effects it would have on her children. Every time Shiphrah attended a birth now, she knew she was gambling her life—and therefore the life of her children's mother—in the hopes that somehow Pharaoh would not discover her deception and have her arrested, or worse.

Although Degana fought hard against the urge to push the infant from its refuge, her body finally made the choice for her, bearing down until the baby slipped free, and everyone in the room went silent.

The new mother looked down at the male infant in Shiphrah's hands and gasped. "No. No. It can't be." She shook her head, panic overtaking any joy she might have in the birth of her child. Her tearful eyes were wide as moons as she looked at Shiphrah. "Take it. You have to take it away."

"I can't…," Shiphrah began.

"You have to," said Degana. "If they find it they will kill it and then maybe all of us. My other three children should not die for this one. Get it away from here."

Dumbfounded by the strange demand, Shiphrah could do nothing but blink up at the woman in shock. "But what would I do with him?"

Degana glanced down at the babe for only a brief moment, her face contorting in what Shiphrah could plainly see was agony before she looked away. The woman was not unfeeling toward the child and was doing her best not to even look at him, knowing it would only break her heart further if she indulged in a longer look at the boy.

"Take him, Shiphrah," she said, before her voice broke into a ragged whisper. "Please."

At a loss for a response, Shiphrah looked up at Puah, whose own face was wet with tears. Her partner took a deep breath, squared her shoulders, and shocked her further by saying, "Of course we will, Degana. Have no fear. He will be safe."

"What could you possibly have been thinking?" chided Shiphrah softly, as she skittered along next to her partner while carrying a newborn tucked in the bottom of a market basket. Her heart pounded as she glanced back over her shoulder, dreading the distinct sight of a tall, broad-shouldered Medjay on the street. Thankfully, no one but three bent-backed old Hebrew women and a group of young children playing a game of stick-and-hoop were close by, but it would not do to tarry out in the open.

"Do you know that some of the women have taken their babies out into the desert?" asked Puah.

"The desert?" echoed Shiphrah.

"Yes. I spoke with two of the midwives from the eastern edge of the city, and they told me that three expectant mothers snuck out into the desert and gave birth in a cave near the tombs."

Shiphrah's mouth gaped at this news.

"It's true," said Puah. A spark of mischief lit her eyes. "And when a group of Egyptian mourners came to bury a body, they heard the wail of one of the little ones and thought it was an evil spirit." The young midwife laughed. "How I would have loved to see them run away in terror."

"So you think we should take this child out into the desert?"

Puah shrugged. "Not necessarily. If too many mothers hide their infants in the same place it would become dangerous. But there has to be somewhere else we can hide him. Someone who would harbor a child not their own."

"Any Hebrew who did so would only be putting their own family in danger," said Shiphrah.

"A foreigner then?" asked Puah.

"Perhaps, but it would have to be someone who would not say anything. How would we know whom to trust?"

"Perhaps Gilah would know of someone?" asked Puah, with a hopeful lift of her brows. "She has so many contacts in the market."

Shiphrah hummed a note of agreement. "Perhaps. But she would have already closed her stall for the day, and I don't know that her husband would be amenable to us delivering a

Hebrew baby to her door. You know how protective Nedjem is of her."

"There has to be *someone* who is desperate enough for a child to keep it secret. Marva said wealthy Egyptians in need of heirs commonly adopt."

Shiphrah suddenly remembered the last conversation she'd had with Sennofre just before he set her free. *"I tried to convince her that we could adopt a child—or ten—like other people we know instead of placing her in more danger."*

Her master had been just that desperate nine years ago, pleading with his wife to take another woman's child as her own because he knew just how ardently she'd wanted to be a mother and was terrified of losing her. And although they had Kafele now, Shiphrah had spent months with Berenice, who'd expressed such a fervent desire to have a large family, and she guessed that the desire that had burned so bright in her had not waned in these years. Could she chance going to Sennofre and pleading with him to take in this little boy?

As if in answer to her silent question, the other statement her former master had made that day came to mind. *"If I can ever be of service to you, Shiphrah, please, come to me. I will ever be in your debt."*

CHAPTER TWENTY

Shiphrah's pulse pounded in her throat, every muscle in her body tight as she made her way toward Sennofre's villa. So far the baby had not made a sound in his basket, lulled to sleep with a full belly of goat's milk. Not wanting to endanger anyone else by asking them to nurse the infant, Shiphrah and Puah had carefully fed him with a small spouted juglet, upon which they'd affixed a soft piece of leather pierced with tiny holes to slow the flow of liquid—before Shiphrah chanced carrying him through a city full of Egyptians. She'd even gone so far as to dress in the garment Berenice had given her all those years ago and prayed that if anyone questioned her, her ability to speak in her mother tongue would allay any suspicion. Although Puah had begged to go with her, saying she could play the part of a handservant, Shiphrah felt it was safest to go alone. If she failed to convince Sennofre, only she would pay the price for this dangerous gamble.

It had been nearly a decade since she'd been in this part of town and much had changed. New buildings had replaced some of the old ones, a variety of monuments had been erected, and the palm trees and flowering bushes along the road leading to the villa where she used to live had grown prolifically. Yet her feet led her directly to Sennofre's door, as if she'd only left his villa last week.

quick

She'd practiced what to say on the way, over and over, hoping that her voice would not tremble when she came before her former master, a man who'd terrified her in those months she'd served in his house. But when she knocked on the door and an unfamiliar manservant answered with a pinch-mouthed glare, every word she'd planned to recite flew out of her head. And to her horror, at the same moment, the infant awoke and let out the distinctive squall of a newborn.

She had only two choices then, to turn and run while praying that no one from Sennofre's villa would care to pursue her, or to gather her courage and follow through.

The first time she'd crossed that threshold, she'd entered as a trembling slave, one who, although she'd made a vow to follow the God of the Mountain, knew little of Him. But in these years among the Hebrews she'd learned so much, had heard all the stories of the Eternal One—from Adam to Noah to Abraham and Joseph—and had come to believe that El Shaddai was far above any other gods. Not to mention, she'd spent all these years fighting against death for the mothers and babies she served and she would not stop now.

This is why you are here, whispered that voice again, the one that had whispered deep within her soul the day she'd met Berenice and again the day she'd seen her and little Kafele in the market. She'd felt the same gentle promptings from time to time during these years among the Hebrews, but this time it was so firm she could not ignore it.

She lifted her chin and looked the manservant in the eye. "I am here to see Sennofre."

"I know of no such appointment." His brow furrowed as he frowned down at the basket in her hand.

The infant had not stopped crying, but Shiphrah pretended nothing was out of the ordinary as she raised her voice. "He will see me. Take me to him."

The man took a step backward, shaking his head, and moved to close the door, perhaps fearing that his master would be angry if he let in a stranger. Shiphrah's stomach lurched painfully. There was nowhere else to go from here with a baby that was now wailing his displeasure. She would be noticed in the street for certain.

"What is going on here?" asked a familiar voice before Thadeo's tall form pushed aside the manservant and filled the doorway. "Shiphrah?"

She allowed her eyes to close for just a moment, inhaling a deep breath of relief as she silently thanked El Shaddai. "Thadeo," she said, "I must speak to your master. It is urgent."

Thadeo leaned toward her, peering into the basket. "Is that a *baby* you are carrying?"

She nodded, praying that the man who'd been so kind to her all those years ago had not changed. "Please. I will only take a few moments of his time."

He smiled, his ebony eyes glinting with humor. "Oh, I have a feeling this might take a bit longer than a few moments."

Then he reached out to take the basket from her and led her down the familiar corridor, ignoring the other manservant's spluttered warnings that the master would be furious at the intrusion.

Thankfully, the infant had calmed by the time they reached the main hall, perhaps soothed by the movement of Thadeo's long strides. But the galloping of Shiphrah's heartbeats had only picked up speed.

When she and Thadeo entered the large doorway, Sennofre was laughing, a sound she'd never once heard in all the months she'd lived beneath this roof, but the moment he noticed the two of them his laughter died away. Nine-year-old Kafele was standing beside him, his arm around his father's neck as he too watched Shiphrah and Thadeo approach the table. Perhaps she should have heeded the warning of the man at the door. It was brazen enough to come to a rich Egyptian's home uninvited, but now she was interrupting his family meal.

"Shiphrah!" Berenice stood from her chair, her tone full of delighted astonishment. "What are you doing here?" Before Shiphrah could explain her presence, a high-pitched cry emanated from the basket in Thadeo's hands. Berenice's eyes went wide. "A baby?" Her mouth gaped as she looked from the basket to Shiphrah. "You brought me a baby?"

All Shiphrah could do was nod, her tongue tied into a knot as she tried to order her thoughts and come up with the right words to convince this family to adopt a Hebrew baby and then lie about his origin.

Shiphrah glanced over at Sennofre, who was still sitting at the table, but he was watching his wife while she reached into the basket Thadeo held out for her and carefully lifted the tiny boy into her arms.

"Oh!" she said, holding his swaddled form close to her chest. "He is so beautiful! Come, look at him, Sennofre."

Her husband complied, trailed by his son, who stood on his toes to take a peek at the infant his mother was cradling and murmuring to in gentle tones. A strong rush of tenderness came over Shiphrah as she took in the sight of the first child her own hands had delivered into the world. Of all the babies whose births she'd taken part in, this one still meant the most. He'd grown so much now, his hair shaved except for the plaited lock of youth that hung nearly to his shoulder. From the length of his limbs, Shiphrah guessed that the tiny babe she'd held once in her hands would one day be similar in build to his imposing father, and just as handsome.

After a few moments of watching his wife coo over the child and his son exclaim over the amusing way the baby's thick black hair stood on end, Sennofre turned to Shiphrah, his brows furrowed as he pinned her with a solemn look.

"Well," he said, in a low tone meant only for her ears, "it seems you've come to collect your debt after all."

The edge in his voice made two things very clear: Sennofre had guessed that the baby was Hebrew. And he knew exactly why she'd brought the child to him.

"I have, my lord," she said. "I have nowhere else to go. I cannot...." Her gaze moved to the child in Berenice's arms. "I won't do what the king commands."

Her former master peered down at her, and she noticed that the shadows that had once lived beneath his eyes no longer marred his face.

"No, I don't suspect you will," he said. "You disobeyed me once too, at the risk of your life. And I can see that in the years since, you've only grown stronger."

"Not stronger, my lord, only more trusting of my God."

His brows lifted. "Ah, yes, your slave god."

Shiphrah wondered if he would mock her now, remembering how he'd said the mud bricks made by the Hebrews held more power. But then again, he'd also been so grateful that he'd asked her to lift his wife and child before El Shaddai.

"I know the king, Shiphrah. I know him well. He will not tolerate rebellion against his decrees. And the vizier will not cease his campaign to cut down the Hebrews."

"Why?" she asked without thinking. "What is the reason for such malice against them?"

He paused for a long moment, deliberating, and she wondered if he would even tell her the truth. Even though he'd freed her, she still was far below him in station. He owed her no explanation.

"There are too many of them," he responded, to her surprise. "Don't you see? Just think if thousands upon thousands of them decided to throw off their chains and rise up. There are a hundred Hebrew men to every overseer, maybe more. There have even been whispers of foreign nations conspiring with them to do just that."

Shiphrah's eyes went wide. She'd never considered that anyone outside Egypt would care about the plight of the Hebrews. Could these rumors be true?

"And then, there are the signs in the sky."

She searched his face, no longer the cowed slave who could not meet the eye of her master. "What signs in the sky would influence Pharaoh to kill babies?"

Sennofre sighed, running his hand over his mouth and chin. "I do not know the exact details, but something in the heavens has convinced the vizier that a child will soon arise from among the slaves who will overthrow the king."

Would this child be the Deliverer so many Hebrews had been praying for? A shiver crept up her spine as a haunting idea arose in her mind.

What if one of the expectant mothers under her care was carrying this child, even now? She'd already been convinced that her decision to disobey Pharaoh was the right one, but the hope of such a thing solidified it further.

"Will you keep him?" Shiphrah asked.

Sennofre's gaze moved back to his wife and son. Berenice had unwrapped the boy from his swaddle, laid him on the table, and was examining his fingers and toes with adoration. Shiphrah well remembered the overwhelming sensation of falling in love with each of her four children at their births and if the rapture on her former mistress's face was any indication, she was already besotted.

"Do you not remember the lengths I went to last time?" he asked. "I would sell my soul to the demons if it meant pleasing her. I've been only too grateful that she has not conceived again in all these years, no matter how much she wanted it. And here you've brought her another child, one who won't endanger her health."

Relief cascaded through her every limb. They were keeping the babe! "You don't fear someone suspecting the child is Hebrew?"

His eyes narrowed, his tone hardening. "No one will question my word."

Of course no one would make such an accusation. Sennofre's standing in this city was far too lofty, and if he did indeed have the ear of the king as he said, no one would dare speak against him. But would a man who was welcome in the courts of Pharaoh keep *her* duplicity a secret?

She did not know how to ask without insulting his integrity. She could only pray for protection, since by coming here and revealing herself to Sennofre she'd made herself even more vulnerable.

"I must go," she said. "My family will be worried."

"You have a family?" Sennofre asked, with such sincerity that she was startled.

"I do." She smiled. "Three sons and a daughter."

"I am glad," he said, his gaze moving back to his own loved ones. "They are everything."

"Yes," she said, tears springing to her eyes as she placed a hand on her heart. "And without your mercy, I would not have them. So thank you, my lord."

He shook his head. "Sennofre."

A smile curved on her mouth at the offer of familiarity. "Thank you, Sennofre."

He dipped his head in acknowledgment of her gratitude. Then, before leaving the room, she took one more look at the new family of four, hoping that her hasty decision to come here would not circle back to bite her later.

CHAPTER TWENTY-ONE

D o you think he will keep the baby's origins a secret?" asked Puah, after Shiphrah had relayed all that happened the night before at Sennofre's villa.

"I have no reason to doubt that he will," Shiphrah answered, her eyes scanning the road ahead for Medjay as they headed back toward their homes. The two women had been summoned earlier to the bedside of a woman who'd sadly miscarried in the night, to check her bleeding and carry the tiny body away to be buried. "He seemed certain no one would question him, but I have heard that favor in Pharaoh's court can be fickle, so I hope that he will keep quiet for the sake of his reputation, and that of his family."

"But can you trust him?"

"I don't know. I hope so. If anything I trust in his adoration of his wife." Sennofre would not take the chance that the babe would be snatched away from her, she was certain of it.

"We also must be careful, Puah," said Shiphrah. "If rumors got out about what happened last night, the Medjay might take a look closer at us. And although we've been fortunate that only Jochebed's babe was born male recently, I have no doubt that the weeks ahead will test our resolve."

"I stand with you," said Puah. "I trust your judgment in all things and will help in any way I can."

"Thank you, my friend," said Shiphrah, reaching out to clasp Puah's hand. "You have been a gift from Adonai. I am grateful every day that Marva yoked the two of us together."

"As am I," replied Puah with a smile, the tiny gap between her teeth making an appearance. "I am honored to work alongside a midwife with your skill and compassion. I can only hope that if El Shaddai finally blesses Micah and me with a little one of our own"—her smile faltered, revealing only a hint of the burden of grief Shiphrah knew Puah carried over her empty womb—"that it will be your hands guiding that child into the world."

Shiphrah halted and turned to her friend. Then she placed both hands on Puah's face. "It would be my immense honor to do so. But for now, count it a blessing that you have not yet conceived. I could not bear to see you forced to give away a child for whom you have prayed for so long."

Puah nodded. "I know. I cannot imagine what Degana is going through right now."

"She made a difficult but brave decision, for the sake of all her children, including that little boy," Shiphrah said, hoping to distract Puah from her own sadness. "Let's go to her now and tell her that he is safe. Perhaps that will assuage a small measure of her suffering."

Arm in arm they changed direction, heading toward the opposite end of the Hebrew quarter to offer a brokenhearted woman a small kernel of hope. But when they turned the last corner near Degana's home, Shiphrah stumbled to a halt at the sight before her.

Two of Pharoah's Medjay were standing on the threshold of the same door Shiphrah had exited last night carrying a male Hebrew infant. As she and Puah watched in shock, the men pushed past Degana's sister with a rough command to stand aside while they searched the home.

Shiphrah's blood seemed to go still. She had no doubt that it was the baby they were searching for, but how did they even know which house to search? Were they monitoring which women were pregnant and near their time? Or were there spies among the Hebrews who had alerted the Medjay when Degana went into labor? No matter how they'd found out such a thing, the implications were alarming to say the least.

A tug of her elbow brought her out of her horrified stupor. "Shiphrah," said Puah in a low voice. "We must go. Now. We could be recognized."

Although she took note of the wisdom of her friend's suggestion, Shiphrah's limbs seemed locked in place and her gaze remained pinned to the open doorway of Degana's home. She'd been so certain that El Shaddai had given her the idea of taking the boy to Sennofre. So sure that He'd quieted the child as she walked through the city and delivered him to a family who would love him regardless of his heritage. But perhaps that had only been foolish hope.

"Move to the side," came a deep-voiced command from behind her and Puah, startling them both into skittering out of the way to press themselves up against the nearest mud-brick home. Two more long-legged Medjay strode past them, their white kilts and gold jewelry shining in the sun.

Shiphrah's gut clenched tightly as she recognized one as the guard who'd taken them on his chariot to the palace and then, before she could turn her face away, the man met her eyes.

Bile surged into her throat. Not only was she certain that he knew exactly who she was, but she had a terrible sense that he knew something about what had happened in Degana's home last night. If so, then she and Puah had no chance of escaping. The two of them could no more outrun Pharaoh's specially trained guards than swim the length of the Nile.

But to her vast astonishment, instead of stopping to arrest her, the man released her from his pointed gaze and continued walking, as if he'd not seen her at all. He and his companion joined the others who'd just left Degana's home, and Shiphrah heard the guard she'd recognized question them about what they'd found inside.

Puah repeated Shiphrah's name with a strangled rasp, her stricken expression reminding her that there was no time to hesitate or pause to wonder why the man had ignored them. Shiphrah reached out her hand to her friend and in silent accord, the two of them spun around and strode away with swift but measured steps. It would not do to bring any more attention to themselves than they'd already done. Pharaoh's men may have left them alone for now, but if fear had gotten the better of Degana or one of her family members during the search, Shiphrah had little doubt they'd be knocking on her door next.

It was three days before the summons came. Three days of startling every time a male voice drifted through the window. Three days of Shiphrah's stomach roiling and muscles clenching whenever a wheeled vehicle rolled by in the street. And three days of wondering which hour would be the last she spent with her children.

And when the fist pounded on her wooden door just after dawn on that third day, she was not surprised at all. She'd not even slept the night before, having tended to another woman who'd given birth to a son. But this time instead of begging her to take the child away when his sex was revealed, the new mother glared at Shiphrah and Puah before having her husband and his brother escort them from the house. Of course she could not blame the woman and was even proud that she'd been so protective of the little one. With such a determined mother, Shiphrah knew he would be guarded well. She only hoped that whoever had informed on Degana was unaware of his birth.

"I will go with you," said Avi, who'd just been preparing to leave the house and head for the construction site. He immediately moved to stand between her and the door, every muscle in his body tight.

"They won't allow it, Avi," said Shiphrah, around the hot coal that seemed lodged in her throat. "You know they won't. There is only room for Puah and me in the chariot anyway, if it's like last time."

The knock came again and the door rattled on its hinges. Still, her husband blocked her way, panic in his dark eyes.

"I must go, husband," she said. "Or they may break the door down, maybe even hurt you or the children."

His eyelids dropped closed, reluctant resignation on his face. "What if...?"

She swallowed a sob. "I know," she said. "But I have no choice."

Very gently, she pushed him aside, took a deep breath, and opened the door.

The same guard who'd fetched her last time stood at the door, a frown on his face. "You have been called back to the palace," he said. His eyes darted over her shoulder toward Avi, who was likely glowering at the man behind her back, before coming back to rest on her. She wished she could ask why he had walked past her the other day, why it had taken so long to come for her, and what Degana had told him, but she knew any such questions would be useless. He was a Medjay, the three golden flies of valor strung about his neck denoting him as highly valued to Pharaoh for his performance during battle. He would have nothing to say to a Hebrew midwife.

Shiphrah glanced over at the chariot, surprised that Puah was not there waiting too.

"There is nothing I can do," said the man, with a bewildering note of frustration in his voice. "I did my best to keep attention away from this quarter, ordered my men to search other areas where I knew fewer women were expecting. But it was inevitable that word would get to the king about Hebrew boys being allowed to live." He shook his head with a grimace, his kohl-lined eyes full of sorrow as he met Shiphrah's gaze. "All I can do now is give you time to say goodbye while I fetch your partner. But then we must go, Pharaoh waits for no one."

It took a few gape-jawed moments for Shiphrah's mind to reconcile the shocking realization that this Medjay, a captain no less, had not only made an attempt to protect her but that it seemed he was grieved at being forced to take her back to the palace now.

"Thank you," she forced out, although the sound was like the scrape of a knife against bone.

He gave her a solemn nod and turned away.

In a daze, she watched him walk toward Puah and Micah's home, wondering if somehow she'd dreamed the entire strange conversation with one of Pharaoh's fearsome guards.

Then Avi pulled her back inside and into his arms, burying his face in her hair. "How do I let you go?" he rasped against her ear. "This cannot be the end."

Shiphrah's ribs felt bruised from the pounding of her heart. "We knew that this was the danger from the beginning. But I do not regret it. I could never have done what Pharaoh commanded me to do."

"I know," he said, pulling back to look into her eyes. "And I am proud of you. So very, very proud of your courage. Our children's children will know your name, Shiphrah, I vow it. And they will bless you for your righteous choice."

She swallowed hard, the idea that she would likely never see the faces of those grandchildren hitting her like a spear to the gut. A movement over Avi's shoulder drew her attention. Marva stood a few paces away, tears streaming down her cheeks.

"Take care of them," said Shiphrah, knowing her mother-in-law understood she was including Avi in the request.

"Until my last breath, daughter," said Marva.

"And tell them…" Shiphrah fought hard to press out the words as she allowed her longing gaze to move toward the fabric-covered doorway where four pieces of her heart slept, unaware that their last moments with her had already come and gone. "Tell them how much I love them."

This time the rap on the door was gentle, and she knew it was Puah standing on the threshold, undoubtedly as destroyed as she was. She took one last look at the man she'd loved for every moment of these last nine years and the woman who'd treated her as nothing less than a child of her own body, before she opened the door to take the hand of her dearest friend, ready as she could ever be to face the king of Egypt and, most likely, her own death at his command.

CHAPTER TWENTY-TWO

The Medjay said nothing to Shiphrah and Puah as they traveled back to the palace, but drove more slowly than he had the first time and gave them both looks of such grieved compassion that it was almost torturous. This man undoubtedly knew exactly what was in store for them, and it obviously gave him pain. She took comfort in the fact that even one of Pharaoh's own guardsmen saw the injustice in his decree and wondered how many other Egyptians felt the same way.

When the chariot shuddered to a stop in the very same courtyard it had before, the guard allowed Shiphrah and Puah to wait beneath the shade of an enormous palm for the rest of the midwives who'd been summoned.

Three more midwives arrived soon after, pale-faced and trembling. Shiphrah and Puah greeted them each with an embrace.

"Where are the others?" asked Shiphrah. Last time there had been eight midwives called before Pharaoh, and now there were only five.

"Orla is in chains," said Amira, the woman who'd arrived without her partner. "She was caught smuggling a male infant out to the desert with its mother. They killed the child, beat the mother, and dragged Orla away. We don't know if she is alive or not."

"Chaya and Zippor escaped," said one of the other women. "In the middle of the night they and their families slipped out of the city. No one knows where they went."

"They were cowards," said Amira, her eyes narrowing. "They complied with the edict."

"You mean...?" Puah began.

Amira nodded sadly. "At least two boys were lost at their hands. May El Shaddai give rest to their little souls. But I think Chaya and Zippor ran out of fear of retribution from the families whose children they sacrificed to their cowardice. A murderer should not be allowed to live."

The other two women remained strangely silent. Shiphrah wondered if they agreed with Amira or if perhaps they too had given in and disposed of Hebrew boys to save themselves from retribution. Yet they were here, were they not?

"Perhaps," said Shiphrah, "we should mourn them as well." No matter how unkind they'd been to her and Puah, she could not fathom the weight of shame and guilt those two women must be carrying after snuffing out innocent lives. She was beyond grateful that she had not given in to fear and suffered the same burden.

The sun dragged across the sky as the women waited, the shade doing little to buffer the heat as the morning wore on. They spoke very little, all lost in their own thoughts so thoroughly that when the guards finally came to fetch them, they startled.

"It is time," said the Medjay who'd delivered Shiphrah and Puah in his chariot. "Follow me."

Unlike last time, when Shiphrah had gawked at the beauty of the painted walls and marveled over the height and girth of the columns in the palace, she barely registered the brilliant colors and the extravagant riches that filled Pharaoh's home. All she saw now were the threatening messages on the murals, the wealth that had been earned on the backs of the Hebrews, and the collapsing distance between herself and the throne. So few steps remained on this journey she'd taken all the way from Midian—one that led here, to this day. This hour. This moment. Had it all been for nothing?

The man who sat on that golden-lion throne—the Lord of the Two Lands who'd commanded her to kill the sons of Jacob—considered himself to be the very embodiment of Horus, and a god himself who took credit for the rising of the Inundation each year to bless the land with fertility. She'd seen the evidence of such boasting inscribed on the very walls of this palace. Like the crocodiles that crouched among the reeds in those murals, Pharaoh meant to consume her, she could tell by the sorrowful gaze of the Medjay captain as he stood by while she entered the great hall behind Puah and the other midwives.

Would the river now finally drag her into its depths for good?

"Stand tall," whispered the captain, just as she passed him. "He values strength. Do not be moved."

She stumbled, eyes going wide as she looked back to this stranger who'd been working in the shadows on her behalf for some reason that she could not even begin to guess. But he'd already turned away, taking up a position near the doorway. The words he'd used were so similar to the prophecy her grandmother Tula had spoken the day of her birth: "*She will stand against the flow of the mighty river and will not be moved.*"

What did that mean? Surely this could not be the time Tula had spoken of. She was only one woman. How would she possibly stand up to the king of Egypt?

As all these things were racing through her mind like an unmanned chariot, she realized that unlike the last time the midwives had been brought before Pharaoh in an empty hall, with only his vizier and a few bodyguards to witness his evil decree, this time a small crowd lined the chamber on either side.

Dressed in a wide array of finely embroidered linens, glinting gold armbands, jeweled bracelets, and wigs decorated with all manner of beads, precious gems, and intricate braiding, the gathering of wealthy Egyptians seemed fascinated with the midwives being herded before them in little more than threadbare woolen tunics, ragged headscarves, and thrice-repaired papyrus sandals. But it was not the ladies with artfully applied kohl around their eyes, nor the men sporting their wealth in the form of sparkling golden breastplates across their chests who caught Shiphrah's attention as she passed between the columns that held up the ceiling of this towering chamber. It was the sight of her former master a few paces away from the throne of Pharaoh.

Sennofre's face was the portrait of disinterest, as if he'd never before seen Shiphrah. Nothing of the man who'd given his former slave leave to call him by his name leaked through the thick mask of indifference.

All the blood seemed to leave Shiphrah's head, leaving her dizzy and disoriented.

Sennofre knew everything. He'd allowed his wife to take the Hebrew baby from her arms, knowing what he was and where he'd come from. Perhaps it had not been Degana or her family who'd betrayed her but the very man she'd run to for help.

How could she have misjudged him so thoroughly? And what did this mean for the child she'd left in his protection? A bolt of dread pierced her straight through, nearly buckling her knees. What if Sennofre had turned the innocent little boy over to Pharaoh's guardsmen to be killed?

Had she guaranteed the death of Degana's baby by trusting an Egyptian to keep her secret?

Her chest ached, breaths labored, as if she were actually struggling to pull air into waterlogged lungs.

As entangled in regret and fear for the child as she was, Shiphrah had not even noticed that the golden throne upon the dais was already inhabited by the king until a royal scribe issued a command for the midwives to prostrate themselves while he listed the five names of the man who claimed to be the very embodiment of the god Horus and ruler of the sky.

With her forehead pressed to the cold tile alongside the other midwives, Shiphrah made one final plea to the God of the Mountain she'd vowed to serve so many years before. *Please,*

El Shaddai. God above all gods. You provided a way of escape for Isaac as he lay atop that altar with his father's knife at his throat, and I beg You to provide a way of escape for us now.

When the women were finally told to stand, the room remained silent for a long while, no one daring to speak while the king glared down at the midwives from his royal dais.

Again, Shiphrah noted the presence of the vizier just behind the throne; but instead of the expression of disgust he'd worn last time she'd seen him whisper into Pharaoh's ear, the corners of the older man's mouth were turned up into a smile saturated with cruelty. Why would an immensely powerful man care to gloat over the arrest of a group of defenseless women?

"When I called you here the first time," began Pharaoh, the sound of his regal voice echoing off the high ceiling, "I gave you midwives a task. You were to deal with the problem before it even took breath."

Speaking of a child, one with a beating heart and pulsing blood and flailing limbs, as a problem to be dealt with made Shiphrah's indignation rise up. She'd been involved in too many births, seen more than a few too-small babes desperately fighting for life after early deliveries, and looked into the eyes of newborns as they took in their new world with awe during their first moments, to question how precious and miraculous each child was.

"I am the Lord of Upper and Lower Egypt, Horus on earth, and it is upon my word that the Nile rises and falls. So *why* have I not obeyed?" snapped the king. "Why have my men found *male* infants among the Hebrews?" His voice grew louder and louder, until he was practically bellowing each word. Indeed, with the reverberation of his displeasure bouncing off the walls, the roof, and the tiled floor, the sound reminded Shiphrah very much of rushing waters barreling through the wadi after a flash flood.

One of the midwives to her left let out a sob, fear getting the best of her as she leaned into her partner, who looked to be barely standing herself under the furious gaze of the man who claimed to have the power over both earth and sky.

But *did* he?

Raising her lashes the tiniest bit, Shiphrah took in the appearance of the man on the throne. She could not tell how old he was, but he was much younger than she'd guessed him to be. He wore the double crown again as he'd done before, but in his agitation, he'd knocked it slightly askew, the cobra at its front leaning to the side in an almost comical fashion. As well, he must have swiped at a bead of sweat near his right eye, because the black and green kohl that rimmed his eyelids was smudged across the upper cheekbone on one side.

She'd seen many images of this king before. Not only on his palace walls but on monuments and carvings all over the city. In every one of them he appeared perfectly formed, his sleek jaw set regally, his every feature symmetrical, his shoulders broad and his waist trim. But in addition to his less-than-perfect kohl and tilted crown, Shiphrah could see that the likenesses which purported to display his divine perfection to his subjects were nothing more than lies.

With a nose that hooked slightly to the side, exceedingly close-set eyes, and a weak chin that did nothing to distract from the visible protrusion of his crooked teeth, nor the paunchy gut below his elegantly embroidered belt, there was nothing about this man that was divine. He was fully human from the tips of his ears to the soles of his feet.

This was not a God who breathed life into the very first man at creation. This was not a God who opened the stores of heaven to deluge the earth. Nor the One who mercifully preserved the life of an obedient man and his family in an ark atop the waters. And neither was this king the One who'd laid waste to Sodom and Gomorrah with fire from heaven.

And if the God of the Mountain, who really *was* all these things, was the One who'd brought Shiphrah safely all the way from Midian to stand before the throne of Egypt, then what cause did she have to fear Pharaoh at all?

The words of the Medjay captain returned to her at that moment. "*Stand tall.... Do not be moved.*"

Was this the moment her grandmother had spoken of? Could she stand firm against the great, but earthly, power of a man who was not the mighty river he purported to be? She'd already come to this palace expecting to lose her life for the offense of saving babies. Why should she not do all she could to save more of them?

THIS IS WHY YOU ARE HERE, came the voice from the center of her soul. But unlike when she'd met Berenice or seen her with Kafele in the market or when she'd stood at Sennofre's door with a babe in hand, the words were not a whisper this time but a silent shout that rang through every fiber of her being.

Jolted by the truth of those words, she spoke without fore-thought, the sound of her own voice strange in her ears. "The babies are born too quickly."

Beside her, Puah flinched in surprise while the King of Upper and Lower Egypt blinked at her with an expression of profound confusion, as if he did not even understand the common language she'd spoken in.

A flicker of movement to the far left of the throne caught Shiphrah's eye as she flailed about inside her head for an explanation of her outburst. An extraordinarily beautiful woman stood there, bedecked in jewels that spoke of nothing less than royal heritage, her curious gaze set on Shiphrah's face. This was a woman who'd never scrubbed her laundry with rocks, sweated over a gape-mouthed oven to bake bread, scoured the fields for dung to fuel her fire, or carried enormous jugs of water on her head from the canal twice a day. And yet she was the very answer Shiphrah had been searching for and the foundation for the lie that was hopefully based in enough truth that Pharaoh would swallow it whole. *Forgive me for what I am about to say, El Shaddai,* she pleaded, *for the sake of Your children.*

"The Hebrew women are strong," she said, standing taller as the captain had told her to do. "Unlike the Egyptian women who have servants to tend their every need, the Hebrew women labor from before sunup to after sundown and have done so their entire lives. So when their time is complete, they give birth with such ease and swiftness that we midwives rarely make it in time to catch the babe."

To Shiphrah's surprise, Puah added to the well-stretched truth, without a hint of warble in her voice. "It is true. Many of them barely pause their work until the final push. By the time we arrive, the baby is either strapped to their backs while they complete their duties, or, as of late, whisked away to places unknown."

The king's eyes narrowed as he regarded the two women, his gaze assessing. Shiphrah wondered if Amira, who'd seemed to have such strong opinions of Orla earlier, might speak up as well, but her mouth remained as silent as those of the other two midwives. Only Puah had had the courage to join herself to Shiphrah's daring deception.

"I have heard this as well," said a feminine voice. Every head in the room, including the king's, turned to find the same high-born woman Shiphrah had noticed before addressing the court with an expression of casual detachment on her lovely face. She lifted her kohl-darkened brows with a regal arch. "Well," she said with a disdainful flick of her wrist toward the midwives before her, "just look at them. They are made for work, are they not? It is why the gods cursed them to be among us and serve us, after all. Their women are practically broodmares. Is it no wonder they press out a child in less time than it takes to call one of these midwives?"

Shiphrah could do nothing but stare at the woman, who for some unfathomable reason was putting her royal weight behind a complete fabrication.

"And how would you know such things?" the vizier interjected, visibly upset. "You are barren."

The young woman flinched at the attack and, regardless that she was a stranger and an Egyptian of the royal house of Pharaoh, Shiphrah's heart clenched at the obvious pain that crossed her beautiful face. But Shiphrah's unlikely supporter recovered swiftly, her gaze going hard as she lifted her chin to address the vizier in a superior tone. "I was well educated by the most learned priests and priestesses in the temple, some of whom are experts in the fields of surgery. You dare question my knowledge of such things? I *am* the daughter of a king, after all."

The vizier blanched at her pointed challenge. Even if he found fault in the princess's explanation, her ancient bloodline superseded his bestowed—and therefore easily rescinded—powers.

Pharaoh lounged back on his throne, one arm carelessly thrown over the corner as he looked down on Shiphrah and Puah as if he were suddenly bored with the conversation. But Shiphrah was under no illusions. He was only toying with them like a great cat. There were claws beneath the surface, ones that would tear her apart if she made one wrong move.

He values strength, came the words of the captain. So instead of cowering like the prey she was, she kept her spine straight and her expression blank and reminded herself that no matter whether he claimed to have command over the mighty river that threatened her now, it was nothing but a ruse. It was the Ruach HaKodesh, the holy breath of Elohim, that hovered over the face of the waters in the beginning, not this man. The knowledge of a truth had been growing in fits and starts from the moment she'd made that vow to El Shaddai in the wadi, had been nurtured by the faithful witness of Marva, and somehow in this moment came to its fullness: there was nothing to fear, because no matter how high the waters rose around her, all life—including hers—was a gift from El Shaddai, to do with as He willed. And if He had brought her here for a purpose, He would not let her drown.

"Perhaps I was wrong," said the king, his voice as smooth as polished marble, "in asking you midwives to fix the problem the vizier—and our learned priests—brought to my attention." He gestured to a group of five men with shaven heads and swathed in the distinct leopard-skin garments of the priesthood. "It is your aim, after all, to deliver a woman safely of her babe." He frowned, his brows coming together in the semblance of sympathy. "And it sounds as if these Hebrew women are much stronger, and perhaps more crafty, than I'd assumed."

Shiphrah was tempted to build on the untruth, concoct details that might further convince Pharaoh that his demand was miscalculated and unjust, but something told her to keep her mouth sealed. Besides, it seemed as though the captain's advice had been wise. She'd stood firm and spoken with decisiveness to the most powerful man in the world, and he'd not had her hauled from his presence or ordered the Medjay to thrust a sword in her belly. She could only stand silently and pray that the king would abandon this senseless assault against the innocent.

"Sennofre," said Pharaoh. The name of Shiphrah's former master on the lips of the king was a jolt to her bones. She barely restrained the gasp of surprise that welled up in her parched throat. "You have a new child, I've been told."

All relief she'd felt when Pharaoh had neglected to call for her immediate death fled in an instant, replaced by a strong charge of hysteria. The feeling of being batted back and forth between lethal paws returned in full force.

"That I do," said Shiphrah's former master, his voice as firm as the floor beneath her feet. "A son."

"Indeed?" The king's brows lifted high. "My congratulations to you. And your wife, she has recovered well?"

To anyone else Sennofre would appear unruffled at the seemingly innocuous question. But Shiphrah had seen him offer the same false smile to his wife as she lay dying in her bed and knew that behind it was an ocean of fear.

"Your felicitations honor me, my king. Although in truth Berenice's health remains unchanged. It has been many years since the birth of our eldest, far too long...." He frowned, palms splayed in a gesture of futility. "However, my wife has begged me for all that time to add to our family, so made"—he paused and cleared his throat—"other arrangements."

Shiphrah's blood seemed to be alive with fire. What did he mean by *arrangements*? And why did he seem to be dancing about the answer when it would be all too simple to point out Shiphrah as the source of the child's appearance in their home?

Pharaoh too seemed to be perplexed by the vague statement. "Meaning?" he asked.

Now Sennofre shifted on his feet nervously, his eyes dropping to the floor for a moment before he answered hesitantly. "I do not wish to embarrass my wife, whom I love with my whole being."

"You *will* answer my question," said the king, "regardless of your wife's wounded sensibilities."

Shiphrah's former master screwed his face into an obvious mask of shamed reluctance as Shiphrah braced for the truth to undo her wild spurt of bravery in front of the king.

"I took a concubine, my king," said Sennofre, his voice lowering, "but only for her sake, and *only* for the purpose of giving her the second child she desired so desperately."

If Sennofre had lifted his hands to the sky and danced a jig before the Pharaoh, Shiphrah would not have been more stunned. It seemed as though telling falsehoods to the king was the order of the day.

Not only had Sennofre not revealed Shiphrah's part in the adoption, but he was claiming Degana's son as his own flesh and blood, a designation that when spoken before Pharaoh himself could not be refuted by anyone else in this court, whether they believed it or not.

"I see," said Pharaoh, blinking a few times, as if he too were shocked that Sennofre would admit such a thing. It must be common knowledge that Berenice was cherished by her husband, for even though it was certainly considered acceptable, and even expected, for rich men to take concubines, there were some among them who remained strictly faithful to only one wife during their lifetimes. His admission of stepping outside the bounds of his marriage to conceive a child had seemingly astounded even the king of Egypt.

Had Pharaoh meant to trap Sennofre into admitting that the baby was Hebrew? And if so, what possible aim could he have had by doing so?

But Shiphrah had no time to contemplate his motives, nor why Sennofre had lied to protect her, because the king abruptly turned his attention back to the midwives.

"The signs in the sky remain clear," he said, as if he'd never paused to speak to Sennofre in the first place. "The Hebrew problem must be dealt with. And where these women have failed, my faithful subjects will not."

The king of Egypt was no longer slouching. He sat tall, his posture for the first time since they'd entered the chamber mirroring that of the many regal carvings meant to display the astonishing might and far-reaching power of the man on the throne. No longer were those vicious claws retracted as his voice rang throughout the chamber.

"Let it be decreed," he said, "that from this day forth, that whenever any person in the Black Land sees a male Hebrew infant, they are either to turn it over to the authorities to be cast into the Nile, or they are to toss it to the crocodiles with their own hands. I am the Lord of the Two Lands, Horus on earth, and my command *will* be obeyed."

At his back, the vizier's triumphant smile blazed like the sun as all his earlier frustration at being admonished by the princess was washed away by the Pharaoh's shocking decree. Shiphrah did not know why this man held such malice against the Hebrews, but it was clear that he reveled in the bloodthirsty command from his king.

The rest of the people who'd been watching this spectacle from the sides of this large hall remained silent, perhaps as stunned as Shiphrah by the cruelty of their king. Her eyes were again drawn briefly to the princess, whose complexion had gone quite pale. The woman's contrived defense of Shiphrah's words indicated that there was a deep vein of compassion in her. She was likely thanking all her gods that she lived within the walls of this palace and would have no opportunity to come across a Hebrew baby in the first place and would never have to be called upon to carry out Pharaoh's awful command.

With piercing intensity, the king of Egypt met Shiphrah's gaze, a vicious glint in his narrow-set eyes. "And now you will see what your disobedience has wrought."

CHAPTER TWENTY-THREE

The days after Pharaoh's shocking announcement were gut-wrenching. Regular raids of the Hebrew areas in the city. Men killed for refusing to allow the Medjay entry to their homes. Infants ripped screaming from mothers' arms. There was no place that seemed to be safe and no end of suffering for the descendants of Jacob.

And through it all, Shiphrah carried the terrible burden of guilt Pharaoh had left her with. He'd sent her, Puah, and the other midwives back to their homes without further censure. Without putting them in chains like Orla. And without ordering their deaths. Because he knew that no amount of torture could inflict more lasting pain than blaming themselves for the horrors that followed.

Even the joy of reuniting with her husband and children when she returned home that day was tainted, the relief that she should have felt tarnished by the knowledge that her audacity may well have cost even more Hebrews their lives.

But there was nothing she could do now except press on, do her job as a midwife, hold the hand of grieving mothers and weep with them, encourage those, like Jochebed, who'd made the bold decision to hide their sons, and spend every spare moment in prayer that someday, somehow El Shaddai would have the final word.

During one such session of prayer, while she and Marva were kneeling together on the roof just after dawn, a knock sounded on the door below. Yanked out of their joint solitude, the two women looked at each other with wide eyes, the memory of the last time such a firm rap had landed on the wooden door of their home fresh in their minds. Had the captain of the Medjay returned to bring Shiphrah back to the palace for a third time? Perhaps Pharaoh had changed his mind after all and meant to make an example of her in front of everyone.

With dread creeping up her spine, Shiphrah carefully made her way over to the parapet and peered over the edge, expecting to see the captain standing at the threshold. But instead of the distinctive striped headdress and broad shoulders of a Medjay at her door, Shiphrah was astounded to recognize the shaven head and deep-toned skin of Thadeo.

He must have heard her swift intake of breath above him, because he tilted his head back and caught her gawking with open-mouthed surprise. With his characteristic reserve he nodded to her and then lifted his brows, a silent question of whether she was going to let him inside. Tempted as she was to call out and ask why he'd come to her home, wisdom demanded discretion. So without a word, she brushed past a bewildered Marva and rushed down the stairs, through the house, to throw open the door.

"I have word from my master," he said, without preamble.

Her eyes flared wide. *Sennofre* had sent her a message?

His gaze flickered side to side, reminding her that his presence in the Hebrew quarter might be deemed suspicious.

"Come in," she said, pulling the door wide and ushering him inside, before poking her head outside briefly to ensure no one had been watching. She breathed easier when she saw that the only witnesses to her unexpected guest were two little girls walking hand in hand down the street and a big, gray cat who stared back at her with golden-eyed curiosity from his perch on the neighbor's window ledge across the way.

She yanked the door closed and latched it tightly before turning to Thadeo, who had already introduced himself to Marva.

"You are the very last person I ever expected to see here," said Shiphrah.

"I guessed that might be the case." A slight smile curved on the man's lips. "But as I said, I came at the behest of Sennofre."

Following her audience with Pharaoh, Shiphrah had decided that the only reason Sennofre had kept his association with her a secret was for the sake of Berenice. If he'd been willing to lie about taking a concubine, thereby exposing her to humiliation, in order to hide the origin of Degana's baby, then her former mistress must be determined to keep the child at all costs. Shiphrah remembered how enthralled Berenice had been from the moment she'd placed the tiny boy in her arms and guessed that she'd only fallen deeper in love with him in the ensuing days. And as Shiphrah had seen with her own eyes, there was nothing Sennofre would not do for his wife. It had nothing at all to do with protecting Shiphrah, but she was grateful nonetheless.

"How is the baby?" she asked.

This time when Thadeo smiled it was with his entire face, an expression of pure affection lighting his dark eyes. "He is well. The mistress barely lets him out of her sight. There are two nursemaids and two wet nurses employed to keep him satisfied at all times. And Master Kafele is entranced by his new brother. He has vowed to share all his playthings with him and to teach him how to read symbols before he is of age to begin tutelage at the feet of the scribes."

Shiphrah's heart thrilled at the revelations. Not only was Degana's son safe, but he was loved and would be provided for in the exact same manner as the child of Sennofre's own flesh and blood. She could hardly wait to share the news with his birthmother. Although it was doubtful that Degana would ever see her son again and would grieve his loss for the rest of her days, at least she could rest in the knowledge that he was alive and well.

"And it is because of little Master Jumoke that I bring you a proposition from Master Sennofre."

Shiphrah smiled at the name that had been given to the infant she'd brought to her former master—beloved child. There was no further question in her mind about whether she'd done the right thing with the boy. El Shaddai had indeed led her on the correct path that night.

"He wants you to know that he and his wife are not the only Egyptians who are desperate for children."

Shiphrah's blood seemed to go still. Was Thadeo implying what she thought he was?

Thadeo spoke slowly as if to imprint the importance of his words. "He said there are a few families he knows that might be interested in similar *arrangements*."

The blatant reference to Sennofre's lie to Pharaoh was as clear as the blue sky outside her window. Her former master wanted to help her smuggle Hebrew babies to safety and place them in Egyptian homes, who would likely use the same explanation of a concubine's pregnancy to hide the truth.

For the first time since she'd walked away from the king's throne room, a burst of excitement sparked in Shiphrah's chest. She'd prayed and prayed for El Shaddai to provide hope to the Hebrew people, even though her heart seemed torn in two over her part in the aggravation of their troubles. Had He provided an answer through the unlikeliest of sources? The man who'd once purchased her at an auction?

Her pulse pounded in her ears as she considered all the dangers inherent in laying her life in Sennofre's hands, along with those of the tiniest sons of Jacob. But if there was anything she'd learned from standing before Pharaoh in bold defiance of his evil command, it was that fear might seem to be a rushing river; it might roar loudly; it might scream and shout and lie about its true power, but it was nothing compared to the omnipotent God who'd carved the path of the mighty Nile with only a word from His mouth.

Still, she had reservations. Not about whether this was the right thing to do, or even if Sennofre could accomplish such things, but about those whose hearts would be involved.

"I will not force any mother to give up her child," she said. "It is not my place to make such decisions. *They* will have to be the ones to ask for help."

"Of course," said Thadeo. "The master only wants to help those who see no other path. None of this will be easy. It may take some gentle convincing on both sides, and perhaps even some silver in the right hands to ensure these arrangements are as discreet as possible."

Shiphrah looked to Marva beside her, who'd been silent throughout this exchange, and the smile that grew on her face was mirrored on her mother-in-law's lips.

"It just so happens," said Shiphrah, the hope in her heart flaming even higher, "that someone once told me to save the silver Sennofre gave me upon my emancipation until it was truly needed. I think such a time has finally arrived."

CHAPTER TWENTY-FOUR

The moment Shiphrah stepped over the threshold and into the street, a chariot clattered toward her. Her heart galloped as the polished spokes reflected the afternoon sunlight, causing her to squint. And just like when Thadeo had arrived at her door unexpectedly, she wondered if Pharaoh had sent someone to take her back to the palace. But instead of halting in front of her house, the chariot driver continued on, heedless of the Hebrews who were forced to skitter out of the way as he turned the corner to head back in the direction of the city.

Perplexed by the appearance of a lone chariot in the Hebrew quarter, especially since the Medjay had already performed another raid just this morning, Shiphrah continued on down the street, willing her pulse to even out as she approached Jochebed's home. The poor woman had been deep in grief, and Shiphrah could not help but feel the blame for the suffering. The compulsion to sit with her, hold her hand, and cry with her had been so strong today that she could not ignore it anymore.

When her neighbor had come to her door early in the morning three days ago to ask Shiphrah and Marva to keep an eye on her son Aaron for a few hours, Shiphrah had thought little of it. Nathanael and Aaron were the best of friends and cheered loudly upon the revelation they would have a long stretch of time to run about and play together.

However, the mask of sadness Jochebed wore that morning had pained Shiphrah. The woman had been working so hard to keep Tovyah hidden over these last two months and it had to be wearing on her, especially after witnessing Elisheba—the woman who'd practically had Shiphrah and Puah tossed from the house after she'd given birth—have her son ripped from her arms and thrown into the river.

Shiphrah had been tempted more than once in the past week to approach Jochebed and tell her of Sennofre's offer, but she had committed to waiting on El Shaddai's direction in this matter and each time it had arisen in her mind, she'd felt a very strong sense that she should be patient and allow Jochebed to come to her if she wanted to find a safer place for Tovyah.

But when Miriam had returned that evening and told Shiphrah that Jochebed had placed Tovyah in a pitch-covered basket and set him afloat on the Nile, and then an Egyptian royal had found him and taken him with her back to the palace, guilt had nearly overpowered Shiphrah.

If only she'd said something sooner, that sweet little boy would not be in the clutches of Pharaoh's family, who could at any moment dispose of the boy once it was made known he was Hebrew. Perhaps he'd even now be safe with an Egyptian family who cherished him the way Sennofre and Berenice did little Jumoke.

She and Puah had already successfully smuggled two more infants to safety. Puah had come up with the brilliant idea to include Gilah in the scheme, and one of those little boys had been spirited up the Nile to Avaris on one of Nedjem's trading boats. Although Shiphrah wondered if perhaps Gilah and Nedjem might even take in one of the babies themselves, they'd declined, not only because Gilah was Hebrew but because they felt they could protect more little ones by using their resources and connections to take part in Shiphrah's and Puah's efforts to save as many lives as possible.

Taking a deep breath to steady herself, Shiphrah knocked on the door of Jochebed's home and was startled when the sound of a baby's cry answered. Had one of the other neighbor's come to call on Jochebed? If so, the sight and sound of someone else's baby surely must be pouring salt on the poor woman's fresh wounds.

But when Miriam opened the door, her young face glowed with excitement. Shiphrah caught sight of Jochebed cross-legged on the ground, rocking her own son back and forth as she nursed him, and Shiphrah could barely muffle the gasp that slipped from her mouth.

"How?" she choked out, sinking to the ground in front of her friend with her eyes latched to the baby. "How can this be?"

The story that flowed from Jochebed's lips was nothing less than impossible. Not only had the woman who found Tovyah in the Nile been from the royal household, but from the description Jochebed gave of her, Shiphrah felt certain she was the very princess who'd stood up for her in the throne room that day.

"But how is he here?" asked Shiphrah. "Why send him back?"

"I have been given the job of nursing him until he is old enough to be weaned and taken to live with her in the palace."

Shiphrah's jaw felt permanently unhinged.

"Look," said Jochebed, using her free hand to slip a golden chain from the neck of her tunic. "She gave me this to prove what my role is and that I should be given access to the palace once a week." The glimmering ornament that hung from the necklace was inscribed with pictures that Shiphrah could not decipher, but she guessed it might contain the name of the princess herself.

"Shiphrah," said Jochebed, her eyes full of tears as she looked down at the tiny boy in her arms, "this is the one."

Shiphrah's brows furrowed as she searched Jochebed's face. "What do you mean?"

Jochebed pierced Shiphrah with an intense stare. "If I tell you, you must keep this quiet, because it will put him in more danger. Someone could say something to the wrong person or even alert the Medjay."

"Of course," said Shiphrah, "I would never do anything that might endanger your son." The words brought back those terrible moments when, in desperation, she'd actually wondered whether she was capable of doing such a horrible thing. Even though she would have never actually gone through with such harming of the child, the reminder dredged up an ocean of regret.

The woman paused, stroking her finger over Tovyah's rounded cheek as his large brown eyes fluttered closed, blissfully unaware of all the panic and pain his appearance had caused.

"Amram had a dream. He believes that El Shaddai has destined this child in my arms to grow into the man who will lead our people out of Egypt one day." Her lashes fluttered and two tears spilled over, trailing down her cheeks where they landed in Tovyah's black curls. "And at first I did not believe him. How could I? But, Shiphrah, I placed my son in a basket and set him adrift on the river and somehow, someway, El Shaddai brought him back to me. My baby will grow up in the palace—under the very nose of the man who ordered his death—educated as a prince and cherished by a daughter of Pharaoh. I have no other explanation, except that Amram's dream was not just a dream after all, but a prophecy. And now I truly believe. Our son *will* one day free all of us from slavery."

Shiphrah returned to her home in a daze, her mind swirling with the astonishing news that if Jochebed was correct, Shiphrah might actually see her children and grandchildren enter Abraham's land of promise with her own eyes.

Now the hesitation in her spirit made sense. There had been a reason why she hadn't been supposed to tell Jochebed about Sennofre's scheme. Tovyah was meant to be raised in the palace, not in the home of some other Egyptian family.

Remembering how the princess had reacted when the vizier had mocked her barrenness, Shiphrah could not help but wonder whether El Shaddai had blessed the woman for coming to her defense that day. Even if she did not know the significance of the child she'd adopted, Pharaoh's daughter had been given a son. And from what Jochebed told Shiphrah of the young woman, her love for Tovyah was already more than apparent, regardless of his heritage. She could only pray for strength for the princess and courage to stand boldly against Pharaoh, or anyone else who might be angry over Tovyah's presence in the palace in the years to come.

"Imma!" called a voice, just as she reached the threshold of her home. Shiphrah turned to take in the sight of Benjamin and Avi approaching, dripping from their dip in the canal.

All thoughts of Jochebed's son were thrust aside by the painful contraction of her heart at seeing her oldest son returning from his first day working alongside his father. Visions of her poor, sweet Benjamin hefting loads of bricks, treading mud and straw, or filling brick molds overwhelmed her as the two of them came near. It was difficult enough to watch her precious child leave at dawn this first morning; how would she endure it for all the years ahead?

But even as she considered the question, the lesson she'd learned in the throne room of the king came to mind. She'd vowed never again to let fear rule her but rather to trust that El Shaddai would provide whatever she, or her family, needed to survive—and to stand firm even when the waters threatened to rise around her.

Tovyah was just a baby now. It would be many years before he'd be ready to lead the Hebrews into battle against the king, but she would continue to seek out every moment of joy she could in the meantime.

Benjamin threw his arms around her waist, looking up at her with a smudge of dirt beneath one eye as he told her about how he'd been given the important task of running tools back and forth between the men who were constructing an enormous wall. Shiphrah's stomach dipped at the thought of him being in the middle of such dangerous labors, but when she looked up at Avi for reassurance, she found him smiling gently at their son.

"It sounds as though you did well today," Shiphrah said, even if her throat burned with restrained tears as she did so. "You be certain to pay close attention to your father's direction and take care as you go about your duties."

"I will, Imma," he said, before asking if he could go eat. Marva had sent a basket full of bread and dried fish with the two of them this morning, but his stomach was likely consuming itself after so many hours without food.

She bent to kiss his forehead, inhaling his familiar, sweaty-little-boy scent before releasing him to go inside, where his siblings greeted him with jubilance and many questions about what he'd been doing with their abba all day long. Instead of following Benjamin inside, Shiphrah and Avi remained in the street, in silent accord that there were things to discuss after such a momentous day.

Shiphrah dragged in a shuddering breath. "Was he safe?"

"Today he was," her husband replied. "In fact Rahotep assigned him the job of running tools between the men because it is the least dangerous of the duties the children perform. And Benjamin is not a careless boy. He's rarely impulsive, so I am certain he will remain aware of his surroundings as I've warned him to do."

Shiphrah nodded, doing her best to avoid imagining all the ways he could get hurt, regardless of how careful he might be. If only Tovyah was already grown and prepared to lead their people into battle against Pharoah's army so her sons would never have to carry bricks or build walls in Egypt but instead grow up in peace and safety in Canaan.

"You look troubled." Avi drew her close and kissed her. "Have you heard more from Sennofre or Thadeo?"

Avi had at first been wary of the offer from her former master, but Shiphrah's certainty that El Shaddai was providing a way to save lives through such an unlikely source had convinced him. He'd vowed to do whatever he could to support her, seeing it as one more way they could fight back against Pharaoh's control over their people.

Shiphrah shook her head. "I am to send a message if any of the women approach me for help. It is too dangerous to contact them in the meantime. Actually, I visited Jochebed today, meaning to sit with her in her grief for a while."

"My heart is so heavy for her and Amram," Avi said, his hold on her tightening. "I wish we could have known what they were planning."

"But that's just it, Avi. It is fortunate we did not."

In low tones that could not be overheard by passersby in the street, Shiphrah explained everything Jochebed told her about Tovyah and his unlikeliest of saviors. By the time she finished telling him of Amram's dream and his belief that their son was the Deliverer the Hebrews had been pleading for these last couple of hundred years, his dark eyes were as round as full moons. He was silent for a long while, studying her face intently. Then a slow smile stretched across his lips and he placed his large, work-roughened hands on her face, holding her with just as much tenderness as he had the very first time they'd revealed their hearts to one another on the roof years ago.

"*Ishti*. My wife," he said, pride undergirding the affectionate term. "Not only did you courageously thwart the king of Egypt with both your words and your deeds, but your hands"— he paused to lift each one, delivering a firm kiss to the center of both her palms—"these precious hands delivered the child who will one day deliver us. Not only will our children's children remember your name, my love, but I have a feeling that many generations to come will speak of your faithfulness."

Heat swept over her cheeks at his effusive praise, but she was prevented from refuting such lofty predictions by the sound of Puah calling her name from twenty paces away as the young woman jogged toward her.

"I just received word that Talia has gone into labor," she said. "Her waters have already broken."

All thoughts of Jochebed, Tovyah, and whatever was going to happen in the future dissipated as she fetched her midwifery bag and followed her partner, wondering if tonight she'd have need of Sennofre's assistance or if this new mother would be spared the grief of giving up a son.

But no matter what Pharaoh said or did, Hebrew babies would continue to be born, and Shiphrah was determined to stand in the gap between his tyranny and each precious life, because there was only one God deserving of her fear and His name was El Shaddai.

EPILOGUE

Eighty Years Later

Most of the children had fallen asleep during the telling of Savta's story, their heavy eyes losing the battle against exhaustion and the lulling tone of their grandmother's voice. Only the freckled girl-child had remained awake to hear the last of the tale just before midnight.

"I thought this story was about me," said the little girl, stubbornly stifling a yawn, "and all of us."

"That it is," said the savta, "because you are the fourth generation of Shiphrah's descendants. The blood of the great midwife who saved many lives, both with her words and with her deeds, runs within the deep rivers of your own body."

The little girl's eyes went wide as she pointed at her chest. "Inside me?"

Savta nodded. "My mother was Ayla, her eldest daughter. And just as she followed in the footsteps of Shiphrah, becoming a knowledgeable midwife, I too inherited the passion for coming alongside laboring women and guiding their little ones into their arms."

"And my imma is a midwife as well," said the little girl with a sagacious nod of her small head. "And someday I want to catch babies too."

The savta exchanged a smile with her daughter, amused at the image her granddaughter had of the calling passed down through the generations of women that came before her.

"That you will," she replied, "but for now it is time to rest. The morning will come all too soon, and we have a long day ahead of us."

Settling onto the floor with her head in her mother's lap, the freckle-nosed girl finally allowed her busy mind to rest. Her savta knew that it would not be the last time she would hear the tale of her great-great-grandmother's courage, but it would be the telling she would remember most.

All around the savta in the little house, other descendants of both Shiphrah and Puah savored the memories of their own connections to the women whose determination and audacity had ensured many generations of Jacob's descendants were not washed from the earth by the cruelty of a man who purported to be a god. Although there had been many innocent victims of Pharaoh's evil decree, hundreds of boys were saved—their bloodlines multiplied many times over among the millions of Hebrews who waited now with sandals on their feet inside homes whose doorways were painted with blood.

However, among those descendants of Abraham, Isaac, and Jacob were a number who did not know of their heritage, who'd been concealed within baskets of reeds, bundles of laundry, and at the bottom of empty water jugs and stealthily delivered to Egyptian homes. All these years later, only El Shaddai knew exactly which child came from the womb of a Hebrew woman who'd broken off a piece of her own soul to save her son's life.

Thankfully within only a few months of his terrible decree, the Pharaoh succumbed to true divine judgment, his life snuffed out just as swiftly and violently as the little ones he had commanded to be tossed to the crocodiles, and the thirst for Hebrew blood abated—even if the heavy burden of slavery did not.

As the children slept, the midpoint of this night of unknown fears reached its fullness. And when the mourning wails of the Egyptians began all over the city, lifting to the heavens like a cloud of despair, the savta was grateful that their innocence buffered them from the truth of the final stroke of El Shaddai's justice. Someday she would tell them that the price for their freedom had been paid for by the lives of the firstborn sons of Egypt and the wages for their forefathers' endless labors satisfied by gold, silver, and jewels pressed into their hands by their former masters. But for tonight, as all of Egypt suffered the pain so many Hebrew women had endured because of Pharaoh's edict, she whispered prayers to the God who'd carried her grandmother from Midian to Egypt. Prayers that the names of Shiphrah and Puah would be forever chiseled on the hearts of the sons of Jacob and that of the Pharaoh who'd tried to wipe them out would be blown away in the wind like so much dust. Both women had been blessed with large and thriving families whose generations would only continue to multiply, whereas the king who'd tried to make them murderers left nothing behind but a legacy of death.

When dawn reached its golden fingers through the window, gently waking the children, they had no idea that their entire world had changed while they slept. But as their mothers and fathers urged them to pass between bloody doorposts in order to emerge into that new reality, and as spontaneous songs of joy broke out among the throng preparing to leave, the descendants of Shiphrah and Puah discovered that the weight of their chains was gone.

During the initial shuffle of organizing wagons and hand-carts and livestock, the freckle-nosed girl found her way to her savta, and with a slight tremble in her voice asked where they were going.

"We are going to the land promised to our forefather Abraham, exactly four hundred and thirty years ago this day," said the savta.

"Is it far?" asked the little girl, her eyes following the gesture her grandmother had made toward the northeastern horizon.

"I have been told that it is less than two weeks' walk. But perhaps with all these people and animals and belongings, it may take a while longer than that."

"But what about the king?" asked the little girl, who'd heard stories of the pharaoh who now wore the double crown of the Two Lands and his refusal to let the people of El Shaddai go, even at the cost of his own people's health and prosperity.

"There is no longer any cause to worry, little one. Because Moses, the man who was once the child known as Tovyah, has proven that the king of Egypt has far less power and might than he claimed and that it is only El Shaddai—also known to us now as Yahweh—whom we have to fear. Yahweh has bested the gods of the earth and sky, the gods of the beasts and the insects, the gods of healing and pestilence, and even the gods of the sun and death itself. He is the same God who brought Shiphrah to Egypt, who preserved her life through slavery, who hid Tovyah in plain sight within the very house of the man who meant to kill him, and who will now fulfill the promises He made to Abraham by leading us to a land flowing with milk and honey.

"Because you see, my sweet child," continued the savta as she curved her hands around the beloved face of her grand-daughter, hands that had delivered hundreds of babes just as those of her own grandmother had done, "this is not the end of our story. It is only the beginning."

AUTHOR'S NOTE

Ihave always been fascinated by the story of Shiphrah and Puah. Even as I wrote my debut novel, *Counted with the Stars*, I spent some time pondering these extraordinary women and what might have inspired their fearless acts of rebellion against Pharaoh. Therefore when given the chance, I was thrilled to use some of the story seeds that were planted in my mind nearly ten years ago in order to bring to life my own imagined ideas about what caused these women to stand so boldly when so much was at stake.

One thing that I discovered in my research was just how important a name was to the ancient Egyptians. They believed that the name given at birth was a part of their personality, as if their essence was actually tied to the word itself and was an essential part of their *Ka,* or life force. If therefore, a person's name was completely erased or forgotten, then their soul would cease to exist in the afterlife. So when we look at Exodus 1 and see that the names of Shiphrah and Puah, two common midwives, are immortalized for all time in the Word of God, I feel as though this was one more slap in the face to the Pharaoh whose true name has been buried beneath the sands of time.

And no wonder God inscribed their names in the Torah. These two brave, audacious women not only refused to take the lives of the Hebrew boys, but they stood proudly (although most likely with knocking knees) and lied to a man who had the power of life and death over not only them but their entire families. In this way they were no different than the many men and women who lied and stole and managed to outwit the Nazis in order to save Jewish lives during the Holocaust—just like my personal hero, Corrie ten Boom, for whom I named my own daughter. Just as Jesus admonished the Pharisees for using the excuse of the Sabbath law not to save a life in Luke 14:5, the untruth Shiphrah and Puah told was justified because it saved the lives of many Hebrew sons and subsequently the many generations that followed them. How wonderful to think that God blessed them both with large families of their own in reward for their refusal to bow to the murderous command of the Pharaoh, which would have cut off so many generations of Jacob's descendants! It's even cooler to think that descendants of Shiphrah and Puah themselves were likely among those who followed Moses into the wilderness alongside the thousands of lives that their foremothers had preserved.

May we all be as brave as these two women in standing up to evil and protecting every life—be it born or unborn—for the sake of the One who breathed life into each one of us from the beginning.

FACTS BEHIND
the Fiction

✦

HOW EGYPTIANS OBTAINED
THEIR SLAVES

War, kidnapping, and debt made slaves of people in Bible times.

At least in one familiar case, jealous older brothers were the problem. A family of ten angry brothers sold their little brother Joseph, favored son of Jacob, to slave-trading merchants headed to Egypt in a caravan (Genesis 37:28).

Egyptians often obtained their slaves that way, purchasing them from merchants importing exotic products such as rare spices and fragrant oils, mainly from Arab lands and beyond.

Egyptians sometimes won their slaves in war. They enslaved captive soldiers. They did the same to citizens of villages they raided on the march home to Egypt.

One Pharaoh named Sneferu (about 2500 BC, a few centuries before Abraham) enslaved 7,000 people at once. He captured them after crushing an uprising in Nubia, now Sudan, a nation on Egypt's southern border.

There's no indication Egyptians launched another campaign like that before enslaving the Hebrews, who had come to Egypt at a king's invitation, as refugees escaping a drought.

THE HARD LIFE OF A HEBREW SLAVE

"Make bricks!" Egyptians ordered their Hebrew slaves (Exodus 5:16 NLT).

One Egyptian painting says a slave who makes bricks from mud and straw is "dirtier than…pigs from working in the mud…. He is miserable."

An Egyptian scroll from the time of Pharaoh Rameses II—the king famous for building cities in the 1200s BC—reports the daily quota of a ten-person team of brickmakers was 2,000 bricks. That's 200 bricks per person. Each brick was handmade from mud mixed with pieces of straw to hold the mud together.

HOW THE HEBREWS BECAME ENSLAVED

The book of Genesis says Joseph, living in Egypt as the king's advisor, convinced his extended family to move to Egypt. He told his brothers, "Bring my father here quickly" (Genesis 45:13 NLT).

MAKING AND
DRYING MUD BRICKS

Joseph's father, Jacob, came "with all his possessions" (Genesis 46:1 NLT). He and his family, all seventy of them, left what is now southern Israel and migrated to the drought-resistant Nile River Valley to escape what the Bible describes as a widespread seven-year drought.

An Egyptian who wrote *Prophecy of Neferti* around the 1900s BC complained about refugees flooding into Egypt. He said, "We're throwing the land away....foreigners fill our land."

Joseph's family stayed 430 years (Exodus 12:40). Somewhere during those four centuries, those seventy Hebrews grew into a group large enough to make the king feel threatened. They didn't just "grow." The dramatic word in Hebrew, the original language of Genesis, says they "swarmed" (Exodus 1:7 NASB footnote).

The king said he worried they might "join our enemies and fight against us" (Exodus 1:10 NLT). So, he enslaved them "to build the cities of Pithom and Rameses as supply centers" (Exodus 1:11 NLT).

HOW PASSOVER GOT ITS NAME

The last supper Jesus ate with his disciples, before His crucifixion, was in remembrance of the last supper His Hebrew ancestors ate in Egyptian slavery more than 1,000 years earlier.

This was the Passover meal, instituted the day before Moses led the Hebrews out of Egypt. It's a strange name for the most celebrated Jewish holiday: Passover, *Pesach* (PAY-sock) in Hebrew. Yet it perfectly describes what happened when God unleashed the tenth plague on Egypt.

Egypt's king, for the tenth time, had refused God's demand to free the Hebrews. As a result, Moses warned the king that God would pass through Egypt and kill the oldest child in every Egyptian family. The Hebrews marked their front doorway with lamb's blood because God promised, "When I see the blood, I will pass over you" (Exodus 12:13 NLT). The blood came from the lamb they slaughtered as the main course for their last meal in slavery.

The king freed them that night, too late to save his own son.

Every springtime, near Easter, observant Jews eat a Passover meal, which is rich in symbolism. The meal reminds all who partake that God has a long history of helping His people—and that He continues to care for them.

PASSOVER MENU

Jewish people call the ritual meal by its Hebrew name: *seder*, which means "in order." That's because the meal follows a carefully ordered script, reminding the people sharing the meal that everything on the table represents something from the time of the first Passover meal.

There's irony here. Jews today slowly eat a carefully orchestrated meal. But their ancestors ate the first Passover meal in such a rush that family bakers didn't have time to let bread dough rise.

Roasted lamb, or just a shank bone. It represents the lamb Hebrews sacrificed for the first Passover meal. Some Jews don't eat the meat, because it also symbolizes the Passover lamb Jews later sacrificed at the Jerusalem temple. Jews didn't eat that sacrifice.

A dip of mixed nuts, fruit, and wine, which symbolizes the mortar Hebrew slaves used when they built Egyptian cities.

Bitter herbs, such as horseradish, a reminder of the bitterness of slavery.

Saltwater dip, a reminder of tears shed in Egypt, by Hebrews as well as Egyptians.

Roasted egg, a symbol of rebirth and of the sacrificial offerings Jews would give to build a worship center—first a tent for the road during the Exodus, and later the temple in Jerusalem.

Flat bread, called *matzah*, a reminder that the Hebrews fled Egypt in a rush. There was no time for yeast to work in the bread dough.

Passover symbols like these vary a bit among Jewish people. But the week-long Passover festival, highlighted by this one sacred meal, is a reminder to all that God loves and care for His chosen people.

THE SEDER PLATE

The Seder plate is the most important part of any Passover
Seder. It's rich with symbolism, meaning, and history. There are
traditionally six main items that go on the Seder plate. Maror
(the bitter herb, usually horseradish); Z'roa (usually a roasted
lamb shank bone); Charoset (a sweet, dark-colored paste made
of fruits and nuts); Chazeret (a second bitter item, usually a
leaf of romaine lettuce); Karpas (typically parsley); and Beitzah
(a hard-boiled egg).

MIDWIFE TRICKS OF THE TRADE

Many Egyptians learned a trade in school. Doctors did. So did religion
teachers. Scribes made a living by helping people who couldn't read or
write. However, midwifery wasn't a formal trade like any of those. Midwives didn't learn how to deliver babies by going to school. There's no
evidence Egyptian midwives were organized into guilds when Hebrews
were slaves in Egypt.

Midwives learned about childbirth from other midwives: relatives
passing down knowledge from generation to generation, friends sharing
experiences, maybe even strangers passing time at the village well.

A SECTION OF THE EBERS PAPYRUS DEPICTING A WOMAN GIVING BIRTH, ASSISTED BY OTHER WOMEN AND THE GODS.

COLLECTED WISDOM:
TECHNIQUES FOR DELIVERING BABIES

Midwives who were new to the trade picked up tips like these from their midwife mentors and tutors:

- **Birthing positions.** Women didn't give birth lying down. They stood. Or they squatted. Or they sat on a birthing stool. Sometimes they sat on two bricks, with a space between them. These positions made fine use of gravity, and they put the midwife in a position to catch the baby.
- **Medicinal help.** One ancient concoction, which was used either for delivery of the baby or to expel the placenta was made by mixing fiber of the mysterious *kheper-wer* plant (whose identification or species is lost to history) with water from a carob plant (a bean that produces a healthy alternative to chocolate) and milk.
- **Olive oil.** The midwife would prepare the woman for the baby's passage by soaking the birth canal with 1 *henu,* or two cups (450 ml), of oil.
- **Invite divine help.** Hebrew midwives may have prayed to God, while Egyptians could have invoked help from many gods. Egyptian midwives sometimes did this by placing on the woman's tummy a small religious object, such as an amulet engraved with an incantation to Hathor, the cow-headed goddess of health. About 700

incantations along with medical treatments are preserved in an Egyptian document called the Ebers Papyrus, written in the 1500s BC, around the time many say Moses likely grew up.

- **Salt the baby.** When the baby was born, the midwife would wash him or her then rub soft, powdered salt over the infant's body. Afterward she would wrap the child snugly in cloth. Midwives taught that salt helped protect the baby by making the skin thicker and stronger and better able to adjust to changes outside the womb, such as fluctuating temperature. The ancients may have borrowed this idea from curing ham and other meat. A salt crust thickens the skin and preserves the meat even in warm weather.

NILE: FLOODS ARE WELCOME HERE

Most Egyptians in Bible times were riverside people who loved seeing the Nile River flood every autumn. In fact, they counted on it.

Floodwaters would sometimes rise 20 feet (6 meters) or more and cover the flood plain with a few feet of water (one to two meters), starting around late August or early September and lasting for about a month and a half.

Instead of destroying crops, this flood nurtured them. When the water receded, it left behind a fresh coat of rich topsoil.

Floods started with summer monsoon rains upstream, in Central Africa. Floodwater broke loose nitrogen-rich silt and

A SCENE OF THE NILE IN ITS FLOODED STATE.

carried it downstream to northern Egypt. The Nile River flows north, into the Mediterranean Sea.

Floodplain fields usually soaked up the water in time for farmers to plant their winter crops. The soaking was thorough enough that farmers in this desert nation usually didn't need to irrigate that season of crops. The Nile River did it for them.

Most Egyptians then, as now, lived within a few miles of the Nile River. Beyond that meandering green swath, there's little more than sunburnt desert.

WATER CLOCKS, A NEW INVENTION IN MOSES' DAY?

Water clocks may have been invented during the lifetime of Moses.

The oldest water clock on record came from the tomb of Egyptian Pharaoh Amenhotep I, who reigned about 1526–1506 BC.

These clocks tell time by measuring how much water has drained *out of* a container (called an Outflow Water Clock) or *into* a container (an Inflow Water Clock). Some were quite simple in design— a conical container with a small

AN EGYPTIAN WATER CLOCK DECORATED WITH A BABOON 664-630 B.C. WATER WITHIN COULD DRAIN FROM A HOLE BETWEEN THE BABOON'S LEGS OVER A MEASURED TIME.

opening through which water flowed—while others were more fanciful, such as the one shown in the illustration.

Measuring lines inside either container show how much time has passed. Clocks like this worked well because water drains at a consistent rate.

Fiction Author
CONNILYN COSSETTE

Connilyn Cossette is a Christy Award– and Carol Award–winning author whose books have been found on both ECPA and CBA bestseller lists. When she is not engulfed in the happy chaos of homeschooling two teenagers, devouring books whole, or avoiding housework, she can be found digging into the rich, ancient world of the Bible to discover gems of grace that point to Jesus and weaving them into an immersive fiction experience. Although she and her husband have lived all over the country in their twenty-plus years of marriage, they currently call a little town south of Dallas, Texas, their home.

Nonfiction Author
STEPHEN M. MILLER

Stephen M. Miller is an award winning, bestselling Christian author of easy-reading books about the Bible and Christianity. His books have sold over 1.9 million copies and include *The Complete Guide to the Bible, Who's Who and Where's Where in the Bible*, and *How to Get Into the Bible.*

Miller lives in the suburbs of Kansas City with his wife, Linda, a registered nurse. They have two married children who live nearby.

Read on for a sneak peek of another exciting story
in the Ordinary Women of the Bible series!

NO STONE CAST:
ELIYANAH'S STORY

by Carole Towriss

Month of Tammuz
Early Summer, AD 30
Bethany, Judea

*B*et-ani. *House of Afflictions.* That's what people called her village.

For Eliyanah, it was a place of joy. Of family. Of love.

The place she would marry her best friend and spend her life with him.

From the rooftop of her small stone and mud-brick house, she looked out over the tiny village of Bethany, still shrouded in dusky, gray light. She sucked in a lungful of fresh morning air. The Mount of Olives lay to the northwest, the desert valley to the east. Birdsong filled the air. The fragrance of ripening apple and grape blossoms rode a gentle breeze. Towering date palms hovered over the nearly dry river beyond the village's walls.

Life in Bethany was perfect.

Thank Adonai no one else was awake this early, because Yana could not hide the smile that threatened to burst from deep within and erupt in laughter. Her heart pounded and her breathing quickened.

Her beloved would return to Bethany today.

She rolled up her mat and laid it against the ledge of the packed dirt roof. Careful not to awaken her *imma*—or Imma's husband—she climbed down the ladder that led to a large square room below, the center section open to the brilliant blue sky. One third housed their sheep in the rainy season, not only to protect the animal but to add its warmth to cold nights when the family slept inside.

The other two thirds contained a cistern filled with water from the river, sleeping benches built into the wall, and pegs to hold extra tunics. A small beehive-shaped bread oven, unused in summer, sat next to a cold firepit.

She retrieved the jar of barley she'd ground yesterday and stepped outside into the courtyard they shared with her *abba's* cousin Simeon and his children. She knelt by the large common oven and poked at the embers, stirring them to life. She placed dried grass on top to encourage a flame and then added dung. When a bright orange fire flared, she poured crushed grain into a bowl and added water and salt, forming circular, flat loaves.

As she mindlessly slapped the rounds of dough to the side of the oven, one after another, she tried to keep her mind from focusing on her beloved's soft brown eyes. The feel of his hand in hers. The low voice that sent a chill down her spine when he whispered in her ear.

After removing each loaf when it had cooked to a deep golden brown, she replaced it with another round of uncooked dough and soon had a stack of hot bread.

She grabbed four of the flatbreads and hurried to the broadroom that ran along the back of the house, where she searched the pottery jars that lined the shelves. She poured out a handful of last year's dates, then placed them in a sack along with a chunk of sheep's milk cheese, a bunch of fresh grapes, and the bread, and tied a string around it.

The sun now hovered fully above the horizon. It wouldn't be long now. She slipped out the door, hurried through the courtyard, and headed for the gate.

"Yana!"

Just outside the gate she froze, and suppressed a sigh. She'd hoped to avoid her cousin Miriam. Yana didn't want to explain why she was rushing to meet Miriam's younger brother.

"Going somewhere?" She smiled. Miriam was only a year or two older than Yana, but Yana always felt like a child in her presence.

"I was hoping to catch you. Can you take this to Eleazar as well?" She handed Yana a small package.

"Well, um..." How did she explain this?

Miriam pulled back one corner of the cloth to reveal two handfuls of pistachios, already shelled. "He loves them, but he can't sit still long enough to eat them." She laughed.

Yana frowned. "That's all?" Not a big meal for someone who had spent the last two weeks with the village's sheep and goats, leading them to fresh grass and water.

Miriam smiled. "I thought you'd be bringing him the rest." She glanced down at the bag at Yana's side.

She knew? How did she find out? They'd been so careful.

"You may have kept it a secret, but he couldn't. Sisters notice when their baby brother wanders around the house smiling for no reason whatsoever."

Oh no. Her ears began to burn.

"Everyone knows, though no one has said anything. Even Abba knows. I'm thrilled. I can't think of anyone better for him than you."

Warmth spread from her chest all over her body. "Truly?"

"Truly. I'd be delighted to have you as a sister." She leaned in and kissed Yana's cheek, then spun around and returned to her house.

Yana placed the pistachios in the bag and hurried along the village's only road toward the northern edge of the village.

She reached the common sheepfold that lay just beyond the last house in the shadow of the tree-covered mountain. In the dry season, all the animals remained together outside the village, and younger girls and boys took turns leading them to the green pastures and cool water in the hills. Eleazar could have given up his turn years ago, but he loved the time alone, wandering in the hills.

She waited, pacing, moving the bag from one fist to the other while keeping an eye on the dirt path that led to Jerusalem.

She heard the sheep before she saw him. She adjusted her head cloth, tucked a stray strand of hair behind her ear, and smoothed her tunic.

And waited.

Finally, his lanky form sauntered down the path, crook in one hand, the sheep following behind him.

Her heartbeat doubled, and she started down the road toward him.

Eleazar's face lit up as she approached. He paused, the flock parting and swooshing past on either side of the couple toward the fold.

She halted before him. "Good morning, Ezi."

He smiled softly. "I love it when you call me that."

When she'd first moved here with Imma, he was eight or nine years old. But she'd only begun to talk, and she couldn't get her tongue to pronounce his name. To her he became Ezi, and even now she rarely called him by his proper name. "Did you sleep well last night?"

A sly grin crossed his face. "Of course. I dreamed of you."

Her cheeks heated. "You can't say things like that."

"Why not? We're going to be married, aren't we?"

"Not unless you speak to Lemuel." She grinned.

"I should probably bathe first, don't you think? I just returned from two weeks with the sheep and goats." He laughed. "I'll do it tonight, I promise."

He glanced quickly at the empty landscape surrounding them, then leaned nearer, his warm breath caressing her cheek. "I missed you."

"I missed you too. I'm glad you're home."

He took her hand and they strolled back toward the village. Just as they reached the last house along the road, Simeon stopped them, his face twisted.

Ezi halted. "Abba, what's wrong?"

Simeon fixed his eyes on her. "Yana, I'm sorry to tell you. Your abba—"

"He is *not* my father." She tried to keep her voice respectful, difficult as it was.

"I know, but he is your imma's husband, and according to the law, he has an abba's authority over you."

"And?" Ezi's voice was sharp.

"He has betrothed you to a man in Jerusalem."

The words ripped through her soul. *No!*

She tried to understand. The message was simple—only a handful of words. But no matter how hard she tried, no matter how many times she turned the sentence over in her mind, it didn't make sense.

Lemuel knew she loved Eleazar. He knew Simeon approved of the match.

"But why?" She searched Simeon's eyes, seeking an answer. An explanation. A reason.

"I'm so sorry, Yana. Your ab—Lemuel has decided. There is nothing I, or anyone, can do."

Ezi turned to her, agony written on his face. "What about your imma?"

"You know exactly what she will say. She would never contradict him."

Life as she knew it, as she had hoped and dreamed it to be, was over.

Yana let the courtyard gate slam behind her and marched toward her house on the left side of the courtyard.

"Yana! Back so soon?" Imma stepped out from the broadroom, a jar in hand.

"You *knew*! You knew and you let me go to him. How... Why? Why didn't you tell me?"

Imma blanched. "Who told you?"

"Simeon."

Her face clouded. "He should have waited. It was not his place to share our news."

"He did it because he cares about me! And Ezi." She stomped around the lower floor.

"I care about you too. More than you realize." She reached for Yana's shoulder, but Yana recoiled.

"Then why make me marry someone I've never met? Never heard of? When you know Ezi and I've been talking about it."

Imma's brows furrowed. "You know I had no say."

"I know you could have a say if you wanted. But you're so afraid he'll leave us. Like my abba did."

"That's enough. Lemuel will leave for his vineyards any mo—" Imma shot a glance toward the ladder.

Lemuel already stood at the bottom, arms crossed. He was an imposing man, taller than most, with broad shoulders, thinning hair, and dark eyes that never seemed to smile.

He glanced from Imma to Yana then back to Imma.

"You told her."

Imma took a step back, her hands up. "No. I wouldn't. You kno—"

"But she somehow found out." He glared at Yana.

"You know there is no such thing as a secret in this village." She held his gaze. No use trying to be nice to him anymore, trying to be polite and respectful so he'd allow her to marry Ezi.

He shrugged. "So you know. Saves me telling you."

"But—"

"No!"

Yana cringed at his shout.

He shook a long, thick finger at her. "There will be no discussion. He is my kinsman, and I've already begun the negotiations. Besides, he is better than you deserve."

The words hit her like a slap in the face. Better than she deserved?

"I've taken care of you for the last six years. Longer than your own abba stuck around." He snorted. "What do you think would have happened to you and your imma had I not married her? Do you think anyone else would have done what I did, marrying a divorced woman with another man's child to raise?" He sneered. "Of course not. One man had already left her. There must have been a reason. No one else would take that chance."

Yana watched Imma's face as he ranted. Imma hung her head. She believed every word this man said. She always had.

"So you will do as you're told. It's your duty to do what is best for the family. This match will help us all."

"How? How does this help us *all*?"

"He is a powerful, respected merchant, a dealer in spices. He has ties with the priests, with other merchants. He has a spacious house with many servants. He is quite wealthy, and he will see that you are well provided for."

"And how does this help *you*?"

"That is not your concern."

"Enormous bridewealth? Is that how it benefits you?"

He stepped nearer, stopping an arm's length away. His dark eyes glared down at her.

Perhaps she had gone too far.

"Yes, he is gifting us with a *mohar* beyond what someone like you could ever expect." His voice was low, controlled. "But even I, as any good abba would, will give most of it to you for your dowry." He turned and left, heading to check on his vineyards.

Imma sat on the sleeping bench built into the wall and patted the space beside her. "Eliyanah, sit down. I need to explain something to you."

Imma's face was calm, but her words frightened Yana. "Imma?"

"Please, just sit."

Yana did as she was told.

"When your father left us, when he *abandoned* us after moving us here from Galilee, my dowry should have remained with me. Although a dowry is meant to be kept by the woman, the husband is allowed to use it as he sees fit, as long as it can be returned to her should he die or divorce her without cause." Imma took her hand. "But your abba had lost ours. We had nothing. You know what could have happened to us. To me. We only survived because his cousin helped us."

She knew. Widows and divorced women led precarious lives in Israel. Those with no family support could easily end up in prostitution. Had it not been for Simeon…

Imma cupped Yana's cheeks with wrinkled palms. "If Lemuel had not married me—" She smiled weakly. "He does care for you, in his own way."

Perhaps. As long as it didn't hurt *him*.

"I want you protected. I don't want to be worrying about you when—" She clamped her mouth shut. "When I'm old and unable to do anything about it."

"But Ezi…"

"My precious daughter, it's rare when a woman can marry for love. Those of little means marry for survival, of themselves and of the family. Even daughters of kings and priests marry to form alliances, to enhance the status of their family." She shrugged. "This man is one of the most successful merchants in all Jerusalem. He could be very useful to Lemuel, and it's important to him to make these connections. What's important to *me* is that you are protected. This man can do both."

Any hope she had of changing Imma's mind flickered and went out. "Yes, Imma."

Imma rose and began to pace. "This man—his name is Oded—is willing to gift us with bridewealth far more than anyone else could, and more than we have a right to expect. Otherwise I would have nothing to give you."

Yana shook her head. "I don't care about that. I am very happy as we are."

"But I care. I don't want you to struggle as I have, ever."

It seemed there was nothing she could do to change Imma's position on this. She saw this marriage as a means to a good and secure life for Yana. She firmly believed she was doing what was best for Yana.

Perhaps she was right.

A NOTE FROM THE EDITORS

We hope you enjoyed another exciting volume in the Ordinary Women of the Bible series, published by Guideposts. For over seventy-five years, Guideposts, a nonprofit organization, has been driven by a vision of a world filled with hope. We aspire to be the voice of a trusted friend, a friend who makes you feel more hopeful and connected.

By making a purchase from Guideposts, you join our community in touching millions of lives, inspiring them to believe that all things are possible through faith, hope, and prayer. Your continued support allows us to provide uplifting resources to those in need. Whether through our communities, websites, apps, or publications, we inspire our audiences, bring them together, and comfort, uplift, entertain, and guide them. Visit us at guideposts.org to learn more.

We would love to hear from you. Write us at Guideposts, P.O. Box 5815, Harlan, Iowa 51593 or call us at (800) 932-2145. Did you love *The Life Giver: Shiphrah's Story?* Leave a review for this product on guideposts.org/shop. Your feedback helps others in our community find relevant products.

Find inspiration, find faith, find Guideposts.

Shop our best sellers and favorites at
guideposts.org/shop
Or scan the QR code to go directly to our Shop

Find more inspiring stories in these best-loved Guideposts fiction series!

Mysteries of Lancaster County

Follow the Classen sisters as they unravel clues and uncover hidden secrets in Mysteries of Lancaster County. As you get to know these women and their friends, you'll see how God brings each of them together for a fresh start in life.

Secrets of Wayfarers Inn

Retired schoolteachers find themselves owners of an old warehouse-turned-inn that is filled with hidden passages, buried secrets, and stunning surprises that will set them on a course to puzzling mysteries from the Underground Railroad.

Tearoom Mysteries Series

Mix one stately Victorian home, a charming lakeside town in Maine, and two adventurous cousins with a passion for tea and hospitality. Add a large scoop of intriguing mystery, and sprinkle generously with faith, family, and friends, and you have the recipe for *Tearoom Mysteries.*

Mysteries of Martha's Vineyard

Come to the shores of this quaint and historic island and dig in to a cozy mystery. When a recent widow inherits a lighthouse just off the coast of Massachusetts, she finds exciting adventures, new friends, and renewed hope.

To learn more about these books, visit Guideposts.org/Shop